HIGHLAND SOUL

HIGHLAND OUTCASTS
BOOK 1

BY
ELIZABETH ROSE

ARE YOU SIGNED UP FOR DRAGONBLADE'S BLOG?

You'll get the latest news and information on exclusive giveaways, exclusive excerpts, coming releases, sales, free books, cover reveals and more.

Check out our complete list of authors, too!

No spam, no junk. That's a promise!

Sign Up Here

www.dragonbladepublishing.com

Dearest Reader;

Thank you for your support of a small press. At Dragonblade Publishing, we strive to bring you the highest quality Historical Romance from some of the best authors in the business. Without your support, there is no 'us', so we sincerely hope you adore these stories and find some new favorite authors along the way.

Happy Reading!

CEO, Dragonblade Publishing

Author's Note

(The Highland Outcasts Series features secondary characters from my MacKeefe Clan. The stories about the characters that are making guest appearances can be found in some of my other series, such as Legacy of the Blade, Madman MacKeefe, Seasons of Fortitude, and Highland Chronicles, amongst others.)

Some of the MacKeefe Clan heroes, heroines, and secondary characters seen in this series are:

Old Callum MacKeefe (Oldest living man in Scotland)

Ian MacKeefe (Callum's son – MacKeefe Clan chieftain)

Lady Clarista (Ian's English wife)

Storm MacKeefe (Ian's son – also a MacKeefe Clan chieftain since they have holdings in both the Highlands and the Lowlands)

Lady Wren (Storm's English wife)

Friends and members of the MacKeefe Clan, and heroes of the Highland Outcasts Series:

Gavin MacKeefe – hero of Highland Soul

Cam MacKeefe – hero of Highland Flame

Nash MacKeefe – hero of Highland Sky

North MacKeefe – twin brother of Nash, and hero of Highland Silver

CHAPTER ONE

Glasgow, Scotland 1363

"ANOTHER ROUND OF drinks for everyone," called out Gavin MacKeefe, raising his tankard high above his head. He and his friends celebrated tonight in the Horn and Hoof Tavern in Glasgow. The battle with the MacGregors was over, and the MacKeefes were the victors, thanks to Gavin and his friends. They'd caught the reivers who tried to steal MacKeefe livestock. Instead of killing the bloody thieves, they'd actually managed to make an alliance. Because of Gavin, Cam, Nash, and North, the MacKeefes had a deal with their enemies in the end.

The MacGregors ended up punishing their own clansmembers who'd tried to steal the livestock, thankful that the MacKeefes had not killed them. Through negotiations, Gavin and the others even convinced the MacGregors to gift the MacKeefe Clan with extra animals of their own. Yes, things turned out better than expected. They saved the livestock and a brand-new alliance was formed.

No blood was shed.

No lives were lost.

Every blackfaced sheep and long-horned cattle from the MacKeefe Clan was safe once again. This truly was a cause for celebration.

"Ye've had enough of my Mountain Magic. No more," scolded the proprietor, Old Callum MacKeefe. Callum was a small, wiry man with long white hair and a cranky disposition. His temper was the biggest thing about him. He was the oldest living man in all of Scotland. Rumor had it that his potent home brew of whisky had been to thank for his long life thus far.

Mountain Magic was so strong that it often knocked a full-grown man on his arse and kept him unconscious for days, unless he was used to drinking it. It was highly coveted, and brought in good money for the clan. It was also the clan's main income. Callum brewed it in secret and distributed it throughout the land. Highlanders, Lowlanders, and sometimes even the English actually showed up at the tavern just to taste this *uisque baugh* – or water of life as the Scots called it.

"Och, Callum, ease up. We're celebratin'," said Cam, Gavin's good friend. Cam was the same age as Gavin at five and twenty years, although Gavin outweighed his friend by at least two stone. Cam was well in his cups also, as the men had been drinking for hours now. "What's all the clishmaclaver about?" Cam continued. Liking the ladies a little too much, he couldn't stop himself from reaching out and boldly pinching a passing tavern wench on her bottom. Then he winked at her, giving her a full-blown smile before pulling her atop his lap and locking his lips against hers in a passionate kiss.

Gavin could see the lust already leaking from his friend's eyes. It surprised him that Cam wasn't already upstairs with one of the tavern whores sowing his oats, like he usually did every time they stopped here. However, Gavin saw trouble brewing. He didn't recognize the girl on Cam's lap as one of the usual whores. As a matter of fact, she looked familiar, but he wasn't thinking clearly now, so he couldn't be sure.

"Mmmph," came the muffled cry of the girl atop Cam's lap. She reached out, pushing against his chest. Then she slapped him hard across the cheek.

"How dare ye!" she spat.

"Let go of her, ye lustful cur!" Callum picked up a wooden

paddle from behind the drink board. The paddle was used in the tavern's kitchen for baking bread, but the old man confiscated it to use as a weapon to hit the drunks instead. "That's Coira, the sister of Aidan MacKeefe's new wife, ye fool! Dinna mess with Aidan because ye ken he is a madman." Callum's thin, bony arms cradled the long wooden pole as he swung it at Cam's head.

"Cam, watch out!" North and Nash, two more of Gavin's friends and clansmembers who were twins, but not identical, blocked Old Callum's swing with their broad bodies and muscle-bound arms.

"What?" Cam looked at the girl in his arms and then back up at the old man. "I didna ken who she was."

Aidan MacKeefe, known as one of the three madmen of the clan, saw what happened and rushed over to protect his sister-by-marriage.

"Keep yer hands off of Coira, ye fool," shouted Aidan, drawing his sword, also well in his cups. "I might have to teach ye a lesson by removin' that hand from yer body so ye willna try somethin' like that again," Aidan threatened him.

"I'm sorry," said Cam, lifting his hands in the air. "I didna ken."

"Aidan, Coira is fine," spat Aidan's wife, Effie. "Leave Cam alone. He is drunk just the same as ye, but one of yer own clan."

"Dinna let it happen again," warned Aidan, slowly slipping his sword back into the scabbard.

"Come on, Sister," said Effie, taking Coira's hand. The three of them headed away to the other end of the room.

"I dinna need this kind of trouble in my tavern," spat Callum, once again swinging the breadboard at Cam.

Nash grabbed the long paddle and held it up high over his head causing Callum to jump to try to reach it. The men all laughed at the amusing sight.

"North, grab that bottle of Mountain Magic for me so I can refill my goblet, will ye?" Gavin peered down into his empty cup. Then he brought a fist to his chest with a loud thump, letting out a long belch. "I'm mighty thirsty."

Callum scrunched up his face and glared at Gavin. "No doubt ye are thirsty, since ye ate every one of my pickled eggs! No' to mention ye followed them down with the last of my salted herrin'. Gavin MacKeefe, ye are naught but a glutton, eatin' and drinkin' me right out of business! Ye are goin' to pay for this, I swear."

"Pay?" North questioned, reaching around the old man to grab a bottle of whisky off the drink board behind him. He spied an ornate silver goblet and snatched that up as well. "We're part of the MacKeefe Clan, Callum," he said with a large smile. "We're family. We're heroes. Besides, we always eat and drink for free!" He inspected the goblet closer, liking what he saw. Gavin recognized North's perusal of the expensive object. It meant he wanted to keep it, just like he wanted everything else. The man was so greedy sometimes. He also envied anyone who had something that he did not.

"Give me that whisky! And put down that goblet. It's no' to be touched." Callum reached out for the items, but North jerked them upward to keep the small man from getting them. In doing so, he stumbled backwards into his twin brother who was still holding the wooden paddle above his head, looking like he wasn't sure what to do with it. Having already had too much Mountain Magic, both of the men swayed back and forth unsteadily. When Nash turned around, the paddle dipped down dangerously, hitting a wall sconce. There was crust of bread stuck to the end of the paddle and it quickly caught the flame. Nash didn't notice. When he lifted it back up again, it hit the thatched ceiling of the tavern, causing part of the roof to catch on fire.

Old Callum's eyes opened wide now, and he shouted at the top of his feeble voice. "Fire! Fire! Someone get water, quick. My tavern's on fire!"

The tavern was crowded with clansmen and even common-ers filling every table. Gavin had been watching a few questionable men from across the room all night long. They kept hanging around, circling like vultures. He didn't trust them in the least. They were either looking for a fight, or deciding what to steal.

"Everyone out!" yelled Gavin, pushing up from his chair. "Someone, hand me a bucket of water. Quick."

"I'll get it," called out Nash, throwing down the paddle and running back to the drink board. A large bucket of water sat waiting for just such emergencies.

North leaned against the drink board while he poured some whisky into the silver goblet. Then he lazily lifted the cup to his mouth, swallowing down the golden liquid. A smile pursed the corners of his lips, and he let out a deep, satisfied sigh.

"It's amazin' how much better the whisky tastes out of this cup." North turned the goblet around and around in his hand, inspecting the embedded gemstones and etchings closely and curiously. It was a very expensive piece. A tavern is the last place it should be. "I've always wanted a silver goblet." He breathed on it, wiping the cup with his sleeve, admiring the piece, not even concerned about the fire. "Perhaps this would be safer with me."

Callum ran around like a crazy man while all of the patrons screamed and stampeded for the door. Chairs and tables were knocked over and the sound of shattering glass filled the air.

"Stop it! Nay. Ye're breakin' everythin'," cried Callum, waving his arms above his head in a frantic manner. "Ye are wreckin' my tavern!"

"Callum, calm down," said Cam, always the voice of reason. "Things can be replaced. These people are just tryin' to save their bluidy necks."

Gavin climbed atop the table, taking a moment to steady himself. It was hot up there and hard to breathe. Still, it was only a small fire on one isolated section. If he moved quickly, he was sure he could put it out before things got out of control.

"Hurry with that water," commanded Gavin, noticing the seedy-looking men hovering around the door now, but doing nothing to help. He was sure he'd seen them somewhere before, but couldn't remember where. He was having trouble thinking and seeing straight at the moment.

"Here ye go." Nash handed Gavin a bucket of water, then bent down and picked up the wooden paddle again. "Ye ken, I can put out the fire without usin' water," boasted Nash. "Let me show ye how to do it. After all, I'm better at things like this than ye are."

It was probably not a good idea to be up on the table when Gavin had drank more of the potent whisky than he should have. He liked his food and drink, and never had the will to stop before he'd consumed too much.

"Get out of my way," Gavin mumbled under his breath, tossing water from the bucket up at the ceiling. When he did so, he didn't realize that Callum was standing right underneath. The water hit the ceiling and crashed down on Callum, soaking his clothes and feet.

"Ye simpkin!" screamed Callum, holding up one foot, looking madder than an angry hornet. Gavin lost his balance and fell from the table atop the old man.

"I've got it, dinna worry," called out Nash, wanting to prove his worth. He poked at the ceiling, causing the thatched part that was on fire to fall to the floor. "North, hurry. Get some more water and put out the flames on the floor."

North took one more drink of whisky, reluctantly putting the silver goblet down on the drink board before running over and picking up another bucket of water. Fires weren't uncommon, especially in taverns. All the lit candles around drunks were dangerous enough that water buckets were placed in every corner for just such emergencies.

Cam came running from the kitchen with several towels next. He beat at the flames as North tossed more water on the fire, causing a puff of smoke to rise up in the air.

"Ian! Ian!" cried Callum from underneath Gavin's large body. "Ian, stop this madness. These fools are tryin' to kill me." He called for his son, Ian MacKeefe, who was the chieftain of the clan. Actually, since the clan had land in the Highlands, as well as claimed a castle in the Lowlands, there were two chieftains, not just one. Ian, and his son, Storm MacKeefe, took turns leading the clan in one or the other of their locations. Ian came running from above stairs, making his way over to them.

"What in the devil's name is goin' on down here?" growled Ian, bending down and pulling his elderly father up off the floor.

Gavin flipped over, lying on his back now, staring at the burned hole in the ceiling. He felt like hell. His head pounded and the room spun as he looked into the angry eyes of their clan chieftain staring down at him. The room was filling with smoke and he started to feel really sick. Men ran around opening the door and windows to air the place out.

"No worries, Chieftain," said Gavin, flipping over onto his stomach, feeling the bile rise in his throat. "We put out the fire. Everythin's under control." No longer able to stomach all the food he'd eaten and the whisky he'd drank, he leaned over, feeling it making its way back up . . . and out. Unfortunately, it all landed on Callum's feet.

"Sorry about that," Gavin mumbled, wiping his mouth with the back of his hand.

"Look at my boots," screamed Callum. "And my roof and my tavern." The old man's eyes bugged out and he looked crazed. Gavin wasn't sure he wouldn't come after him with a knife next.

"Ye men should be ashamed of yerselves," scoffed Ian, trying to console his father at the same time.

"We didna mean for any of this to happen," spoke up North. "We were just havin' a little celebration and a wee dram of Mountain Magic, that's all." He patted his chest, then look down at the floor, turning in a circle. "Where's that silver goblet?" he asked.

"Ye fool. Ye lost Storm's goblet that was gifted to him from the king," spat Callum, his face getting even redder and his eyes turning to slits now.

"Losh me. Was that really Storm's goblet? Ooops." North

continued to look around the floor. "Well, I'm sure I left it here somewhere."

"The thieves must have taken it," groaned Gavin, lying back down on the dirty, wet, burned rushes.

"That's it. I've had enough," ground out Callum. "Ian, lock these drunken fools away in the dungeon of Hermitage Castle. It is where they belong. At least there, they canna cause any trouble. Lock them up, I say. Every single one of them."

"Lock us away?" asked Cam with a snort. "Whatever for? We no' only saved the livestock from reivers, but made a new alliance and also put out a fire tonight. Callum, we just saved yer bluidy tavern."

"Ye caused the fire in the first place, in case ye've forgotten," sniffed Callum, crossing his bony arms over his chest.

"Ye boys are drunk," said Ian. "Ye need to sleep it off. Ye're upsettin' my faither."

"Mayhap we are drunk," agreed Nash. "But it's no' our fault. Callum's Mountain Magic is just too potent."

"Bein' well in our cups isna a crime," added his brother, North.

"Ye are all guilty of breakin' the rules." Callum glared at them intensely.

"Rules?" asked Gavin from the floor. "What rules?"

"My faither has his important rules of the tavern that canna be broken," explained Ian. "Ye boys are MacKeefes. Ye should ken about them."

"Och, those silly rules." Cam waved his hand through the air. "What are they again?" He looked over at the twins and they just shrugged.

Gavin did remember something about this but, for the life of him, he couldn't remember the details at all. They all thought those silly rules made up by the old crazy man were naught but an ill jest.

"What rules, ye ask?" Callum's face scrunched up and he spun on his heel and hobbled back to the drink board at a near run.

Then he reached up and pulled down a shade that was attached to the back of the kitchen door. There, written on the parchment were a bunch of rules with numbers besides them." "These rules," he snapped, hitting the parchment with his open palm.

"Ye ken, no one ever paid any attention to those," said North, picking up an overturned chair and sitting on it. He proceeded to put his feet up on the table, leaning back with his hands behind his head.

"I wouldna do that if I were ye," Ian mumbled under his breath.

"No feet on the tables . . . rule number two!" Callum picked up a long wooden spoon and slapped it against the list of rules.

"What? Really?" North laughed, but then shut up when he realized the man was serious. He slowly slid his feet off the table.

"Ye, North MacKeefe are also responsible for stealin' and losin' my grandson's silver goblet," continued Callum.

"That was an accident," protested North. "And I was only . . . borrowin' it."

"Well, ye broke rule number five." Callum thunked the spoon lower on the list. "No one touches or drinks from Storm MacKeefe's silver goblet, given to him by the king."

"Bid the devil, North," said Gavin with a deep chuckle. "Ye stepped into a real mare's nest breakin' rules number two and five both. That's a true crime." He chuckled, finding the situation amusing.

Nash and Cam laughed along with him.

Gavin moaned and flipped over on his back, covering his eyes with his arm, still lying on the floor.

"Dinna laugh, Gavin MacKeefe," came Callum's crackly old voice. "Ye are responsible for breakin' my number one rule."

"Me? Really?" Gavin slid his arm off his face and lifted his head slightly. "What is number one on the list?" His eyes flashed over to his friends and then back to Callum.

"Ye wasted my precious Mountain Magic," Callum informed him.

"Nay, I didna," Gavin protested, shaking his head and lifting a finger in the air. "I may have drank a little more than my share, but I assure ye it wasna wasted."

"Really?" Callum looked down and held up one foot, pointing out the fact that a lot of that Mountain Magic was wasted when it came back up and landed on his boots, thanks to Gavin retching on him. "Rule number seven is that no one is allowed to vomit, urinate, or defecate inside the tavern walls."

"That wasna done on purpose," Gavin told him in his defense. "I couldna help it."

"If ye hadna been such a glutton, it wouldna have happened at all," answered Callum. "And neither would ye have soiled my boots. Look at them. They're ruined."

"They're no' ruined, Callum. Just clean them. Besides, dirtyin' yer boots isna a rule," mumbled Gavin.

"Nash, come here," instructed Callum.

"Me?" Nash's eyes darted back and forth. "What for?" He seemed like he was starting to get a wee bit worried.

"I want ye to read rule number nine to Gavin."

"Och, is that all?" A sense of relief washed over Nash's face and he headed across the floor. Once in front of the list, he bent over and read it aloud.

"Rule number nine," he said, seeming much too smug in Gavin's opinion. "It says right here, my friend, that no one is to ever step on or soil Callum's Cordovan leather boots."

"It does no'," spat Gavin, finally getting up to see for himself. Nash and Cam bellowed with laughter. Sure enough, when Gavin read rule number nine, he realized that it wasn't a jest, after all.

"Damn it," he swore, not believing his ill luck.

"What are ye two fools laughin' for?" asked Callum, sneering at Nash and Cam.

"What do ye mean? Dinna look at us," said Cam. "We didna break any rules." He slapped his palm to his chest.

"Like hell, ye didna." Callum poked at the list again with the end of the wooden spoon. "Right here, rule number three. No touchin' or pinchin' or kissin' the lassies unless they are whores."

"Now wait a minute. That's no' fair," complained Cam. "I didna remember who that lass was. After all, Coira is new to the clan. I canna remember everythin'." Cam lifted his palms in surrender.

"Ye didna really do that, did ye?" mumbled Ian, shaking his head and closing his eyes.

"Aye, he did," said Nash, only making matters worse and getting a nasty glance from Cam. Nash started coughing from laughing so much. He cleared phlegm from his throat, and spat it in the rushes on the floor.

Callum's eyes followed and Gavin knew it wasn't going to be good. The old man took one bony finger, running it down the list. Then he stabbed at something written near the top of the list and the bottom of the list as well.

"Uh oh," said North, as they waited for the next accusation.

"Rule number six is no spittin', which ye just broke." Callum lifted a brow.

"What? Everyone spits," said Nash, looking very nervous. "Right?" he added softly.

"And ye also broke rule number four," stated Callum.

"I didna kiss any lassies," protested Nash, shaking his head.

"That's rule number three, ye fool," grumbled Cam. "I should ken."

"No one is to damage anythin' inside my tavern," explained Callum.

"I didna," squeaked Nash.

"What's that?" Callum pointed at the piece of burned thatch from the ceiling, now lying on the ground still smoldering.

"I put out the fire," said Nash, looking confused.

"Ye took a good chunk out of my roof with yer pride and paddle," stated Callum.

"Aye, but he did it only to put out the fire, and save the tavern from burnin' to the ground," said North, coming to his twin brother's rescue.

"Blethers, Callum," said Nash, shaking his head. "Isna that what the entry fee is for? To pay for damages that might occur?"

"Ye boys dinna pay entry fees, if I must remind ye." Callum was not going to back down. The old man had more spunk than all of them put together. "Plus, ye all drank so much that I'm sure I'm goin' to be broke after repairs."

"Now, Callum . . . really? After all, we're part of the clan," said Gavin. "Werena ye the one who said clansmembers are like family and dinna have to pay entry fees, or pay for food or drinks?"

"It doesna matter." Callum angrily yanked on the shade and released it. It snapped up with a twang, flipping around in a circle. "Ian, they broke the rules and they need to be punished. They are now outcasts of the MacKeefe Clan."

"Outcasts?" all four men said at once.

"Ian, please," begged Nash.

"That's right, boys," agreed Ian with a nod. "Ye will all have to find retribution by carryin' out a mission of Callum's choice. Only then will ye be allowed back into the clan."

"That's no' fair," wallowed North. "We were only cele-bratin'."

"Lock them up until I decide their punishment," ordered Callum with a satisfied nod.

"Ian, ye are chieftain, no' Callum," said Cam. "Dinna let him tell ye what to do."

"Aye, I am chieftain," agreed Ian. "But ye all ken that if it wasna for my da, the clan would be broke. This tavern brings in most of our clan's income. I made a deal with my da that if the proceeds from his Mountain Magic went to the clan, I would honor his wishes where his tavern is concerned."

"Oh, hell, just let me make the Mountain Magic and we willna need him," spat Nash. "I willna abide by any doitit rules."

"Ye canna make it," Gavin reminded him. "No one can but Callum. He is the only one who kens how to brew it, and he's never told a soul."

"That's right. Now, on yer feet and to the door," said Ian, looking very pale. He wiped his brow with the back of his hand and let out a sigh.

"What? Where are ye takin' us? I dinna want to leave," complained Cam.

"Ye heard my da." Ian leaned an elbow on the drink board, looking ill. Gavin hadn't seen much of him lately and he wondered if the man was keeping up appearances, but was really ailing from something. "Ye boys will be locked up for now so ye dinna cause any more trouble."

"Locked up?" North looked over his shoulder as Callum directed him to the door. "Ye're no' really goin' to imprison us, Chieftain, are ye? No' in the dungeon of our own castle. That's unthinkable."

"I have no other choice," said Ian in a soft voice, following them to the door. "I am a man of my word. Now, get movin'."

"Where's Storm?" asked Gavin, knowing that Ian's son who was also chieftain wouldn't let this happen to them. Storm was fair and also their friend. "Storm will put a stop to this absurd nonsense. We want to see him right now."

"Ye'll see him soon enough," said Ian. "My son is on an errand for me but will be back at Hermitage Castle in three days' time. Now, I suggest ye get movin'. My guards will escort ye there."

"Three days?" whined North. "Ye're no' goin' to really leave us in that nasty dungeon that long, are ye?"

"When Storm returns, he and I will talk with Callum and yer missions for retribution will be decided," explained Ian. "Now, I'll no' hear another word about it."

Gavin's head spun and he felt like retching again. From heroes to outcasts just that fast, now he and his friends were nothing more than prisoners of their own clan. The worst part about all this was that an old crazy man would decide their fates. Gavin had no doubt that whatever punishments the old coot thought up – he and his friends were doomed.

━━━◆·◦◇◦·◆━━━

CHAPTER TWO

"**O**PEN THE BLUIDY cell door and let us out," shouted Gavin, his deep voice echoing off the cold, stone walls of the dungeon of Hermitage Castle. His long fingers wrapped around the rusty iron bars and he shook the locked door with angry fists. If his teeth hadn't been clenched, he was sure they would have rattled in his head from the jolting movement.

"It's no use, Gavin, give it up," complained his good friend, Cam, sitting on the dirty floor with his back propped up against the wall. The dungeon was attached to catacombs that snaked around underground, with tunnels leading deep and far, and even all the way to the other side of the border. It was a nasty place, and feared by all.

Cam pulled his blond hair back into a queue, tying it with a leather band. Next, he pulled off one boot and rubbed his foot. Spotting a rat sneaking through the bars, he quickly hurled his boot at it. Missing the rat, the boot ended up hitting North instead.

"Och, what was that for, ye fool?" North rubbed his knee. "I'm no' the one makin' all the ruckus. Ye should have thrown it at Gavin instead."

"Arrrrg!" bellowed Gavin, kicking at the locked door of the cell, and then cursing. "We've got to make noise if we're ever goin' to get out of here. We've been locked up for three days now. This is insane."

"Ye heard Ian tell us that they are waitin' for Storm to return." Nash stood in the shadows. He used an object to clean under his nails. "By the way, I agree with Cam, Gavin. Ye're makin' so much noise ye're goin' to wake the dead." He cleaned off the object against his green and purple plaid – the colors that depicted they were from the MacKeefe Clan.

"We've got to get out of here." Gavin paced back and forth like a caged lion. "It's just no' right that we've been imprisoned in our own castle when we really didna do anythin' wrong. We are heroes, no' outcasts!"

"I agree," remarked Cam from the floor. "However, we're in here, and that crazy old man is out there, decidin' our fates."

Clan MacKeefe was from the Highlands. They had a camp in the Grampian Mountains near Oban. However, they also had holdings in the Lowlands, near the border. Years ago, they managed to secure Hermitage Castle, taking it back from the English. That's where they were now.

"There's nothin' we can do about it until Storm returns," continued Cam with a yawn, crossing his arms over his chest. "Ye ken we'll rot here until Callum cools off."

"Aye," agreed North, rubbing a weary hand through his long brown hair. He and Nash looked very similar, but were not identical twins. They both had long brown hair, but Nash was a little shorter, and his face was more rounded than North's. Nash's eyes were also hazel, while North's were silver. Their mannerisms were quite different as well. "I now regret drinkin' so much of Old Callum's Mountain Magic. If I had kent he was goin' to shove his silly rules in our faces, I never would have done it."

"Me, too," agreed Nash. "But Callum has never done anythin' like this before," he pointed out. He continued to clean his nails.

"I think he's been upset about somethin' lately," said North.

"He does seem more ornery than usual." Cam nodded in agreement.

"I think our chieftain, Ian, is ailin'," said Gavin. "He looked ill and in pain to me."

"That would make sense," said Nash with a nod. "Callum is worried about his son."

Gavin stopped in his tracks and looked over at Nash, surveying what he was doing. "What's that?" he asked.

"I said that would make sense."

"Nay! I mean . . . what's that in yer hand, Nash?" Gavin couldn't believe his eyes. He hurried over to him and gripped Nash's wrist, holding it up for the others to see. "I dinna believe it." A dirk reflected in the dim glow from the light of the torch burning outside the cell. Gavin's jaw ticked in aggravation and he tried not to explode. "Ye have a bluidy dirk," he said through his teeth. "Ye've had it all along."

"Aye," Nash answered. "It's the one I always hide in my boot. Ye ken that."

"He has a dirk?" asked North from the front of the cell.

"Aye, he has a dirk," Gavin repeated, his fingers gripping tighter around his friend's wrist now. "Yet, he didna think to mention it to us three days ago."

"What?" This news actually got Cam off his arse. He jumped up and headed over to them.

North watched from over by the door. "Brathair, we could have used yer blade to pick the lock and get the hell out of here by now. I canna believe they missed yer blade when they removed all of our weapons before throwin' us in here."

"Leave me alone. All of ye." Nash pushed Gavin, and pulled his hand back, still clenching the small blade. "It doesna matter. We're outcasts now with nowhere to go. If we had used it, we'd be on the run for the rest of our lives." Nash bent over to replace the dirk in his boot. But before he could stand back up, Gavin tackled him and brought him to the ground, punching Nash in the face.

"Blethers, Gavin, ye're goin' to hurt my brathair." North dove atop the pile, struggling with both of them. A sea of green and purple plaid got tangled around their legs as they rolled over and over in a heated struggle, fighting for the blade.

"Stop it," said Cam, but of course they didn't listen. So, Cam put his fingers in his mouth and whistled loudly to get their attention.

"What is it?" growled Gavin, looking over his shoulder, but continuing to fight. His long, black hair fell over his eyes. With a shake of his head, he flipped it back over his shoulder.

"Fightin' isna goin' to get us out of here," stated Cam, not even getting excited. Sometimes, Cam was a little too calm and Gavin didn't think it was normal for a Highlander to act this way. "I hate to say it, but Nash is right. That dirk is of no use to us in our situation."

"Then mayhap I'll use it to slit the fool's throat instead," shouted Gavin, his anger out of control now. Never would any of them intentionally hurt each other, but three days in the bowels of the castle with very little to eat or drink was making Gavin insane. His stomach growled, and his mouth was so dry that he could barely swallow. God, he needed whisky.

"Get up, all of ye," a low voice split the air. They all turned their attention to the cell door, not even having heard anyone approach since they were so busy fighting each other.

"Storm!" cried Gavin, jumping to his feet. "We're more than happy to see ye."

"Finally. Get us out of here," added North.

"Callum is playin' silly games and yer da is goin' along with it," explained Cam.

Their other chieftain and laird, Storm MacKeefe, stood outside the cell with one of his guards. He, at one time, had long, bright blond hair, but through the years it had slowly started to show signs of gray. "Unlock it," he commanded with a nod, and the guard did as ordered.

"Guid. Ye're lettin' us out." Gavin was the first one to the door.

"No' so fast." Storm held up his palm and stepped into the cell, stopping in the doorway to keep any of them from exiting. "I ken ye four dinna feel ye deserve to be here and, honestly, I have to agree."

"Then what's the problem?" asked Cam anxiously. "Let us go."

"I canna do that," said Storm, pressing his lips together and shaking his head. He genuinely looked sorry.

"Why no'?" asked Nash. "Ye're our laird as well as Ian. Besides, ye're our friend."

"I am, but I am also outvoted two to one by my da and grandda."

"Callum isna our chieftain. He has naught to say in the matter." Gavin was adamant about this.

"Actually, he does," said Storm with a shrug of his shoulders. "Ye see, he is the decidin' vote whenever my da and I disagree on somethin'."

"This is crazy." Nash slapped the wall. "This has never happened to any of our other clansmembers. Why us? Why now?"

"Leave us," Storm said to the guard with a nod of his head. Once the guard left, Storm moved further into the cell to talk to them quietly so as not to be overheard. "I didna want anyone in the clan to hear this, but my da hasna been feelin' well lately."

"He's no'?" asked North.

"I thought so. How bad is it?" asked Gavin.

Storm shook his head. "It's no' guid, I'm afraid to say. He's seen several healers, and even the old gypsy, Zara, but none of them can seem to help him. He grows weaker every day, and some days it seems he forgets he is the leader of this clan. All he wants to do is sleep and rest. My mathair has been worryin' so much that I'm afraid her health might be sufferin' next."

"Och, we had no idea," said Nash. The moods of the men in the cell suddenly became sullen.

"I've made him a promise to keep things in order in case of his death," Storm explained.

"Death?" gasped Nash. "Is Ian really dyin'?"

"We dinna ken," Storm answered. "Ye see, no one can figure out exactly what is wrong with him. Anyway, I didna want to worry him further, so I agreed to do anythin' I can to ease his mind and lift his spirits. My poor mathair tries to hide it from me, but she cries all the time."

"So keepin' Old Callum happy is the way to ensure some peace for Ian and Clarista both," said Gavin, seeing where Storm was going with this.

"I'm sorry, boys. Just bear with it. I am doin' everythin' I can to help ye. I've had a talk with both my da and grandda. If ye each complete a mission of Callum's choice, ye'll be happily welcomed back into the clan."

"Damn it, Storm," spat Gavin, hitting the bars of the cell, making them rattle. "This isna fair and ye ken it."

"They're just makin' an example out of us, and I dinna like it," Cam agreed with Gavin.

"Please, just do it and dinna cause trouble," said Storm. "It will be over soon. It will also be the best thing for ye, as well as for the rest of the clan," explained Storm. "We dinna want to do anythin' to upset my da further."

"Ye mean Callum," scoffed North, looking the other way.

"What is it we have to do?" asked Nash curiously.

"If Callum is decidin' our fates, there is no doubt it will be somethin' stupid," spat Cam.

"Now, that's no' fair either," said Storm with a scolding look.

"Sorry," grumbled Cam. "I just want out of here."

"We all do," said Gavin. "Storm, can ye at least assure us that whatever Callum decides as our punishments, it willna be too . . . too humiliatin'?"

"Aye," agreed Nash. "After all, everyone just started to see us as heroes."

"Well, we wouldna want to ruin that reputation now, would we?" asked Storm with a chuckle. Storm MacKeefe was a legend throughout the land, and he was used to being a hero. Gavin wasn't sure he understood how they felt. "I'll do my best," said Storm. "Now, let's go up to the great hall where I will start the trial."

"Trial?" Gavin's head snapped up. "Ye canna be serious. We're bein' tried for spittin' and drinkin' too much whisky?"

"Aye. We didna commit any real crimes," added Nash. "We didna even kill any of the MacGregors."

"Dinna worry, I'll take care of everythin'," Storm assured them. "My da just wants all to go smoothly, so that is what we'll do. Between ye and me, I think he just wants to instill fear into the rest of the clan. Then, once he's gone – if he dies, no one will even think to cause trouble."

"Do ye really think Ian is goin' to die?" asked Nash once again.

"I hope no'," Storm answered.

"Does anyone else think it's odd that Ian is the one dyin' when Callum should have been dead long ago?" Cam scratched at the stubble on his cheek and looked the other direction.

"Ye ken the old man is goin' to live forever." North added his thoughts to the conversation.

"Dinna forget, that is my grandda ye boys are talkin' about," Storm said, stopping their idle chatter.

"He's right. Let's go." Gavin pushed past Storm and led the way out of the cell. "I just want this done and over with so I can get somethin' to eat and drink."

ONCE UP IN the great hall, Gavin and his friends lined up in front of Storm who sat on his dais chair, ready to try them. His father sat on one side of him, and his wife, Lady Wren, on the other. Old Callum stood over to the side with a rolled-up parchment under his arm. Gavin recognized it as his silly list of rules from the tavern.

The hall was filled with members from their clan, all wanting to know just what was going on. Hushed conversations amongst them told Gavin that they were as confused about this whole thing as he was.

"We'll get started," said Storm, holding up his arm to quiet everyone.

After a small speech announcing what the men were guilty of, Callum made a big show of unrolling the parchment by dropping one end to the ground.

"Here's the list of rules of the Horn and Hoof Tavern," said Callum, holding it up above his head, while the other end touched his feet. "These four boys have broken almost every one of my rules."

"That's what they're bein' tried for?" someone called out.

"That's absurd," said someone else.

"Quiet!" shouted Storm, getting up out of his chair. He looked over to his father, and then back to the crowd. Ian sat quiet with his face turned downward. Gavin noticed that he'd lost weight. He also seemed dazed or confused. Gavin wasn't even sure the man was listening. "Men, how do ye plead to the charges that are brought up against ye?" asked Storm.

Gavin glanced over to his friends. Each of them was looking at the ground, not saying a word. Then he looked back over at Ian, wondering what would happen to the clan if their chieftain died. The crowd behind him grew louder. Now he could see why they were doing this to them, even if he still didn't agree with it. If Gavin and his friends denied these charges, it could get ugly with the boisterous crowd. They were being used as examples, and it was important that Gavin and his friends showed their leaders respect.

"Guilty," Gavin called out, causing his three friends to look over in utter confusion. He nodded to them, and then spoke under his breath. "Remember what Storm told us," he said. "Let's be a good example for the rest of the clan."

Cam let out a breath and spoke next. "Guilty, my laird."

This was followed by North and Nash saying they were guilty as well.

The crowd suddenly became quiet.

"All right then," said Storm, nodding at his grandfather. "Grandda, do ye want me to tell them yer decisions?"

"Aye," said the old man, struggling to roll up his list of rules.

"Gavin, ye are sentenced to spend time in the village, helpin' the cordwainer," announced Storm.

"What?" Gavin almost laughed aloud, thinking how ridiculous this sounded.

"Ye're goin' to help make me a new pair of boots." When Callum pointed to his feet, Gavin realized for the first time that he was barefooted.

"But yer boots can be cleaned and repaired," stated Gavin.

"I dinna care. I said I want a new pair of Cordovan boots. Do ye hear me?"

"All right," said Gavin, not sure how to answer. "However, my laird, I dinna ken how to make shoes. I only ken how to fight."

"Ye'll be taught," Storm assured him. "There has been trouble between the cobblers and the cordwainers lately. The cordwainer's daughter has asked for our help."

"Och," said Gavin with a smile, thinking he'd have the chance to spend time with a bonnie lassie. "All right, then." He looked over at his friends and smiled. "That's no' so bad," he whispered.

Callum cleared his throat and Gavin turned back. The old man wasn't finished yet.

"The cordwainer's daughter, in return for our help, has agreed to keep ye away from the tavern, and from havin' even a drop of whisky while ye're there," added Callum.

"Now wait a minute." Gavin was becoming very concerned with this statement. "No whisky? At all?"

"Ye heard me," spat Callum. "No' a drop."

"Nay. I dinna like this." This took Gavin by surprise. He heard his friends chuckling softly from next to him.

"Ye heard my grandda's decision," said Storm. "It is final."

"Well, how long will I be there?" questioned Gavin, knowing his protesting wouldn't do a thing to stop this now. He could only hope he wouldn't be there long at all.

"I'm no' sure," said Storm. "It could be a sennight, or mayhap a fortnight or more. It all depends on how long it takes ye to stop the trouble between the guilds, and also to make my grandda a new pair of Cordovan leather boots."

Gavin groaned. "So now I need to settle a dispute between shoemakers as well? That could take forever. Besides, how do I ken they'll even listen to me? I'm just one man."

His friends looked way too amused, and this truly bothered Gavin. Instead of enjoying this, they should be supporting him right now.

"Ye're right," said Storm. "Therefore, yer friends will go with ye. There is power in numbers." This shut up the other three men quickly. None of them understood what was going on. Finally, Cam spoke up.

"But this isna our sentence, it is Gavin's," he reminded their laird.

Storm called Callum over to him. With Ian, they discussed something between the three of them in muffled voices. Then Storm finally looked up.

"Cam, Nash, and North, we've decided yer sentences willna be finalized until Gavin has completed his," Storm told them.

"Sounds good," said Cam with a smile and a nod. "I'm in no hurry."

"Well, guid luck makin' those shoes, Gavin," said Nash, still sounding much too happy.

"We'll save some Mountain Magic for yer return," added Nash's brother.

"Fine. Let's just get this over with," complained Gavin. "When do I leave?"

"First thing in the mornin'," Storm told him. "All four of ye will be goin'."

The laughter stopped.

"But ye said our punishments will be decided later. After Gavin is finished with his," Nash reminded him.

"That's right," said Storm. "However, I think ye boys misunderstood me."

"I am no' goin' to the village. Forget it," North was furious about this.

"Me, neither," said Cam. "I'm stayin' right here to wait. Either that, or I'm goin' back to our Highland camp."

"Ye are all outcasts now," Storm reminded them. "Ye canna stay here, and neither can ye go to the MacKeefe camp until ye finish yer sentences and are invited back into the clan."

"No trouble. We'll stay out in nature then," said Cam.

"Right. I like sleepin' under the stars," added Nash.

"We can hunt for our own food," added North. "That's no' a problem."

"Nay. That's no' the way it works," Storm told them, shaking his head. "Ye three will go along with Gavin and stay somewhere in the village until his sentence is finished. If ye dinna like that decision, then ye will go back to the dungeon and stay there to wait for his return."

"That's right," came Callum's crackly old voice. He lifted his chin and made a sour-looking face.

"Well, what will it be, boys?" asked Ian, finally speaking up. "We need yer decision."

They all grumbled and then finally decided.

"I'm no' goin' back to the dungeon," said Nash.

"Me, neither," added his brother. "I dinna want to sleep with rats."

"Guid," said Storm. "And how about ye, Cam? What is yer decision?"

"Well, since there are no bonnie lassies in the dungeon, I guess I'll go to town as well."

"Then it's settled," said Storm. "Ye four will leave in the mornin'."

"All right. Then I have plenty of time yet today to get some food and whisky." Gavin's stomach growled as he spoke.

"Well, no' really," Storm answered. "There is somewhere

else ye need to be."

"Please. No' back to the dungeon," Gavin pleaded.

"Nay," answered Ian. "Ye will go about the castle collectin' all the shoes that need to be repaired. Then ye and yer friends will pack them on the wagon and ye'll take them with ye to the cordwainer's shop on the morrow. Gavin, they'll all need to be repaired before yer sentence is complete."

"Ye want *me* to do it?" asked Gavin in disbelief. "I told ye, I dinna ken how to fix shoes."

"Then ye'll need to learn," Storm told him. "Now get movin'."

"You can start with the garrison and then the servants' quarters," spoke up Lady Wren. "And then please stop in the ladies' solar when you've finished." Lady Wren was English and noble. She had a way about her that when she spoke, one listened and did not argue with her.

"Aye," said Gavin. "Thank ye, Lady Wren."

"Go now and start collectin' the shoes," said Storm. "Hopefully, ye'll have all of them ready to go by mornin'."

"When can I get the shoes from the cooks?" mumbled Gavin, turning away, wanting nothing more than to stop by the kitchen first. His stomach growled once more and all he could think about was how badly he needed some food and drink.

━━━◆·◦◇◦·◆━━━

CHAPTER THREE

D AVITA, DAUGHTER OF the town's cordwainer, pushed the needle through the tawed leather of the turn welt shoe. Sniffing and wiping her eye with the back of her hand, she tried her hardest to hold back her tears. Her mind wasn't on her work. All she could think about was her poor father. Her eyes darted over to the window at the front of the shop as she once again checked, but still didn't see the man that the castle said they were sending to help her in her time of great need.

It bothered her that he wasn't here yet. It was already midday. Hermitage Castle was held by the MacKeefe Clan, so she knew they'd be sending one of their Highlanders. She just hoped it wasn't one of the wild and crazy ones, since the clan seemed to have a lot of those!

Her thoughts drifted in distraction, making her careless. When she took another stitch to repair the loose leather separating from the sides of the shoe, she accidentally pricked her finger.

"Ouch! God's eyes," she cried out, feeling the pain. The action ended up drawing blood. Lifting the tip of her finger to her mouth, the taste of tangy iron on her tongue soured her senses and caused her body to tense. Immediately, it brought back memories of the horrible image of two days earlier.

When her father hadn't returned to their cordwainer's shop by nightfall, she'd gone out looking for him. After searching for hours, she finally found him beaten and unconscious, having been left for dead in a ditch. He'd been covered in blood from head to toe. The horrific image was still embedded in her mind, and would probably be for the rest of her life. Davita sewed him up, much like she was doing now with the shoe she repaired.

"Daughter, are ye cursin'? Ye ken I dinna like it when ye do that," came the weak voice of her father from the back room where he lay like an invalid upon his pallet.

"Sorry, Da," she apologized, now wishing she had bit her tongue and stayed quiet instead. She didn't want to do anything to upset her poor father after what he'd been through.

"What happened?" came his gruff voice.

The man was devoted to his work, even more so since the death of Davita's mother three years ago. His despair was only muted by keeping his hands and mind busy at all times. He never liked sitting still. She was sure it was driving him mad having to stay in bed right now. Although he was hurt and weak, it was crucial that he stay put and rest so he wouldn't risk breaking his stitches. His ankle was also broken and the bones needed healing. Since they had no healer in town at the moment, she'd had to set his ankle as well.

If she didn't assure him right away that she hadn't been harmed, he'd hobble off the pallet and make his way to the workroom at the front of the shop, wanting to help her. He'd already attempted to do it more than once in the past two days, not caring that he had his arm in a sling and his lower leg and foot wrapped in boards and cloth bindings.

"I'm fine, Da. Honest, I am," she called out, taking a deep breath and releasing it, trying to sound chipper instead of scared. Truth be told, she was very worried. Things were not going well with the business lately. They were way behind in their work, and many of the nobles had threatened to cancel their orders. Besides that, the town's cobbler and his apprentice had been giving them a hard time lately. The cobblers were only supposed to repair shoes, not construct new ones. Plus, they weren't allowed to use new leather. The cordwainers were in charge of making new shoes, with new leather. The problem was that the customers liked her better, and had been bringing their shoes to her to fix instead of taking them back to Clyde. They weren't happy with his work lately at all. She couldn't turn away these people, but in not doing so, she'd created trouble.

"I'm comin' out there, to make sure ye're all right," she heard her father mumble.

"Nay. Stay put. Ye need yer rest and shouldna be movin' about. I dinna want yer stitches breakin' open. Plus, yer broken bone needs to heal."

"Bah! I need to find those ruffians and make them pay for what they did to me," he told her, sounding like he was about to go off on a rampage, complaining. Or possibly even right out the front door. She wasn't sure how he thought he was going to find the culprits since it was dark when it happened, and he'd told her that he never even saw who jumped him.

Davita needed to stay strong – not only for her injured father but also for her younger siblings. Her sister, Aila, was two years younger than her. At sixteen years old, Aila already had eyes for the boys. She'd been spending a lot of her time outside the local tavern. Often, Aila showed more skin than she should, and was always altering her clothes trying to attract the attention of the opposite sex. What she didn't understand was that she was asking for trouble. Men who drank wanted the comfort of a whore. She needed to keep Aila away from the tavern. Her sister was proving to be a real handful, and her father was always too busy to even notice.

Archy, her nine-year-old brother, on the other hand, had a habit of stealing and was proud of it. They were not a wealthy family, and Archy decided if he wanted something and couldn't afford it, he'd just take it instead. It was becoming a real problem. Davita didn't know what to do about it. She didn't want to see him ending up on the gallows or perhaps being punished by having his hand cut off if he was caught. Davita worried night and day, and never had a good night's sleep anymore. She barely ever slept at all.

Thinking it best, Davita kept this information about her siblings from her father. He had taken to the bottle since her mother's death and didn't seem to care much what his children did. Davita was the closest one to him. Therefore, she felt it her duty to keep him from getting upset. He never accepted the death of his wife, and now with the turmoil that came with his own near death, things just kept getting worse.

If only she had more time, she might be able to keep her siblings from ending up as a whore and a thief. She might even be able to stop her father's drinking. If she didn't do something to help her family soon, they were all going to end up in a bad way. That is why she'd sent a message to the castle asking for help. She couldn't do this alone.

Her town was small and not really under the protection of the castle. Still, the MacKeefes aided them when they could. Davita had taken it upon herself to care for her family, but that left no time at all for her. She always felt tired and weary, and couldn't remember the last time she'd eaten a decent meal. When she did manage to drift off to sleep, she had nightmares and woke up screaming and in a cold sweat.

How much longer she could keep this up before she broke down?

"I just pricked my finger, that's all, Da," she told him, trying to keep her voice from wavering. "Please, just stay on the pallet. There is no need to get up. I am more than capable of carryin' on the business until ye recover."

"Where's my whisky?" he complained. "I need somethin' to drink."

"We canna afford it, Da," she told him, not wanting him to know that she'd hid every bottle and wasn't about to go out and get him more.

Her father did have a journeyman who used to help him. But last year, the man was thrown from his horse on one of his deliveries. He'd hit his head on a rock and died. Davita stepped in at that time, since she had always helped her father in the shop ever since she was a child. The art of shoemaking had always fascinated her. Through the years, she'd incorporated some creative touches on the shoes that the customers really seemed to like.

Davita was the one who was responsible for the ornate stitching of butterflies and flowers on the silk shoes of the nobles. It was also her idea to add fancy toggles to the boots, or to use colored thread instead of black or brown. It made their work more desirable. Plus, it was better than the customers just going to the cobbler's down the street.

"Ye didna remember to use the thimble, did ye?" he called out, sounding disappointed with her. "How many times do I have to remind ye? Use yer thimble."

"I have my thimble," she told him, searching the floor. Finally finding it, she plucked it up from atop the leather scraps. A knotted-up thread stuck to it and she blew it away.

"Davita, I hope ye were at least wearin' the thumb leather. Ye ken ye need to protect yer hands."

"Dinna worry," she called over her shoulder, snipping the thread and placing the large shears down on the worktable. She never covered her thumb with the strip of protective leather, because it was bulky and hard to complete intricate work with her thumb wrapped up. "Everythin' is fine," she told him once again, struggling with the shoe to pull it off the wooden last – the shoe form, shaped like a foot. After removing her work, she used a long wooden stick to turn the shoe right side out, therefore hiding the stitches and exposing the neater side that would be seen by all.

A bell jangled over the door, taking her attention. Quickly throwing down the shoe she'd been repairing, she jumped up to greet her customer.

Her body froze when she saw the cobbler, Clyde, and his apprentice, Gregor, standing in the doorway. They had both been giving her father a good amount of trouble lately. She highly expected that they might be the ones who even robbed and injured her father as well, but she couldn't prove it. Her stomach clenched. Being in such close quarters with these two questionable men was not to her liking.

"What do ye want?" she spat, crossing her arms over her chest, wishing them gone.

"Now, is that any way to greet a fellow tradesmen? We came to see yer faither," said Gregor, the younger of the two men who was still a good ten years older than her.

"Where is he, lass?" Clyde boldly walked in, picking up the shoe she'd been repairing, and inspecting it closely.

Davita's eyes flashed over to the door of the back room. She prayed her father wouldn't walk out now. She didn't want these men to see him in his condition, because she wasn't sure they knew how bad off he really was. She'd been trying to keep it a secret. "H-he's sleepin'," she told them. "If ye havena heard, he was beaten and left for dead in a ditch just three days ago."

"Really." Clyde looked up and smiled, showing broken, blackened teeth, making Davita want to retch. "Now, isna that a shame."

"Aye, such a shame," said Gregor, starting to laugh. Clyde shot him a nasty glare and Gregor cleared his throat and pretended to cough instead.

"This shoe looks like the one I repaired for the butcher's wife just last month," said Clyde, holding the shoe out for her to see.

"Mayhap it is. Why does it matter?" she asked.

"It seems odd that she'd come here instead of back to see me if there was a problem."

Davita didn't want him to know that she'd promised the butcher's wife fancy toggles and a small stitched rose on each toe if the woman provided them with some meat in exchange. She only did it to help her family and because they could barely afford food lately.

The woman heartily agreed, and Davita realized it wasn't just for fancy shoes, or to help her and her family. No, Clyde had been threatening the townsfolk to bring their shoes to him, and had even stolen several of her father's best customers lately by making up lies. "Mayhap if ye had fixed it right the first time, she wouldna have to seek me out," she snapped.

"Seek *ye* out?" Clyde raised a brow and looked over to his counterpart.

"I – I meant my faither." Davita's gaze dropped to the floor. She busied herself swishing around the discarded leather scraps with her toe. "Seek out my faither is what I meant to say."

"Of course ye did, lass." Clyde obviously did not believe her. "I can only say that I hope ye're no' the one doin' the cordwainer's work now that he's . . . incapacitated. I mean, after the death of his journeyman and all last year, he has been strugglin' to get his work finished on time."

"I didna think he could even work with a bottle of whisky clutched in one fist," added Gregor.

It pained Davita to listen to this but, deep down, she knew it was the truth. Her father had been slowing down and slipping for a long time now. Davita had been the one to pick up the slack and help him save face – and the business, before they lost it all.

"What difference would it make if I was helpin' him?" she asked. "We have orders to fill, and there is much work to be done here. It doesna matter who completes it."

"That's where ye're wrong," snapped Clyde.

"Ye're a lass, if we must remind ye." Gregor wiped his nose in his sleeve. "Ye ken the cordwainer's guild doesna allow a lassie to be doin' the work of a man."

"The cordwainer's guild allows a widow to take over her husband's business if he were to die, so I dinna see the difference," she told them.

"The difference is that ye are Graeme's daughter, no' his wife," said Clyde. "And Graeme is still alive. There are rules about these kinds of things." Davita noticed him smirking and wanted to slap the smile right off his face. He was enjoying taunting her, a little too much.

"That's right," said Gregor. "A man has to do the work, and if no', the business will be shut down."

Davita stood up to these men, not letting them intimidate her. "The guild's dues are supposed to go toward helpin' a family in need if the cordwainer should get sick or injured. I'm sure the guild will understand."

"Understand what?" asked Clyde. "That yer faither is a drunk and can no longer do his job? I hardly think they'll support that! If only they kent."

"Please, dinna tell them that. Ye two ken I dinna have a mathair. She's been dead for years now," said Davita, not knowing how to respond. "I have helped my family in every way I can. Ye have to understand this."

Gregor clucked his tongue. "Tsk, tsk, what a shame. And with yer faither's arm and leg broken, it looks like he willna be able to do his work after all for quite some time."

"It's only a sprained arm, and it's his ankle that is broken, not his leg."

"Ah, so that is what's wrong with him," said Clyde, making her wish she'd held her tongue. She didn't want to give these two any further information because they would just use it against her. "That's why we're here," Clyde continued. "To tell ye that we will be takin' care of all yer customers now, since yer da canna do it."

"Nay!" she cried, one of her worst nightmares coming true. "I willna let ye."

"It will only be until yer faither is healed, of course," Clyde tried to assure her, but she didn't believe him at all. She knew all these men wanted was to steal their customers and to put them out of business.

"This was yer plan all along, wasna it?" she retorted. "Ye are tryin' to steal all of my faither's business. Ye will never give the customers back, so dinna think I believe that ye will."

"Well, unless ye have a man who can make and repair the

shoes, I guess ye have no other choice but to send yer customers to us. That is, now that yer faither canna do the work," said Gregor, with no remorse at all in the tone of his words.

"I think mayhap we'll have to put a sign on the door. We'll alert the customers to come to our shop instead." Clyde tossed the shoe up and down. "What a shame for yer family, Davita. But dinna worry, lass. We'll tend to everythin', and fill the new shoe orders for the nobles as well."

"Ye'll do no such thing," she spat through gritted teeth, her body shaking now. "Both of ye, get out!" She snatched the shoe away from Clyde, holding it possessively to her chest. Through the window, she saw a wagon pull up with four burly Scotsmen inside. She breathed a sigh of relief. This had to be the help from the MacKeefe Clan that she'd requested. The corners of her mouth pursed upward, and a renewed sense of hope washed through her.

"Ye have no choice," growled Clyde.

"That is where ye're wrong," she told him, seeing one of the men heading toward the door. "Here comes the man now that I've hired to make and repair shoes in my faither's absence."

"What?" Clyde and Gregor both turned around to look as the bells atop the door jangled when it opened.

"Losh me! He's a stinkin' Highlander," spat Gregor.

"He kens nothin' about shoes," growled Clyde. "I doubt that the barbarian even wears them."

"The MacKeefe Highlander is a man, so that fulfills the obligation of the guild," Davita stated. "Besides, I will teach him everythin' he needs to learn." She felt much more confidant now than she did a few minutes ago. "So as ye see, I will have a man doin' the work and ye will no' get any of my faither's business, after all. Now go, before I have the Highlander throw ye out of here with brute force," she threatened. "And I assure ye, that willna be pretty."

The Highlander entered as Clyde and Gregor hurried to leave.

"Hullo?" The man stepped into the shop, his large body filling the small area. His face was in shadow. "I've been sent here by Laird MacKeefe to make shoes," he announced, causing Clyde and Gregor to stop in their tracks.

"Wait a minute. I recognize ye," said Clyde, craning his neck to see the man's face. "Ye're that Highlander that always comes to our tavern and gets so drunk that ye fall on yer arse on the way out the door."

"Aye, it's him, all right," agreed Gregor. "He's naught but a drunken fool." They both laughed and quickly left the shop.

"What was that all about?" asked the man as he turned back to face her. She could see his features clearly now as he stepped forward and the sunlight streamed in through the window. Long, black hair hung past his shoulders. He had a sculpted face, and a straight, strong nose. The most remarkable feature about him was his mesmerizing dark blue eyes. They reminded her of a midnight sky filled with stars.

His shoulders were wide, his chest sturdy. And his saffron leine was opened slightly at the top. Davita spied a small amount of curly dark hair on his chest. He wore the MacKeefe colors of green and purple on his plaid. He was a handsome man indeed, but his physical features couldn't outweigh the fact that what Clyde and Gregor said was true. Sure enough, she recognized him as well, and wasn't happy about it.

"God's eyes, nay. Please tell me that ye are no' the man they sent to help me," she blurted out, feeling filled with despair once again. Every time this man came down from the Highlands, he visited the tavern across the street with his friends. He never knew when to stop eating and drinking and making merry. This man had also been the cause of many fights when he was well in his cups. The last person she wanted to help her was someone who was nothing but a troublemaker.

"Aye, my name is Gavin MacKeefe, and I am here as prom-ised."

She remained silent.

"Is there some sort of problem, lass?" Gavin scratched the stubble on his cheek in thought. Looking over his shoulder, he glanced back at the door seeming highly confused.

Davita was angry as hell. "No wonder they told me if they sent help I had to agree to keep ye away from the taverns and whisky. Is this some sort of ill jest?"

Laird MacKeefe had indeed promised to send someone to help her. However, the only thing this man would be able to help her with was drinking her father's hidden whisky.

"Did I hear ye mention whisky, Davita?" her father called out from the back room. "Och, guid, ye found my bottle. Bring it here, will ye, Daughter? I thought I heard voices. Is someone out there with ye?"

Davita slowly lowered her body atop the wooden stool. Leaning forward, she buried her face in her arms against the table, closing her eyes in surrender. She hadn't thought things could possibly get any worse in her life, but the arrival of Gavin MacKeefe proved her wrong!

CHAPTER FOUR

GAVIN STOOD IN the doorway, not even sure he was in the right place since there was another shop down the street with a sign shaped like a shoe outside of it as well. Since most peasants couldn't read or write, a wooden sign depicting what the proprietor sold or did hung in front of every shopkeeper's door. "Is this the cordwainer's shop?" he asked, but the girl kept her head down on the table instead of answering. She wasn't even moving.

Nash and North walked up to the shop carrying an oversized metal trunk lined with wooden slats. Cam held the door open, assisting them as they entered.

"This is bluidy heavier than I thought it'd be," complained North. "Who the hell would think that shoes could weigh so much?"

"Och, that's probably the stones in the bottom that give it the weight," explained Nash. "I put them in there."

"What in God's name did ye do that for?" complained his brother. "What were ye thinkin'?"

"I did it to take up room," Nash answered proudly. "Storm told us once the trunk was full we could get somethin' to eat. Since Gavin was moanin' how hungry he was, I thought it would help speed the process along nicely."

"Nash, sometimes ye can be such a dolt that I'm ashamed to say ye are my twin brathair," griped North.

"Just put it down anywhere," instructed Gavin, waving toward a spot next to the door.

"God's teeth, it's small in here." North's back hit against something as he tried to make the sharp turn without dropping the trunk. A wooden tree pole holding shoes dangling from its arms fell over. It hit the floor with a loud crash.

"Nay! Be careful," shouted the girl, jumping up, finally responding to their arrival. "Ye fools are goin' to ruin the shoes. Those are for the nobles." She righted the shoe tree and started collecting the shoes into her arms. "Dinna put that trunk here," she spat.

"Damn it, North, ye really ken how to make an entrance," remarked Cam, walking in holding the hemp lacing that held one pair of shoes together. It dangled lazily from his fingertips.

"By the rood, ye can help us, and stop bein' so lazy, Cam," complained North.

"I am helpin'," he said, holding up the single pair of shoes. "Where do ye want me to put these, Gavin?"

Nash and North still stood there holding the heavy metal trunk that was so full it would barely close.

"Hell, forget about that, where do ye want this?" asked Nash. "It's heavy and I'm goin' to drop it."

"Heavy?" asked Cam. "Ye are turnin' weak, Nash."

"I'll show ye weak." Nash let go of his side of the trunk and it hit the ground hard. The force of it made North drop his side as well and, unfortunately, it landed on his toe. North let out a string of curses, jumping up and down, holding his foot.

"What is all the bluidy cursin' about?" came a voice from behind them. Gavin turned around to see a man with his arm in a sling holding on to the doorframe as he exited a back room. One crutch was clutched under his arm, and he leaned on it for support. His ankle must have been broken, because it was wrapped with wooden boards serving as a splint all the way up to his knee. "I dinna like cursin'," said the man, losing his balance, his body starting to lean.

"Faither!" cried the girl, running to him, but Gavin got there first. He scooped the man up in his arms to keep him from falling and getting hurt.

"Put me down, ye fool! I dinna want a man holdin' me," screamed the girl's father.

"Blethers, I'm sorry," apologized Gavin. "I was only tryin' to help. Cam, get a chair for the man, quickly," he told his friend with a nod of his head.

Cam slid a chair over to him, and Gavin gently placed the man atop it.

"We need another chair for his hurt leg," instructed Gavin, taking a stool from Nash next. He slid it under the man's wrapped leg, gently propping it up.

"Ah, that's better. Thank ye, Son," said the man, looking and sounding truly grateful, although his breathing seemed labored. "I canna get around like I used to since the accident."

"Hrmph," snorted the girl, looking disgusted. "If ye can call it an accident."

"What happened?" asked Gavin curiously. "Did ye take a spill from yer horse, perhaps?"

"Nay," the girl answered for him. "My faither was beaten and knocked unconscious and left for dead in a ditch days ago."

"Och, nay. I'm sorry to hear that," Gavin answered.

"Who the hell are ye?" asked the girl's father, almost making Gavin chuckle since the man made a big stink about cursing and now he was doing it himself. "Ye look like Highlanders to me."

"We are," said Nash proudly. "We're from the MacKeefe Clan."

"Or used to be, anyway," mumbled Gavin.

"Faither, I contacted the castle and asked them to send help," the girl told him. She looked over at Gavin. "I am Davita, and this is my faither, Graeme. Faither, this man is Gavin MacKeefe."

"I'm here with my friends," Gavin told them, introducing the others. "This is Cam, Nash, and North. I've been sent here to help ye, and that's what I intend to do."

"It was his sentence at the trial," Nash spoke up, making Gavin want to hit him. They didn't need to know all the details. Somehow, he figured if they did, it would only make things worse.

"Och, so I suppose it has somethin' to do with drinkin', since I was instructed to keep ye away from whisky and the taverns," said Davita in a knowing manner.

"What? No whisky?" The girl's father sounded shocked and even more disappointed than Gavin felt. "What is goin' on here?" the man demanded to know.

"Are ye two twins?" asked Davita, looking at Nash and North. "Ye look so much alike."

"Aye, we're brathairs and twins, but no' identical," explained North.

"That's right," said Nash. "I'm the handsome one."

"Gavin, ye might as well tell them everythin', since they're goin' to find out eventually," commented Cam.

"I suppose ye're right," said Gavin with a sigh, not really wanting to let them know because the whole thing seemed ridiculous and embarrassing to him. Still, he really didn't have a choice now. "We are Highland outcasts," he explained. "We did some things that were against the rules of Old Callum MacKeefe at the Horn and Hoof Tavern in Glasgow. Because of it, we need to prove ourselves before we can be accepted back into the clan."

"Ye must have done somethin' horrible to get a sentence sayin' ye canna have whisky," stated Graeme.

"Forget the whisky," interrupted Davita. "These men must have really wronged their clan if they were banished."

"Well, no' really." Gavin's eyes flashed over to his friends. "All we did was anger the chieftain's faither."

"I dinna understand," said Davita.

"The old man is crazy," said Nash, making a face and tapping the side of his head with his index finger.

"It's true," added Cam. "Now, we all have missions of his choosin' before we can be redeemed."

"Did ye . . . kill someone?" The girl stepped closer to her father and her hand went to his shoulder. She had a look of fear deep down in her bright green eyes. When she moved, the firelight from the nearby candle spilled across her face. It was still daytime and light came in through the window at the front of the shop. But these small homes were void of many windows and needed candles burning for extra light all day long. It was hot and dingy and dirty in the place. The room was stuffy and smelled strongly of leather. Gavin and his friends filled the room just with their bodies. Their heads almost scraped the low ceiling. As like the other shops in town, this one seemed to also have a second story. The shops were built so close together that they were touching. The second floors stuck out further than the first.

"We've killed lots of men," stated Nash. "We're Highlanders, lass."

"In battles. We only kill in battles . . . in self-defense," Gavin said quickly, throwing Nash a stern glance that silently told him to shut up. He did not want these people thinking they were barbarians. If they rejected him, he'd have to go back to Hermitage Castle and get another punishment from Callum to redeem himself. That would take up too much time. All he wanted was to serve his sentence quickly, and be able to drink again.

"So, did ye hurt someone, or destroy someone's home in a raid?" she asked.

"Nay, nay. It was nothin' like that."

"Well, it must have been somethin' or ye wouldna be here lookin' for redemption," the girl continued. She refused to drop the subject.

"By the rood, all I did was have a little too much to eat and drink," he told her, knowing how stupid that sounded, but it was the truth.

"That, and then he deposited it all atop Callum's boots," said Nash, not able to hold back a chuckle. Gavin didn't bother to respond to him. The truth was on the table now, and he couldn't hide it.

"Aye," said Gavin. "Now I have to help make a new pair of Cordovan boots for Callum as part of my sentence."

"I dinna understand. Are ye . . . all here to help us?" asked the girl. "I only asked for the assistance of one man, no' four. We are no' wealthy, and I canna pay ye. I hope ye understand that."

"No' them. Just me," said Gavin with a sigh. "And we dinna need to be paid. Just redeemed."

"Aye, this is Gavin's punishment, no' ours. We're only here for support," said North with a nod.

"Now, that's no' the way I see it." Gavin shook his head. "Ye three are here because we're outcasts and ye chose to stay here instead of in the dungeon. It was the lesser of two evils. Ye may as well tell them the truth about everythin' since we are bein' so honest."

"Stay here?" asked Davita, her eyes growing wide, darting from one man to the next. "All of ye? Och, nay. Ye canna stay here." She shook her head furiously and held up a halting hand. "The shop is small and there is only room for my family. Ye'll have to find somewhere else to go."

Just then, the door opened and a young woman and a boy walked in.

"Whoa. Are ye Highlanders?" the boy asked, his eyes filled with admiration as well as a little mischief.

"We are," admitted North.

"I've never met one of ye close up before," said the boy with a wide smile. "I've heard stories about how wild Highlanders are. And mean. Ye're no' goin' to yank off our heads and rip out our insides and eat them, are ye?"

"Archy, stop it!" Davita hurried over to the boy and put her arm around his shoulders. "This is my brathair, Archy, and my sister, Aila," she told the men.

"Ye four are sure big . . . with lots of muscles." Aila's eyes scanned down their chests, one by one. She grinned and the tip of her tongue shot out to lick her upper lip.

"Aila, go to the baker at once, and see if they have any old bread they are willin' to get rid of to feed these men," instructed Davita. "Archy, ye take their horse and cart to the livery and ask the stablemaster to house it for them. Also ask if these men can sleep in an empty stall."

"Now, Daughter, that is no way to treat our guests," scolded her father, yawning, and looking very tired. "Especially since they came here to help us. We must have some whisky around here to offer them." His eyes searched the room once more.

"Nay, Da. We are out of whisky," the girl told him impatiently, but Gavin didn't believe her. He knew that tone of voice. He'd often heard it when someone was trying to keep the brew away from him.

"Davita, ye can take those shoes ye repaired back to the butcher's wife," said her father. "Bring back the meat they promised us in exchange. Ye and Aila can make up a pottage with the meat and the leftover root vegetables we have in the cellar. It's the least we can do, to feed these men."

"I would love some pottage and whisky," said Gavin. He felt famished and craved food and drink to the point that he could no longer think straight.

"Da, are ye forgettin' somethin'?" asked Davita. "Gavin canna have whisky. I promised Laird MacKeefe I would keep it from him in exchange for his help with the shoes."

"That's nonsense," spat her father. "No man should be deprived of such a thing."

"Nay, she's right," Gavin finally admitted, not wanting the girl to get in trouble. "As part of my sentence, I canna have it. However, that pottage does sound invitin'. Only, I'd like it thick with oats added to it. And also plenty of fresh bread instead of crusts that are so old and hard, we canna bite them."

"I'm sorry, but we canna afford all that," said Davita, her green eyes looking up at him in desperation. If he wasn't mistaken, he saw a tinge of fear in her gaze, as well. She looked tired and pale. Very little life filled her eyes and he wasn't at all sure that she wasn't ill.

"I dinna expect ye to pay for our food or drink or lodgin', lass," said Gavin, plunging his hand into the money pouch hanging from his side. He dug out several coins and held them out to her in his open palm. Her eyes dropped to the coins and stayed transfixed, but she did nothing to take them.

"I – I canna take that," she said, her eyes closing as she let out a sigh. Then they opened again and drifted back up to meet his gaze. Green swirling pools of innocence stared into him, touching his very soul. He felt the girl's huge concern. It was as if she were drowning in a loch, and too proud to reach out her hand to let someone help her. It also seemed as though she could see straight into his mind. It unnerved him. Gavin never let anyone know what he held deep inside, and he certainly didn't want to expose all his secrets to a mere stranger. Not even if she was a bonnie lass.

"Why no'?" he asked in a low whisper. His words caught in his throat. He cleared it, not wanting to sound as if he were affected by just looking at her, even though he was. Those mesmerizing eyes still stared at him . . . into him . . . touching his heart in a way that he had never felt before.

"I willna take money from . . . from . . ."

"A Highlander?" he asked. "A drunk? Or just outcasts in general?" Gavin broke the connection between them by quickly looking the other way.

"I dinna want it. I dinna even want ye, but I have no other choice," she told him, cutting him to the bone. It made him feel so . . . rejected. So lonely and unwanted. It wasn't that different to another feeling he had from something that happened when he was a boy that scarred him deeply. It was a time when he lost everything and everyone he ever loved. It was something he wanted desperately to forget because it made him feel vulnerable. Gavin worked hard to be strong, and he didn't like to feel that way around anyone – especially a woman.

"I'll take it if she willna," said Archy. Davita's brother reached up for the coins, but Gavin snapped closed his fingers over the money and held his hand high above the boy's head. Archy laughed, thinking it a fun game. He jumped up, trying to touch it.

"Archy, stop it! That's no' nice," scolded Davita, sounding more than perturbed by her little brother's actions. She acted like the boy's mother, instead of his sister. That made Gavin question where their mother was, since he hadn't met her yet. Figuring it wasn't the right time to ask, he decided he would approach the girl about it later.

"Well, I'm tired, and done for the day." Cam yawned and stretched his arms above his head. "I'm goin' to relax in the tavern until the food is ready." He turned and headed for the door.

"I'll take ye there, if ye'd like." Aila's face blushed. Cam looked back at her and smiled.

"All right," he agreed, never turning down an offer from a bonnie lass.

"Nay, ye willna," shouted Davita to stop her younger sister from leaving with this man. The last thing she needed was for Aila to go into the tavern with a Highlander on her arm. It wouldn't look good and would only court trouble. Davita had enough problems in her life, and this kind of behavior needed to be stopped quickly. "Sister, ye need to go to the butcher and give his wife these shoes." She scooped up the pair of shoes she'd repaired and handed them to Aila. "Get the meat we need, and then stop at the baker's on the way back for the fresh bread and oats. I'll need ye to help me prepare the meal."

"Och, Sister, ye never let me have any fun."

"Get goin'," said Davita, pointing at the door.

"But ye ken as well as I that none of the vendors will give us food on credit anymore."

What Aila said was true. They'd been struggling lately getting all the work done, and collecting the payments. Until they caught up, they wouldn't be able to pay for the food. Their bill was already high, and that is why Davita took to doing trades instead of paying for things outright. Any leftover money was needed for supplies since the prices had risen drastically lately on tacks, nails, string, and leather.

Davita's eyes wandered back to Gavin. He smiled at her and held out his hand again, opening his fingers and offering her the money. Pride ate at her, but she had no choice. With all these mouths to feed, she would have to take what the Highlander offered. For now. Once they started filling orders again, she would pay the man back, as well as pay all of her outstanding balances.

Her hand slowly reached out, and she plucked the coins from his palm, one by one so she wouldn't actually have to touch his skin. Once more, her eyes met his and, this time, she felt timid when he perused her. Her body warmed and an odd tingle drifted up her spine. She didn't understand it at all. It frightened her.

"Get some whisky, too, while ye're out," commanded her father, snapping her out of her semi-like trance. It immediately broke the connection between her and Gavin. The tingle dissipated and, for that, she was glad.

"Nay. No whisky, Da. We have a little wine and plenty of ale. That will suffice." Davita handed the coins to her sister. "I hope this will be enough."

"It should be," said Gavin, lowering his empty hand to his side. "If no', I'll give ye more."

Gavin's kindness touched her heart. She'd been so angry and distraught when he'd entered her shop that she didn't realize until now how nice the man truly was. Then again, she didn't want to think about that. She had problems to solve, and so many shoes to make and mend. Her body felt heavy. It was like all the weight of the world was on her shoulders. All energy had been drained from her because she needed sleep and hadn't been getting much at all. Still, unless this man was truly part of the solution, he was only going to prove to be another distraction. That was some-thing she surely didn't need or want. She could only hope that wouldn't be the case.

Trying hard to push all idle thoughts from her head, Davita struggled to remain focused. Her family needed her. Her customers needed her, too. Davita's eyes roamed back to the Highlander once again, and this time when his eyes met hers, it made her heart flutter. It had been so long since Davita thought of herself that she really didn't understand why she was reacting this way. Could it be that she needed something in her life besides food, a roof over her head, and to take care of her father's shoe business? Perhaps so. But even if this were true, there was no way she really needed this drunken Highlander named Gavin.

CHAPTER FIVE

A N HOUR LATER, Davita was still waiting for her siblings to
return. She'd tended to a few customers who came into the
shop, and now she put ointment on her father's arm and leg,
checking and rewrapping his wounds.

"I wish ye would let me start workin' on the shoes," said
Gavin, pacing back and forth, watching her. He'd hovered over
her, eying everything she did. It made her feel uncomfortable.

"No' yet," she told him. "I have to teach ye, and I'm afraid
there is no time for that today. I have too much to do."

"Then let me help ye," he suggested. "I am capable of doin'
more than ye think."

"There ye go, Da," she told her father, washing off her hands
in a basin of water. "Yer wounds are no' festerin' and neither are
they infected. Thank God, that ye dinna have a fever."

"Then why do I feel so much pain?" her father complained.

"Yer ankle is broken, and yer arm sprained badly," she told
him. "Besides, ye had a lot of cuts and bruises. Remember, ye
almost died."

"I need some whisky for the pain." He stirred atop the pallet,
whining. "Davita, get me some whisky."

"I will make up an herbal remedy to help with the pain.
However, I will need Archy or Aila to go out and hunt down the
herbs I need first, since I dinna have them all growin' in the
garden. I wonder what is takin' them so long?" She threw down

the towel and hurried out of the room with Gavin at her heels. "Where are those two? Their errands shouldna have taken half this long."

"I can get the herbs for ye," he told her. "Or I'll ask my friends to help. I'm sure they're just drinkin' in the tavern anyway. I'll go get them." He headed to the door but Davita rushed after him, meaning to stop him. She grabbed the sash of his plaid that was thrown over one shoulder. In doing so, it was pulled down, and his leine opened further. When he turned toward her, she could see the exposed part of his chest.

"Nay, ye canna go into the tavern. I canna allow it," she told him.

He looked down to her hand gripping his plaid, not saying a word. Then his eyes slowly trailed up her arm and to her face.

"Lass, if ye wanted me to undress, all ye had to do is ask."

Her fingers opened, and she released him. She wasn't sure how to react to his comment. Part of her wanted to slap him. Another part of her found it curious. She couldn't stop herself from wondering how he would look without a tunic. Thankfully, she spied her siblings out the window. They were strolling along slowly, talking with the two of Gavin's friends who were twins. One of the twins carried packages while Aila held on to his arm, smiling up at him. The other twin – Davita couldn't remember which was which since to her they looked so much alike – walked with Archy. Her little brother talked to him excitedly with his arms waving wildly in the air.

"There they are. Finally," she said with a sigh, pushing past Gavin, opening the door for them. "Where have ye been so long?" she scolded. "It has gotten so late."

"Davita, I got to ride the horse before it was stabled," Archy told her excitedly. "And then Nash let me brush it down as well."

"Ye were supposed to take it to the livery and come right back," she said to her brother. "Because ye didna listen, ye will do the dishes after we eat, now."

"Dinna ye think ye're bein' a little hard on the boy?" asked

Gavin, bothering her that he would even make such a judgment when he didn't know a thing about them.

"Nay. He needs to learn to obey," she told him. Then she turned to talk to her sister as the group walked into the shop. "Aila, ye were supposed to go to the butcher and baker and come right back so we could start the meal. Da needs to eat if he is goin' to heal. Where were ye this long?"

"I was showin' North the town," said Aila with no urgency at all in her voice. She looked starry-eyed but, then again, she looked that way around every man. "After all, I thought it only proper to show our guest around."

Aila wouldn't know proper if it stared her in the face. "Ye didna go into the tavern, did ye? I told ye no' to."

"We only went in for a moment to talk to Cam," explained North.

"Aila, how could ye?" snapped Davita.

"I didna see any harm in it," said her sister. "I've been in there many times before." She slapped her hand to her mouth, surely not meaning to divulge this information to Davita. It didn't matter. Davita had known.

"Somethin' could have happened to ye," Davita told her sister.

"I was with her to protect her, so ye need no' worry," said North, smiling at Aila.

"Men, we are guests here and it wouldna be wise to go against the wishes of our hostess," said Gavin.

"I'm no' yer hostess. Ye are only here as part of yer sentence, if I must remind ye," she snapped, instead of thanking him or being grateful. "Give me the food, please." She reached out to take it from North, but Gavin's hand shot out and his fingers closed around her wrist.

"NAY. I'LL COOK our supper," Gavin told her. "Nash and North, I think ye'd better disappear until it is time to eat."

Davita's mouth opened, about to protest, but Gavin stopped

her from objecting.

"If ye'd like to join me at the hearth, I willna turn ye away. However, I willna hear another word about it either. I insist on doin' somethin' around here, and that is final."

Confusion filled Davita's eyes, and he watched her look from one person to another. They were all looking back at her, not saying a word. Then her arms wrapped around herself, reminding him of a butterfly being protected in a cocoon.

Finally, she spoke. "Archy, please show Gavin to the hearth and stay with him in case he needs somethin'," she said softly.

"I'll help him, too." Aila started to move toward Gavin.

"Nay," said Davita. "Aila, I need ye to go out and find herbs for me. I have to make a potion to help ease Faither's pain. I will give ye a list."

"I ken somethin' that will ease his pain," said Nash, finding one of the bottles of whisky she'd hidden in a boot. He held it up and smiled.

"Nay. What are ye doin'? I dinna want Da to find this." She snatched it away from him, glancing over her shoulder at the door to the back room.

Gavin's gaze settled on the amber liquid, and his craving for it became strong. It was too risky to keep it here, even hidden, now that he knew about it. He wasn't sure he'd be able to control himself. One sip of the brew and he'd only need more. Too damned bad it was part of his punishment not being permitted to have any.

"I suggest ye let my friends take it somewhere and dispose of it," said Gavin. "I am no' guid with temptation, so it is best that it doesna stay in this shop."

"I agree," she told him, shoving the bottle into North's hand. It was more than half-full. Damn, that whisky would go good with a hot bowl of pottage about now. Gavin's mouth salivated just thinking about it.

North pulled out the cork, sniffed the bottle, and then took a swig. "No' bad," he said, shrugging his shoulders. "But it's far from bein' Old Callum's Mountain Magic."

"Let me try it." Nash reached out and took the bottle and repeated the action of his brother, making a satisfied sound, smacking his lips. "Yep, he's right, Gavin. It's no guid at all." He proceeded to take another long draw.

"That's no' what I said," protested North, finally realizing what his brother was trying to do. "Och, he's right. It was no guid, Gavin. Ye wouldna want any."

"Take that out of here. Now," Gavin growled. "And if either of ye take another swig from that bottle in front of me, I swear ye'll be pickin' broken glass from yer teeth. Archy, take me to the hearth."

"Aye," said the boy, anxiously leading the way.

DAVITA NOTICED THE longing in the Highlander's eyes when he looked at the bottle of whisky. The way he clenched his jaw and gripped the packages told her he was fighting a strong desire. For all she knew, his large hands could have smashed the bread. Perhaps she was wrong in keeping the whisky there in the first place. But honestly, she was under so much pressure lately, that a good nip of the brew was the only thing that helped her to get even a little sleep at night. She needed it to relax, just as much as her father, or this Highlander did. Still, was it selfish, she asked herself? Was it really a need or just a desire? Davita was so tired that she could no longer tell the difference.

After giving a list of the herbs she needed to her sister, she looked around the shop at all the shoes waiting to be repaired or constructed. They were so far behind in their work, that it was frightening. The repairs didn't take that long, but she had orders for new shoes that were very time consuming. Without her father's help, she would never get caught up and be able to fulfill all the orders.

Spying the trunk of shoes brought by the Highlanders from the castle, she walked over and flipped open the lid, gasping because there were so many. Did Laird MacKeefe really think she was going to repair all these shoes in return for lending her a man? Plus, the Highlander had told her he was supposed to make a new pair of Cordovan leather boots for Callum MacKeefe as part of his punishment. Cordovan leather was expensive. They didn't even have any in the shop right now. She would never be able to afford it until she started getting caught up on the work, delivered the shoes, and collected the money.

Tears filled her eyes as she picked up a pair of shoes and sat down at the workbench to repair them. She busied herself with her work, trying hard not to think about the Highlander preparing food at her hearth while she did the work of a cordwainer. How was she ever going to tend to her father, her siblings, and her customers as well? And now that Gavin had arrived, she would need to repair another trunkful of shoes and teach him to make boots all within the short time he'd be here. It was impossible. She couldn't do it.

Putting a shoe atop an anvil, she used a small hammer to nail the sole back on. Her thoughts weren't on her work, but on her worries. Gavin was supposed to be the answer to her problems, but that was never going to happen.

Not sure how long she worked, her mind was on the Highlander, her troubles, and also the delicious aroma that filled the air. Did Gavin even know how to make pottage? It was a simple dish, but she thought all Highlanders knew was how to use a sword and fight. Battles were what they were skilled at in their lives. She was sure that their talents did not lie in domestic jobs such as making a meal.

"The food is ready," came Gavin's deep voice from behind her, causing her to jump. The shoe slipped from the anvil and hit the ground.

"Och, ye scared me," she said, leaning over to pick it up. His hand got there first, and her fingers brushed over his skin. She expected his hand to feel rough like leather, but it didn't. Instead, it felt surprisingly smooth. A slight tingle of excitement flitted through her, having touched this rugged, handsome man.

Quickly, she pulled her hand back, holding it to her chest, and sat upright.

"Yer work is fine," he said, inspecting the shoe before handing it back to her.

"I only repaired the sole. It was nothin'." She felt a rush of heat pool in her cheeks. He was standing so close to her that his plaid rubbed up against her. The scent of wood smoke and herbs drifted from his body.

"Ye seem distraught, lass. Are ye all right?"

"I'll be fine." She sniffed and quickly wiped a stray tear from her cheek with the back of her hand. Davita kept her eyes on the shoe rather than looking at him. It was safer that way, and easier not to lose focus.

"Davita, it is no' hard to see that ye are takin' on the responsibilities of too many people. Where is yer mathair? Mayhap she can help."

"I lost my mathair years ago. She became ill and never recovered."

"I'm sorry," he said, gently placing his hand on her shoulder. He stood behind her, and his presence filled the room. "I ken it is hard to lose a mathair."

"Oh, so ye lost yer mathair, too?" She turned her head slightly and glanced up at him from the corners of her eyes.

"I no' only lost my mathair, but also my faither and siblin's. I came to the MacKeefe Clan as a homeless child, and was taken in with open arms."

"I'm so sorry. I had no idea. How did it happen?" She turned on the chair, and when she did, his fingers slipped off her shoulder. With it, went the warmth and comfort, as well as the excitement that she'd experienced if only for a minute.

His eyes turned cold now, and she could tell he was remembering the past. His jaw clenched and his whole face turned stonelike. Whatever it was that had happened to his family still affected him today.

"We are no' talkin' about me, lass. I am concerned about ye."

"Dinna fash yerself. I will be fine." She got up from the stool, putting down the shoe.

"Will ye? It didna take long for me to see that ye have the weight of the world on yer shoulders. Ye canna keep playin' mathair to yer siblin's, and caregiver to yer faither, while tryin' to keep from losin' the business."

"I dinna have a choice." She turned and raised her chin to him. "They need me. I have to do it."

"What about ye, lass? Who will take care of ye and yer needs?"

"I – I dinna have needs."

He chuckled heartily. "We all have needs. From what I've seen, ye have more than anyone I ken."

"That's no' true. I dinna have needs. No' any."

"Really?" He reached out and lifted her chin with the tips of his fingers. "Look into my eyes and say that if ye want me to believe it."

"I – I dinna have needs," she said, looking into his blue eyes, saying the words but not meaning a one. Instead, she felt so mesmerized by him that she could barely breathe. Was this Highlander really standing so close to her and actually touching her chin?

"I dinna believe ye. Ye have needs but dinna want to admit it."

"I have a roof over my head, food to eat, and a family I love," she told him, hearing the quaver of her voice. The warmth of his hand as he cradled her chin felt sensuous and inviting. "I dinna need anythin' else." Her eyes dropped to his strong mouth and she found herself staring at his lips, wondering what it would feel like to kiss him.

"Perhaps ye're right," he said. "But even if ye dinna need somethin', it doesna mean ye dinna desire it."

"I am no' sure what ye mean." Her eyes flashed up to his again before settling back down to his mouth.

Then his thumb gently brushed across her bottom lip and her

eyes closed as a wave of strong desire flowed through her. Before she could open her eyes again, she felt his warm, wet lips pressed up against hers as he gently kissed her.

Her eyes shot open and she pulled away. It surprised her more than repelled her. She had thought a Highlander would have a forceful kiss, but his was gentle and caring.

"What did ye do?" she asked in a mere whisper. Her hand went to her lips as she savored his essence upon them.

"I – I'm sorry, lassie." He stepped back and held up his open palms. "I guess I got caught up in the moment, that's all. I didna mean to offend ye."

"I'll say ye did. I'm no' that kind of girl, no matter what ye may think."

"I'm sure ye're no'. It's just that we were talkin' about needs and wants . . . and then I saw ye starin' at my mouth. I thought ye wanted to kiss me."

"Davita, can I eat? I'm starvin'," said her little brother, running out of the small kitchen at the back of the shop. There was an upstairs as well, but it was used as a sleeping area. The room downstairs that held her father was usually a storage room, but Davita had moved most of the storage upstairs to make a downstairs bedroom for her father after his accident.

"Go find yer sister, and stop at the tavern and tell the Highlanders as well," Davita told Archy.

"I dinna want to go," he whined. "I want to eat the pottage. I'm starvin' and it smells so guid."

"Ye heard her, lad. Now do it," commanded Gavin in a deep voice.

Archy looked up and nodded. "I'll be fast." He ran out the door.

"I need to check on my da." Davita started to walk away, but Gavin reached out and grabbed her arm to keep her from going.

"Was I wrong?" he asked.

"Wrong about what?" She pretended not to know what he meant, but she did.

"Did ye want to kiss me or no'? Wasna that why ye were lookin' at my mouth? Am I right?"

"I dinna ken what ye mean."

"I think ye needed it as well as desired it. How long has it been since ye've had a man?"

That shocked her, and she jerked away from him. "I told ye, I am no' that kind of a girl. Now, enough of this silly talk about wants and needs. We need to eat before the food gets cold."

She walked away, leaving him standing there, and didn't look back. Aye, she had wanted to kiss him, but couldn't admit it to him. She didn't want to tell him that he was right. Besides, the last thing she needed right now was a romantic encounter with a Highlander who was only here as part of a punishment, and only for the next week or two at most.

Need. Want. Desire. The words burrowed into her brain as she made her way to her father's room. That lonely part of her deep inside had been brought to life by a mere kiss. Confusion clouded her mind, and her worries seemed to triple. She only needed the man so the guild would be satisfied and her family wouldn't lose their business. The last thing she wanted was a romantic encounter with Gavin MacKeefe!

Then again, mayhap he wasn't wrong. Perhaps she did desire him just a little, after all.

❖ CHAPTER SIX ❖

"HERE IS SOME pottage, Archy," said Davita, scooping some of the food into a bowl and handing it to her little brother. She broke off a piece of bread and gave it to him as well.

"This smells great!" said Archy, carrying his food to the table, staring at the bowl and being careful not to spill it. "Better than yers, Sister."

"Now, dinna say that before ye've even tasted it," Gavin said with a chuckle, feeling pain in his stomach since he was so hungry. He'd only tasted the pottage once or twice while making it to see if it needed more herbs and spices. He'd been tempted to eat a whole bowl or two earlier, but forced himself to wait for the others.

Davita handed food to her sister, and then poured out some for her father. Gavin's friends stood in a line by the kettle, eying up each dish of food as it passed by. He swore she saw them salivating. He certainly was. This was one of the best batches of pottage that Gavin had ever made. He couldn't wait to eat his fill.

"I will take my da's food to him. All of his movin' around lately has made him even weaker. The rest of ye, just help yerselves," said Davita.

She left with the food and as soon as she walked away, Gavin's friends grabbed bowls and nearly fought each other to get to the kettle first.

North managed to secure that spot, and filled up a heaping

bowl of pottage, so full it almost ran over the rim. Then he grabbed a huge chunk of bread and sat down at the table next to Archy.

Nash filled up his bowl next and sat down as well.

"Save some for the rest of us," complained Gavin, seeing that Nash's pottage was overflowing. Gavin filled a pitcher with ale and brought it to the table.

Cam sat down next to Aila with his full bowl, taking the last of the bread.

"Oh guid, ye are sittin' by me." Aila batted her lashes and moved closer to him.

"Aye, I like sittin' next to such a bonnie lass," said Cam, flashing her one of his flirting smiles that he used when he wanted to get a girl into bed.

"That's my spot," growled Gavin, not wanting Cam near the young girl.

"There's another spot on the other side of her," remarked Cam.

"That's for Davita. Now move."

Cam groaned but picked up his food and moved to the head of the table.

"This isna half-bad," said Nash, shoveling down the pottage.

"I helped him make it," said Archy proudly. "Gavin put in a lot more spices than Davita ever does. Herbs, too. That's why it's so guid."

By the time Gavin picked up a bowl and finally made his way to the kettle there was only a tiny bit left. He stared open-mouthed at the bottom of the pot, his heart dropping in his chest.

"Ye all call me the gluttonous one?" he snapped. "Ye barely left enough food for a mouse."

"I'd give some of mine back, but it's all gone," said North, holding up the bowl and drinking the contents from the side.

"Mine, too." Nash put his head down and ate quickly.

Cam looked up and shook his head. "Sorry, but since ye get the guid seat at the table, I'm no' sharin'."

"Never mind," he spat, scraping the bottom of the kettle to get the last of the pottage. It wasn't much, but at least it was food. He was so hungry right now, that he would eat a raw rat and not think twice about it.

Just as he was making his way to the table, Davita walked out and sighed. "Da isna feelin' that guid," she told him. "However, he did eat his food fast which surprised me. He never eats fast when I cook. Oh, well. I only hope the meal will help him. He ate everythin', and then fell fast asleep. At least it gives me hope that he will get stronger and recover." She put the empty bowl down on the table. "However, he keeps askin' for whisky."

"Why dinna ye just give him some?" asked Gavin, getting a glare from her. "For the pain, of course."

"He tends to have a problem with the brew, drinkin' too much. Just like some others."

Gavin knew she meant him, but he didn't respond. She still looked angry with him for kissing her and he didn't want to make her any more upset.

"Thank ye," she said, taking the bowl of pottage from his hands and sitting down next to her sister. "It looks delicious."

Gavin stood there empty-handed, feeling like he was going to faint. So now, he was left with no food at all, because Davita thought it was for her. His friends all chuckled, knowing he hadn't gotten any.

"Are ye no' goin' to sit down and eat, or are ye already finished?" Davita asked him, taking a mouthful of the pottage. "Mmmm, this really is guid. Ye surely ken how to cook. I'm impressed."

"He's already done," said North, making Gavin want to hit him.

Now, how could he tell her he never got any food? If he did, she'd give him hers, and he didn't want her to do that. He needed to look after her. She needed to eat.

"Is there any more bread?" she asked, looking around.

"North has plenty and wouldna mind sharin'." Gavin reached

out and ripped the bread out of North's hand just as he was going to take a bite. He handed it to Davita.

"I only need a little," she said, tearing off a small piece and handing the rest back to North. "I'm sure ye boys are hungry."

Before North could take it, Gavin grabbed it from her, ripping off a chunk with his teeth. "The boys were finished, and just leavin'," he told her.

"What?" asked Cam, looking up from his food. "Nay, I'm no'. I'm still eatin.'"

"They are goin' to find pillows and blankets, since I'm sure ye dinna have enough for everyone," finished Gavin.

"Oh. About that," said Davita, scraping the bottom of her bowl and licking the remnants off the spoon. His eyes fastened to the sight and he wasn't sure what he wanted more . . . her or the food. "I dinna think this place is big enough for all of us to spend the night."

"Nonsense," said Gavin. "We dinna need much room."

She looked up at him and let out a sigh. "Mayhap ye dinna *need* room, but I am sure ye will *want* more." She stressed the words need and want purposely, most likely referring to their conversation about the kiss.

"Sister, they can sleep upstairs with me and Archy," said Aila. "There is plenty of room for all the men now that ye have been sleepin' with Da down here."

"When I want yer opinion, I'll ask for it," snapped Davita, and a silence fell over the room. "Fine, they can stay," she finally agreed. "But all the Highlanders will sleep in the work area and no' upstairs. Understood?"

"We'll find what we need, and be back." Nash let out a belch, and followed it with a drink of ale. "Come on, men."

They started to leave the table but Gavin cleared his throat. "Are ye forgettin' about the dishes?"

"Davita said Archy has to wash them," Aila supplied the information.

"Aye, but they willna walk to the wash bucket by themselves." Gavin nodded to the dirty wooden bowls.

"He's right, men," said North, picking up his bowl. "Clean up." He walked over and handed it to Gavin, and left. Nash followed him, doing the same. Then Cam walked up, having the nerve to scoop the last of his food into his mouth right in front of Gavin. Gavin's eyes devoured the bowl and he couldn't help but let out a small groan. Then Cam placed his bowl on top of the others in Gavin's hands, making a tower of dirty dishes.

"We'll be back later," Cam called out over his shoulder.

"Aila and Archy, ye two sleep upstairs like usual, and I will stay with Faither down here, as I've been doin' since his accident," said Davita, getting up and handing the rest of the empty bowls to Gavin, stacking them atop the others. They were so high that they started to lean. Now they were just underneath Gavin's nose, and he could still smell the tasty pottage. It was driving him crazy. "Aila, I need ye to help me change Da's bandages, and clean his wounds," Davita told her sister.

"All right," said the girl, getting up and following her into the downstairs room. That just left Archy and Gavin standing there.

"That's a lot of dirty bowls," said the boy. "I dinna want to wash them all. That's more than we usually have and it's no' fair."

Gavin put down the stack and picked up an empty bucket, handing it to Archy. "Go get some fresh water at the well, and I'll help you with them."

"Really?" he asked.

"Really."

"Ye're no' bad for a Highlander." Archy ran from the room to get the water.

Gavin walked back over to the kettle, using a spoon to try to scoop out the burned parts on the bottom of the pot. He was bringing the spoon to his mouth with some charred remains when Davita walked out and took it away from him.

"Och, dinna eat that burned part. It's no' guid for ye." She dropped the spoon into the kettle, and stacked all the dirty dishes atop it, making Gavin's heart sink. "Thank ye again for makin' the pottage. I think it turned out quite nice, dinna ye?" She turned and opened up a cupboard, pulling out a jar of ointment and some clean rags.

"Well, I really canna say."

"Stop bein' so modest," she said, giving him a quick smile that almost melted his heart. "I think mayhap ye'll be able to learn cordwainin', after all."

"When do we start?" he asked.

"In the mornin'. Right after I make Faither's herbal potion, and we break the fast."

"Aye," he said, his stomach growling already just thinking about the next meal . . . or any meal at all.

She left. Archy ran back in, looking very excited. The bucket was filled with water. Since he moved so quickly, some of it spilled on the floor.

"Slow down, lad," Gavin said, grabbing the bucket from the boy before he spilled it all.

"Gavin, ye'll never guess what I found at the well."

"Water?" he asked with a chuckle, starting to wash the dishes.

"Nay, I found a toad. A big, fat toad." He dipped his hand into his pocket and pulled it out to show it to Gavin. "I always wanted a pet and now I have one."

"Well, if ye're goin' to keep him, ye'll need to give him a name," said Gavin.

"I'm goin' to call him . . . Hamish," said the boy, petting the toad and nodding.

"Archy, what is that?" Davita walked out of the back room with Aila at her side.

"It's Hamish. My new pet." When Archy opened his hands to show them the toad, it jumped out, landing on Aila before falling to the ground.

Aila screamed and held up her skirt. Then she jumped up on the wooden bench, trying to get away from it.

"Hamish!" cried the boy, hitting the ground, trying to catch the toad but it hopped away, toward Gavin.

"Stop yer screamin', Sister. Ye are goin' to wake Da," Davita told Aila.

"Make him get rid of it, Davita. I hate that horrible, ugly thing. I'm scared," cried Aila.

"It's just a toad," said Gavin, reaching down and picking it up as it hopped near his foot. "See? It willna hurt ye." He started toward Aila and she screamed again.

"What's wrong?" called out her father from the other room.

"Nothin', Da. Everythin's fine." Davita looked back at her brother. "That better be gone before I get back. Come, Aila, it's time for bed." She helped her sister from the bench.

"But it's my pet," cried the boy. "I dinna want to get rid of it."

"Get rid of it or I swear I'll put it in our next pot of stew." Davita slammed the door to her father's room as her sister disappeared quickly, climbing the stairs.

Gavin looked back at the boy and he seemed like he was about to cry.

"Here," said Gavin, handing the toad to him. "Take it."

"I dinna want to get rid of Hamish. I never had a pet before. I love him."

Gavin let out a deep breath. He was so famished that those frog legs were calling to him. "I'll tell ye what. If ye promise to keep the toad outside, I willna tell the lassies that ye didna get rid of it."

"Will ye help me feed it?"

"Nay. It's a toad and it will feed itself. However, it'll need a place to sleep and feel safe or it willna stay outside the door."

"How will we do that?" asked Archy, his spirits lifting.

"We need to make a toad house."

"Is there such a thing?"

"There will be when we're done. Are there any bowls that are mayhap broken that ye dinna use often?"

"There's one that I dropped and cracked and hid in the cellar so Davita wouldna punish me."

"Go get it."

The boy ran over to the corner of the kitchen and pulled open a wooden door with stairs leading down to an earthen cellar. He was back in a moment with a wooden, cracked bowl that had a chip on the side. He handed it to Gavin.

"This will work nicely." Gavin pulled out his dirk from his waistbelt, causing the boy's eyes to open wide. Archy held the toad protectively against his chest.

"Dinna hurt Hamish," the boy begged him.

"Dinna worry, I willna hurt ye or the toad," Gavin told him. "I am only goin' to make the door a little bigger on Hamish's house." He used the knife to cut a horseshoe-shaped hole near the rim. Then he turned the bowl over and laid it on the table. "There is Hamish's home."

"I like it," said Archy, happily.

"Now, place it in the garden, but try to hide it so Davita willna notice. Put Hamish inside for the night. He will live there, but come out when he is hungry to find insects to eat."

"Thank ye," said Archy, taking the new toad house in one hand and the toad in the other and heading out the door.

Gavin turned and continued washing the dishes.

"Where is my brathair?" Gavin heard from behind him, realizing Davita had returned. "Archy is supposed to wash the dishes, no' ye."

"Well, I'm helpin' him," said Gavin, turning around to see her in her nightdress. It was buttoned up to her neck, but she still looked fetching.

"Oh, he must have gone to get rid of the toad. Guid."

"Aye, he took the toad outside," said Gavin, not really lying.

Davita yawned. "I will put my pallet out here by the hearth to sleep, so my da can get a guid night's rest. He has overdone it, and is verra tired. However, I'll stay close enough to his door in case he needs me. I will still be able to hear him callin'. I'd like ye and yer friends to please stay in the workshop area tonight."

"Aye," he answered. "When I finish the dishes, I'll get yer

pallet for ye, Davita."

"Why, thank ye, but I dinna need ye to do it. I can do it myself."

"I ken ye dinna *need* me to do it, but I *want* to do it," he told her, stressing the words that she'd thrown back in his face earlier.

"Whatever ye *desire*," she said with a flash of a smile.

"Mmmm," he answered, feeling so hungry that he thought he would retch. "Ye canna even imagine what I desire right now and how badly I really want it." He turned and left to get her pallet from her father's room where she'd been staying. If he waited until he was finished with the dishes, he'd probably end up eating them, hoping to find a scrap of food left.

DAVITA SWALLOWED FORCEFULLY, feeling her heart about beating from her chest. Did Gavin just mean what she thought he meant? He looked at her and made a lusty noise, then admitted that he wanted her badly. Perhaps she shouldn't have been so bold as to walk out in her nightdress. But it covered her completely, and was not at all revealing, so she didn't think it mattered. Did Gavin just want to kiss her again, she wondered, or did he want something more?

She paced back and forth, not knowing what to do. Were she and her siblings really safe in the house with four lusty Highlanders sleeping here? Mayhap she was tempting them. She hoped this wasn't a big mistake, letting them stay, after all. What had she been thinking?

"Och, this is no' guid," she said, turning and walking across the room, wringing her hands in worry. She had her virtue to think about, as well as that of her sister's. Plus, these men were most likely going to be a bad influence on her little brother. Archy already had sticky fingers. What other bad things were they going to teach him?

"What's no' guid?" asked Gavin, walking up with her pallet stuffed with straw over his shoulder. He plopped it down on the ground in the kitchen.

"I was just talkin' to myself. I didna mean a thing by it."

"All right," he said.

Archy ran in the back door and stopped abruptly when he saw his sister.

"Did ye get rid of the toad like I told ye to?" she asked him.

"Ye put the toad outside, right lad?" Gavin asked before he could answer.

"Aye." Archy's eyes darted back and forth and he looked very uncomfortable.

"Then finish the dishes and go to bed," instructed Davita.

"I'll do them. There are no' many left," said Gavin.

"If ye insist. Go on to bed, Archy."

Her brother ran up the stairs to the second level.

"Guidnight," called out Gavin, making Archy stop to turn and look at him. Gavin winked. "I'm sure everyone will sleep better now."

She didn't know what he meant by that, and thought it odd he winked. It didn't matter. He was probably just trying to get Archy to like him by offering to do the dishes.

Davita helped Gavin and the dishes were finished quickly.

Then the front door opened and Gavin's friends came in. Both of them went to meet them.

"Did ye find pillows and blankets?" asked Gavin.

"No one will give us any, since we're Highlanders," Cam answered. "I think mayhap I'll go spend the night with a whore in the tavern. At least then I'll have a bed."

"Cam," warned Gavin, his eyes darting over to Davita.

"Och, sorry, lass." Cam waved a hand through the air. "I'll just stay here and sleep on the floor."

"We did manage to get three woolen blankets from the livery, but the stablemaster wants us to bring them back in the mornin'," Nash informed them, handing one to Cam and another to North. Gavin didn't get one.

"I'm bushed," said North, removing his weapon belt and then starting to remove his plaid.

Davita gasped when she realized he was undressing.

"Leave it on," commanded Gavin. "As long as we're guests here, the only thing we'll remove is our weapons, our shoes, and our leines."

"But I was hopin' to roll up my plaid and use it as a pillow," complained Nash.

"Take it or leave it." Gavin gave him the ultimatum. "Ye can always go back to Hermitage Castle and sleep in the dungeon if ye dinna like it."

"I'm no' goin' back to the dungeon. I'm stayin' here." Cam yawned and stretched, and removed everything but his plaid and lay down. The others did the same.

"There's no' much room in here. I'm sorry," apologized Davita. "Where will ye sleep, Gavin?"

"I'll find a place. Dinna worry. Now go on to bed, and in the mornin' ye can start teachin' me all about shoes."

"All right. Guidnight," she said, heading back to the kitchen. Gavin turned and made his way to the door.

"Where are ye goin', Gavin?" mumbled Cam with his eyes already closed.

"Dinna worry about it. I have somethin' important I need to do. I'll be back later."

DAVITA HEARD THE bells jangle above the door as she headed back to her pallet, preparing to sleep. Curious, she wanted to know who would be entering or leaving at this hour. Barefoot and in her nightdress, she hurried back to the shop area, peering into the darkness, trying to see what was going on. The men were all lying on the floor in the dark, as far as she could tell. She didn't notice anything amiss. Just as she was about to go back to her pallet, she spied movement from outside the front window.

Tiptoeing over to the window in the dark, she looked out to see Gavin in the moonlight. He headed over to the tavern, being met by two whores who escorted him inside. Her heart dropped. Was he looking to fulfill his desires with a whore since she turned him away?

She headed back to bed, trying to convince herself that it didn't matter. After all, she barely knew the man. Then she had another thought. He might be going there to sneak some whisky. If he did, Laird MacKeefe might find out. If so, their deal could be called off. If she didn't have Gavin here, the guild would come after their business for sure.

"I canna let him do it," she whispered, hurrying over to a hook on the wall, throwing a cloak over her shoulders to cover her nightdress. "I am supposed to keep him away from whisky," she said to herself. "By God, that is what I'm goin' to do. And whether he needs it or desires it, I will keep him away from the whores as well."

◆•◇•◆

CHAPTER SEVEN

"I NEED FOOD. Lots of it, and make it fast!" Gavin slid onto a high stool at the drink board in the tavern across the street from the cordwainer's shop. It was a place to go to get drinks as well as food. And like the Horn and Hoof, it had rooms upstairs where paying customers could enjoy the tricks of whores.

"Gavin, nice to see ye again," said Keithen, the proprietor of the tavern, shining a tankard with a rag. "I was wonderin' when ye were comin' back. Yer friends were in here earlier." He poured some whisky into the tankard, filling it more than halfway. Then he pushed it across the counter. "The first one's free," he said with a smile. "That's because ye've always been one of my best customers."

Gavin's eyes drank in the sight of the whisky, his thoughts already devouring the alcohol. His tongue shot out and he licked his lips, imagining the taste of it. This was something he wanted more than anything right now. He needed it, desperately! His hand snaked out for the tankard, stopping and wavering right above the cup. Then, instead of picking it up, he pushed it away.

"Nay. Just give me some ale," he told the man.

"Some ale?" Keithen laughed. "Ye have some sense of humor tonight, Gavin. Ye always drink whisky, and plenty of it. Everyone kens that."

"Nay, I mean it. I just want ale and some food. Plenty of food. I dinna care what ye have, just give it all to me. And hurry."

"All right, calm down," said the man, looking at him as if he thought Gavin had gone crazy. "Here's an ale. I'll tell the cook to fix ye up a feast, since I ken what kind of appetite ye have." He took back the whisky and slid a tankard of ale across the drink board instead. Then he plunked the whisky bottle down in front of Gavin. The sight of it tempted him like an apple in the Garden of Eden. "This is just in case ye change yer mind, guid friend."

"I willna." Picking up the tankard of ale, Gavin's eyes remained fixated on the bottle of whisky. His desire became stronger and it was getting hard to ignore. That whisky was calling to him like a siren of the sea.

As soon as Keithen left, the two whores who'd escorted him inside came back to join him. He'd known their pleasures before but, tonight, he wasn't interested in them. Ever since he'd kissed Davita, it was all he could think about. Her innocence, her determination, and her devotion to her family and business, were refreshing and intriguing. He'd never known a lassie to take on so many roles. The girl cared for everyone, and never even seemed to stop once to think about herself. She truly was amazing.

Gavin liked being around her family as well. Even if they weren't perfect, it didn't matter to him. He hadn't known that feeling of togetherness since he was a young boy. Gavin had been a loner since earlier childhood and had convinced himself he didn't miss being with his true family. But the truth was, he missed it more than he could even say. Since he'd arrived at the cordwainer's shop, he'd been questioning a lot of his beliefs. Something about being here shook him up, making a part of him come back to a life that had died long ago.

Being around Davita and her family made him remember the good times he'd had before his family was killed and he was left as naught but an orphan.

"Ye look lonely tonight, Gavin," said the whore named Red, named for her flaming red hair and lips. She reached out and pushed a lock of his long, black hair behind his ear, but not before taking a moment to rub the ends of the strands against her lips while she purred like a cat.

"We can make that lonely feelin' go away verra easily," said Violet, the other tavern whore. "Ye ken what we mean." Her breasts were trussed up and spilling out of her bodice. Her long, black hair sometimes looked like it took on a tinge of purple. Both girls were alluring, but in a whole different way than Davita.

"No' tonight, lassies." He lifted the tankard and took a big swig of ale. It felt good as it slid down his throat, but not nearly as comforting as whisky. His eyes settled on the bottle once again. Just one sip would be enough to suffice the urge. Or would it?

"Come upstairs with us," Red coaxed him, tugging on the end of his plaid.

"Nay," he answered. "I'm waitin' for my food."

"Ye can bring the food, too." Violet giggled, rubbing up against him. "It could be a lot of fun, if ye ken what I mean."

"Lassies, I am tryin' to change," he told them, pushing their hands away. "Now please, leave. Ye are only makin' it harder."

"I'll bet we are." Red's hand slipped atop his lap. Then her fingers closed over his manhood, causing him to get an erection. Damn, this needed to stop! Any other time he would have gladly gone above stairs with both of them at once. But now, all he wanted was something to eat, a lot more ale, and a good night's sleep. Why didn't these two just leave him alone?

DAVITA HURRIED ACROSS the street, wearing a cloak covering her nightdress. She'd pulled the hood up to cover her loose hair as well. She didn't take the time to put on shoes, and now wished she had. The feeling of dirt under her bare feet made her cringe. It was probably a mistake to have left the shop in her bedclothes, she realized, but she hadn't wanted to waste precious time changing. She needed to stop Gavin before he did something he'd regret. Or that she'd regret, anyway.

Pushing open the door to the tavern, she clutched the cloak to her neck and slowly ventured inside. She rarely came in here, because there was no reason. The only people who inhabited places like this were drunkards, troublemakers, and whores.

"Hey, wee lass, come on over here," a drunk man called from a stool across the room. That was followed by a few whistles from some of the other men who noticed her enter the establishment.

Davita ignored them, and made sure not to make eye contact. All she could think of was her little sister being in here, and that was a scary thought. The place was dark and smelled like sweat and alcohol. The dirty rushes crunched under her feet as she moved forward, making her wish she was back in bed instead of in this den of the devil. Hurrying past a group of drinking men, she scanned the area, looking for Gavin. Then she spotted him over at the drink board, and stopped dead in her tracks. He had a tankard held up to his mouth and a bottle of whisky was directly in front of him. Two whores were at his sides, pressing up against him and kissing him behind the ears. Her heart sank in her chest, and she felt a stab to it that felt like a knife. Biting the inside of her cheek, she tried to keep from crying out.

Furious to see this, she stormed over to the drink board, ready to give Gavin a piece of her mind. Too mad to even be frightened right now, she reached out and yanked the whore with black hair away from him. "Stop that, ye hussy," she spat. The girl stumbled, and her friend came to her aid.

"He's ours, bitch. Go work another area," warned the whore with red hair.

"Work?" she asked in question, then realized exactly what they meant. "Och, nay," she said, shaking her head. "Ye have it wrong. I – I'm no' a whore," she protested, horrified to even say the word aloud.

"Davita? What are ye doin' here?" asked Gavin, thumping down the tankard in front of him. Confusion painted his expression. "And why are ye wearin' that in here?" he asked, his eyes scanning her from head to toe.

She realized that her cloak had fallen open, exposing her nightdress to everyone there. She quickly clutched the material, trying to hide her intimate apparel. "I think the real question is, what are ye doin' in the tavern, Gavin MacKeefe?"

"What?" He made sour face and jerked back his head.

"Let's teach her a lesson for tryin' to steal our customer," Violet told her friend, pulling Davita's hood down, exposing her long, unbound hair. Stale air flowed freely around her, and Davita suddenly felt exposed and very vulnerable.

"Nay! Leave me alone. I told ye I'm no' a whore." When Davita tried to push the girl away, the redhead yanked off her cloak next, exposing her bedclothes to every man in the tavern.

"She's a whore all right," called out one of the drunks. "Look at what she's wearin'."

"She's barefoot, too," added another man.

"Ye're ready for bed," said the girl with the black hair. "Ye lied. Ye most certainly are a whore, and tryin' to steal our business."

"Violet, Red, leave her alone," Gavin said in a low voice, surprising Davita that he knew the whores by name. Then again, a man like him wouldn't be a stranger to any tavern. When he got off the stool, Davita's eyes opened wide. There was no mistaking his attraction to the whores, because his huge erection tented out the wool of his plaid at the groin.

"Oh!" she cried, unable to speak more, or to even look away. The man was big . . . and she couldn't help imagining just what lie under his plaid.

The whores laughed. "We told ye he was ours," said the redhead.

"Gavin likes the two of us at once, but we willna allow a third. Sorry," said the one named Violet.

"H-he does?" This was the last thing Davita wanted to hear. Suddenly, she felt foolish for coming in here at all. Gavin was obviously here for a reason, and there wasn't a thing she could do to stop him. Her cheeks burned with embarrassment. Never should she have followed a Highlander into a tavern. Lesson learned.

"Now wait a minute," said Gavin, raising his hand in the air. "Davita, this isna what ye think."

"Really." She crossed her arms over her chest, trying to hide. "What's that on the drink bar?" she asked with a nod of her head.

"It's whisky," Red answered for him.

"Ye ken ye are no' supposed to drink whisky, Gavin MacKeefe," Davita reminded him.

The whores laughed. "It will be a cold day in hell when Gavin rejects whisky," said Violet. "It's all he ever drinks."

"I didna have any," Gavin said in his defense. "I was drinkin' ale, I swear."

"Do ye think I'm daft?" she asked him. "I see the bottle of whisky right in front of ye."

"Aye, but I didna drink any."

"Prove it!" Davita threw down the challenge, not liking his lies, and wanting to prove that she wasn't fool enough to believe him. "Let me taste what's in the tankard, and then I'll ken for sure."

"I canna."

"Why no'?"

"Because there is nothin' in the tankard, lass. I drank it all. It's gone."

"Then explain them." She nodded at the whores.

"Och, Davita, I'm no' here for their pleasures, no matter what ye think. I dinna want them at all."

Her eyes settled on the bulge under his plaid. "Another obvious lie. I have eyes, Gavin, and can see for myself how much ye both *need* them and *want* them."

"I swear, I came in here for food and ale only."

She lifted her chin and scanned the drink board where he'd been sitting. "I dinna see any food."

"No' yet. They're makin' it," he explained.

"I see." This was getting tiring. How many more lies could he make up? Why was she even wasting her time talking about this? Why did she even care? "Tell me, then. What did ye order?"

"I ordered some of everythin', since I'm so hungry."

That had to be the biggest lie he'd told her yet. "Hah!" she spat. "Now I'm certain ye're lyin' since ye just ate ye fill of pottage at my shop, and couldna possibly still be hungry."

"Nay, I didna eat any. My friends ate it all. I gave what little was left to ye. Davita, ye have to believe me. I didna have even a spoonful of pottage, only a bite or two of bread."

Some of the drunkards in the tavern strolled over, calling out to her again. Emotion welled up within her. She had enough problems in her life, and didn't need this drunkard, this randy Highlander, causing problems for her as well. Suddenly, she felt like crying. Davita couldn't stay here anymore. Not wanting to cry in front of everyone, she swore to herself to remain strong. Turning on her heel, she ran from the tavern, hearing Gavin calling out from behind her.

"Davita, come back! Damn it, lass, listen to me!"

She didn't stop until she got back to the shop. Running inside, into the darkened room, she tripped on something and landed atop one of the sleeping men. The Highlander cried out and jumped up, grabbing his sword in two hands.

"Nay, dinna hurt me," she begged from the floor as the bells above the door jangled and Gavin rushed in right after her.

"What is goin' on down here?" Aila came down the stairs from her bedroom with a lit lantern in her hand. She looked over at them, rubbing one sleepy eye.

"God's eyes, Nash, put down the sword before ye hurt someone," shouted Gavin, only managing to wake up Davita's father and brother now.

"Davita? Davita, are those bluidy Highlanders accostin' ye?" Her father hopped out of the bedroom on one leg, not having bothered to use his crutch. Archy hurried down the stairs to see what was happening.

"Damn it," shouted Davita's father as he lost his balance. His arms flayed wildly, but it was of no use. He fell to the ground. "Arrrrrgh," he cried out, sounding very much in pain.

"Da!" Davita jumped up. "Let me help ye."

"Nay, let me," said Gavin, pushing past her and reaching out for her father.

"Dinna touch him," she spat, hitting Gavin with her fists.

"Davita, why are ye hittin' him?" asked Archy.

"Someone, light the candles so we can see what the hell we're doin'," growled Gavin, helping the man back to his pallet to lie down.

"I will." Archy ran around, lighting candles in the shop, enabling everyone to see clearly now.

"What is all the shoutin' about?" Cam finally woke up, and North started to stir as well.

"What hurts?" Gavin asked Davita's father.

"Everythin' hurts, ye fool. I need some whisky to dull the pain."

Gavin turned and faced Davita. "I ken ye've got whisky hidden in here somewhere. I suggest ye give him some right now."

"That's yer answer to everythin', isna it?" she snapped. "Whisky and whores."

"Whores? Where?" Cam asked from just outside the bedroom door, stretching and yawning. "Did I sleep through it?"

"I am no' givin' my da whisky," protested Davita.

GAVIN PULLED DAVITA into the other room to talk to her privately, without the others hearing.

"Look, I dinna ken what yer problem is with me, but dinna let it get in the way."

"Get in the way? Of what? Those two whores, back at the tavern that ye kent by name?"

"Stop it, Davita. I told ye I didna want them, and neither was I drinkin' whisky."

"Right. Ye were waitin' for food. Invisible food, that is."

"I was waitin' for food, no matter what ye believe."

Just then, the bells above the door jangled and Keithen walked in, carrying a large platter of food. It contained a chicken drumstick, a pork chop, a pile of cooked vegetables, and a chunk of brown bread. The entire thing was covered with gravy.

"Gavin?" asked Keithen. "Ye left before yer food was ready, so I brought it over. I hope this is enough. If no', I'll get ye more. Do ye want to eat it here? I brought more ale as well." He held up a pitcher in his other hand. "Sorry that Red and Violet wouldna leave ye alone after ye asked them nicely. The girls have trouble with the word nay."

"Thank ye," said Gavin. "And yes, I'll eat it here."

"Y-ye were tellin' the truth?" Davita looked up at him with wide eyes.

"Of course, I was," he snapped. "Now, get the whisky for yer faither, because I think he broke open his stitches and is in a lot of pain. Someone is goin' to need to sew him back up."

"Oh, my poor da." Davita ran over to a large trunk in the corner and reached behind it, pulling out a bottle of whisky. "Archy, give this to Da. Aila, get some towels and a needle and thread and some fresh water. I'm goin' to have to sew him back up."

"Gavin, can ye take this?" asked Keithen, nodding to the food and ale. "I need to get back to the tavern."

"Nash, pay the man for me," said Gavin, taking the food and ale and setting it down on the workbench.

"Me? Why? Are ye goin' to share it with me?" asked Nash, sounding suddenly hopeful.

"Did ye and the others share any of the pottage that I made with me?" asked Gavin in return. "Now pay the man and haud yer wheesht."

"Fine," mumbled Nash, picking up his money pouch and handing some coins to the tavern owner.

"Come back to see us, any time. Ye've been missed," Keithen told Gavin, pocketing the coins and leaving the shop.

"Gavin, I'm sorry I didna believe ye," Davita apologized, placing her hand on Gavin's arm.

"There will be time for this conversation later," he growled, not happy at all by the turn of events tonight, when all he'd wanted was to relax. And eat. "Right now, we need to help yer faither."

"Nay, I'll do it. Dinna fash yerself about it," she told him. "Please, sit down and eat somethin'. I'm sure ye are hungry. I'm sorry that ye didna get any of the pottage. Had I kent, I would have given ye mine."

"That's why I didna tell ye."

"Davita, hurry," called out Aila from the bedroom. "He's losin' a lot of bluid."

"Losh me. Nay!" cried Davita, hurrying to the room.

"Let us help ye," called out Gavin.

"Nay, please stay here. All of ye. I have my siblin's to help, and dinna need ye." With that, she slammed the door to the room, leaving the Highlanders standing there, not knowing what to do.

"Well, how do ye like that?" asked North, still sitting on the floor. "She doesna need our help."

"She needs it, but doesna want it," Gavin corrected him.

"Either way, I still dinna understand what is goin' on." Cam sat down and reached out for the plate of food.

"Leave it," warned Gavin in a gruff voice, causing Cam's hand to stop in midair. "I am goin' in there to help her or just support her if need be. But I warn the three of ye that this food and ale better all be here when I return, or heads will roll. Do ye understand?"

"Aye," said Cam, shrugging and slowly heading back to bed.

"Why did I have to pay for the food when North was the one who ate most of the bread and pottage?" asked Nash, still fretting about that.

"Was Davita really outside in her bedclothes?" North asked, still half-asleep, scratching his head.

"Aye. She came lookin' for me in the tavern," explained Gavin.

"Ye went to the tavern without us?" Nash sounded sorely disappointed.

"Were Red and Violet there with ye?" Cam wanted to know.

"Why dinna ye three stop with all the questions and go back to sleep? I need . . . and want, some peace and quiet," Gavin told them, thinking about his conversation with Davita.

"What about the food?" North wanted to know.

"If I were ye, I'd forget about that food and no' mention it again." Gavin headed to the bedroom.

"If this is his punishment, then I canna wait to get mine," Gavin heard Nash say to the others from behind him as he entered the bedroom. Once inside the dimly lit room, Gavin saw Davita sewing up her father's broken stitches. The man was squirming around, moaning, and making it difficult for her to work.

"Hold still, Da. I need to sew ye up again, and ye arena makin' it easy," Davita told him, sounding like she was losing her patience with her father.

"I dinna want to hold still. I want to ken what the hell is goin' on around here." The old man was ornery and not cooperating in the least. Aila tried to hold him down on one side with Archy on the other, but it wasn't working at all.

"Give me that bottle," Gavin said in a low voice to Archy, seeing the whisky on the floor next to the bed, but out of Graeme's reach. The boy gave it to Gavin, and he held it out to the man. "This should ease yer pain, Graeme."

"I dinna want whisky. I want to ken what is goin' on here," the man shouted, and then cried out in pain. He was very angry. Gavin knew the man wanted and needed the whisky, but was just upset that he didn't know what was happening in his own home.

"Well then, I'll just have to drink this all myself, I guess." Gavin looked over at Davita and winked. Then he pretended to drink as he held up the bottle to his mouth.

Damn, the scent and the tingle of the brew touching against his lips had his senses reeling. Thankfully, his ploy worked. If it hadn't, Gavin wasn't so sure he wouldn't have actually taken a sip, after all, since it was so close to entering his mouth.

"Give me that," squawked Graeme, yanking the bottle away from Gavin, and drinking. Finally, he started to calm down. "Now, will someone tell me what all the ruckus was about?"

"It was my mistake," said Davita, finishing sewing him up while he drank. "I didna believe Gavin, when I should have."

"About what?" he asked.

Davita cut the thread, and washed off her hands, glancing over at Gavin instead of answering.

"Have some more whisky," Gavin coaxed the man, knowing Graeme was in a lot of pain. Hopefully, he would fall asleep or pass out soon. It would be the best thing for him.

Thankfully, after a few more draws from the bottle, Graeme's eyes started to close partially. In a few more minutes, he had actually fallen asleep. Gavin took the nearly empty bottle from the man's hand and set it on the table. He held a finger to his lips, motioning to the others to keep quiet.

"Aila and Archy, go upstairs and back to sleep," Davita whispered. They all left the room and Gavin closed the door behind them.

Instantly, the sound of three snoring men filled the air. Davita and Gavin exchanged glances and smiled.

"Let me warm yer food up for ye," she offered.

"Nay, go back to sleep," he told her. "I will eat it cold. I'm too hungry to wait for ye to warm it."

"Do ye really think I can sleep with all this noise?" She stretched out her arms, motioning to his friends.

"Aye, ye're right. I have a better idea." He grabbed the food and ale, and led the way through the kitchen and out the back door. Gavin sat down on a small patch of grass next to Davita's garden, and she did the same.

"Are ye sure I canna warm that up for ye?" she asked again,

trying to take care of him the way she served the others.

"Nay," he said, picking up the pork chop and holding it up to his mouth. "I'm so hungry I could eat dirt right now and no' care." He was about to take a bite, but then held it out to her instead. "Would ye like some, Davita?"

"I would never deprive ye of yer food after all ye went through to get it, but thank ye just the same."

He took a bite, savoring the flavor, eating everything quickly and, of course, wanting more. But there would be no more food tonight. He picked up the ale and drank it down, then lay back in the grass, staring up at the bright stars in the sky.

"Do ye feel better now that ye've had some food?" she asked.

"It barely helped, but it's better than nothin'."

"Shall we go back inside, then?"

"Ye can. I'm goin' to stay here a while and just look at the stars. Have ye ever really looked at stars and wondered where they came from?"

"Nay, I dinna suppose I ever have."

"Lay down with me, Davita," he said, then corrected himself, before she got the wrong idea. "To look at stars, only."

"All right," she agreed, laying on her back and looking up at the sky. "I never took the time to realize how beautiful they are."

"I love sleepin' under the stars. I prefer it to sleepin' inside," he told her.

"Why is that?" she asked, curiously.

"I suppose it all started when I was a boy. But it all ended when I was nine years old."

"Tell me about it. I'd like to hear about yer life."

"There's no' much to tell. My family was attacked on the road by bandits one day when I was just a lad. They'd stopped so I could relieve myself behind a bush. By the time I made my way back to the wagon, we were bein' robbed. My mathair, my faither, and my sister and brathair were all bein' . . ." He felt himself getting choked up, remembering that horrible day. He couldn't bring himself to tell her they were murdered as he watched from behind a bush, too frightened to even try to help. They were all killed that day. Aye, they were now dead.

"So they are dead," she said for him, and he nodded slightly.

"To this day, I canna bring myself to say the word. For some reason, it is as if I say it aloud, it will make it final. By never saying the word, it is silly, but it is like a last spark of hope that it is naught but a bad dream. The only problem is, I never wake up."

"I'm sorry," she whispered, closing her hand over his.

"I used to always look at the stars with my family. We traveled a lot and slept outdoors."

"So that brings ye comfort," she stated.

"Aye, I suppose it does. Somehow, it makes me feel like they are still with me. I ken it sounds stupid. It is just somethin' I did as a child, and have never been able to stop."

"Didna ye have other family to go to . . . afterwards?" she asked, choosing her words carefully.

"Nay. No' really. Ye see, my faither was a mercenary. He hired out his sword to the highest bidder. He was hired to kill, and because of it, he was an outcast and not wanted by his own people."

"Did ye belong to a clan then?" she asked him.

"I dinna ken. I dinna remember a clan or even much at all. I just remember one night while we were all star gazin', my da told us the truth. That was right after he decided to give up bein' a hired sword. It was because of the love of my mathair. He wanted to start over and raise his family in pride. But he never got the chance."

"So, yer family was always on the run, then, I suppose."

"Aye. We were. We lived with gypsies sometimes, and at other times we stayed hidden in the Grampian Mountains, all by ourselves."

"Wasna that lonely? Didna ye miss bein' around others?"

"Ye canna miss somethin' ye never had in the first place. I learned to rely on myself. I appreciated nature, and found solace bein' with the animals and plants instead of with people in a clan."

"How did ye end up with the MacKeefe Clan then?"

"Ian MacKeefe, our chieftain, and some of the MacKeefes approached as this was happenin' and killed all the bandits. However, they were too late to save my family. They found me and took me with them, back to their clan after they'd buried my family. They never forced me to answer questions that I didna want to answer. They accepted me with open arms, and that was all that mattered. From that day on, I was a MacKeefe. And although it took years, I finally felt like I had a family again."

"Dinna ye ever wonder about yer old life and who ye really were before?"

"It doesna matter. All that matters is who I became."

"Ye are a strong man, Gavin, and I respect ye for it."

"Nay, I dinna see it that way at all. But I do see ye as a strong woman, Davita, and that impresses me."

"Really?" she asked softly, sounding as if she were touched that he'd said it.

"Well, it canna have been easy to lose yer mathair and take on so many responsibilities. Especially at such a young age. How old are ye, anyway, lass?"

"I am eight and ten years of age. How old are ye?"

"I am five and twenty, but sometimes I feel much older. Tell me, how did yer mathair die?"

"It was a contagious illness that took her life, and only in a matter of days. The rest of us were lucky no' to catch it. It really angered and saddened my da that he lost her. He was never the same afterwards. Ever since my mathair's death three years ago, my da seems to have lost his spark for livin'. He turned to the bottle rather than to have to deal with his pain."

"So ye stepped in as role of mathair when ye were only five and ten years of age? Really?"

"Aye. I did. I had to. I saw my sister and brathair goin' in the wrong directions, but my faither had taken to drinkin' so he never noticed. I was the one who had to step in and discipline them."

She shivered, and Gavin put his arm around her.

"Come closer, and use my body warmth," he told her. "Unless ye'd rather go inside?"

She didn't answer at first, and he honestly thought she was going to leave him. Then, instead, she leaned in to him, snuggling up against him and closed her eyes.

"What do ye mean that yer siblin's were goin' down the wrong road?" he asked, curious.

"Aila is too interested in boys," she said sleepily. "She's been loiterin' around the tavern, and I dinna like it. She's also befriended those whores and I dinna want them to influence her."

"What about yer brathair? He seems like a normal lad."

"Archy keeps stealin' things from the other townsfolk. I fear he'll be caught someday and sentenced to death." She yawned, and snuggled up closer against him.

"That's no' guid," he said, putting his arm around her and lightly rubbing her shoulder. He heard a croak, and turned his head to see Archy's pet toad hopping by.

"What was that?" asked Davita, her eyes popping open. She tried to turn her head to see. He had to do something to distract her, since if she saw the toad she'd probably cook it up for supper.

"I didna hear anythin'," he said, leaning over and kissing her gently on the lips.

"Mmm," she said, kissing him back, and then resting her head on his chest.

"Get out of here," he whispered, trying to shoo away the toad with his hand.

"What did ye say?" she asked, sounding sleepy.

"I said, isna it beautiful out here?"

"Aye, it is. I'm glad I stayed. I feel much better. Thank ye, Gavin."

Gavin could see now why Davita was always so worried, after what she'd just told him. Having a drunkard for a father, a randy sister, and a thief for a brother would make anyone concerned. She was truly stronger than he'd even thought. He had to help her. Not only from losing the business, but also from having her family fall apart at the seams. The only problem was, he didn't know how. He barely remembered his siblings or parents, so this was all an area that he had no experience in at all.

It was only a matter of a few more minutes before Davita's breathing slowed and he knew she'd fallen asleep. He leaned over and kissed her atop the head, pulling her closer to him. The moonlight shone down upon her satin skin, and he swore her hair glowed. She was truly an angel.

Gavin looked up at the stars once more. But this time, he didn't feel so lonely. With Davita at his side, it helped fill the emptiness in his broken heart. Mayhap it was fate that he was sent here to help her, he decided. Perhaps it was not really a punishment, after all, but rather a reward.

✦•○◇○•✦

CHAPTER EIGHT

"**G**AVIN, GET UP," said Cam, kicking at Gavin and waking him from a sound sleep.

"What?" Gavin opened one eye and then the other, the sunlight about blinding him.

"Are ye goin' to sleep all day?" asked Nash.

"What are ye doin' sleepin' in the garden, anyway?" North wondered.

"He probably wanted to be close to the vegetables and herbs in case he got hungry." Nash laughed at his own jest.

"Is it day already?" Gavin stretched, realizing that Davita wasn't lying next to him. He sat up and looked around. "Where is Davita?"

"Was she out here, too?" asked Nash.

"Ye spent the night together?" Cam looked interested in knowing more.

"No' like that, ye fools." Gavin stood up and brushed the dirt off his plaid. "We were just lookin' at stars. That's all."

"Suuuuure ye were," Cam answered, grinning from ear to ear.

"Dinna ye three have somethin' better to do?"

"We came to wake ye because Graeme took a turn for the worse durin' the night," said North.

"He did?" Alarmed, Gavin headed for the house. "We need to help him. Mayhap I should have put whisky on his wounds if they were infected."

"Gavin," Cam said, as they hurried after him.

"Wait, I just had a thought," said Gavin, stopping in his tracks. "Mayhap there are herbs in the garden that will help to heal him." He turned on his heel to go back, but North grabbed him by the arm.

"What are ye doin'?" asked Gavin, shaking himself free. "Why are ye tryin' to stop me?"

"We're tryin' to tell ye that it's too late," said Cam.

"Is he . . . is he?" Gavin swallowed deeply, not able to say the word dead. Strange, since Graeme was not part of his family, and that only happened when he tried to talk about his late family.

"He's no' dead yet, but pretty darned close to it," North reported. "Davita and her siblin's have been cryin' at his bedside most of the night."

"Why didna anyone wake me?" Gavin's heart pumped furiously in his chest.

"Davita wouldna let us," said Cam.

"Well, why didna ye three help her? I canna imagine what she is goin' through."

"We would have helped, but she didna want us," said Nash.

"She needed ye. She needed me. Damn, why didna anyone wake me?" Gavin turned and hurried back to the house.

"The man's wounds have become infected," Nash told him. "Plus, it looks like he broke his sprained arm last night when he fell. He is in bad shape."

"Why didna someone call for a healer?"

"They dinna have one in the town right now," Cam told him. "Their healer died months ago, and no one is trained to take his place."

"We need to get Graeme help."

"Gavin, let it go," said Cam softly. "Face it, the man is goin' to die."

"Nay! I refuse to give up. Davita needs her faither, and her siblin's do too. They already lost their mathair and I willna let them lose their da as well. They dinna deserve to be orphans."

"Ye mean . . . like ye?" asked Nash, causing silence between them.

Finally, Gavin spoke. "Cam, get the horse and wagon. Nash, find me a bottle of whisky."

"Och, Gavin, this is no time to be drinkin'," said North.

"It's no' for me. We're goin' to take Graeme to Hermitage Castle."

"What for?" asked Nash.

"The castle's healer can help him. Plus, Lady Wren is skilled in such things."

"I'm no' sure Ian is goin' to like that," said Cam, not showing much emotion in his voice at all.

"Aye. Plus, we're outcasts and no' welcome there right now, or did ye forget?" asked Nash.

"I dinna give a rat's arse if we're welcome or no'." Gavin wasn't going to let anyone or anything stop him. He would help Davita and her family, no matter what the consequences were for him. He no longer cared about himself. Now, his focus was on Graeme, and that was all that was important. "There is a dyin' man in there that needs our help and, by God, we are goin' to help him. North, come with me to carry Graeme to the cart."

"I'll get the wagon," said Cam, heading off.

"I'll get the whisky," said Nash, rushing off in the other direction. North followed Gavin to the bedroom where crying could be heard before they even entered.

"Davita, I'm here to help." Gavin rushed into the room, stopping in his tracks when he saw the pale man lying motionless on the bed. His eyes were closed and his mouth was open, as if he were gasping for his last breath. It looked like the life had nearly been drained from him already. His friends were right. It didn't seem like there was much hope that Graeme would live. Still, Gavin had to try to help him.

Aila knelt on the floor, holding one of her father's hands. Archy sat on the edge of the bed holding the other. Davita stood at the foot of the bed, dabbing his infected wounds with a cloth and an herbal remedy. The two younger siblings cried, but Davita's face was stone-like with no expression at all.

"Lass, I'm here," he said, resting his hand on Davita's shoulder. He looked down at the man's leg and grimaced silently. It didn't look good at all.

"It's all my fault," she said in a soft voice. "If I hadn't come after ye last night, my da never would have fallen. He's goin' to die now, and only I am to blame."

"Stop it," he commanded, but she just continued wallowing in her self-pity.

"I should have done more for my faither. If I had, mayhap I could have saved him."

Gavin put his hands on Davita's shoulders now, and turned her around toward him. "Look at me," he commanded in a stern voice. Slowly, her eyes lifted to meet his. The look of despair and sadness within them was almost too unbearable to take. "Ye did yer best. Ye need to realize that."

She shook her head and her eyes traveled back to her father. "My best wasna guid enough, Gavin."

"Ye're no' a healer, lass. No one expects ye to be able to do what they do. This man needs help from someone who kens about these things."

"Oh, Gavin, I dinna want to lose both my parents. What am I to do?"

"Ye are goin' to do nothin'," he told her. "My friends and I will take yer faither to the castle. We have a healer there. Plus, Lady Wren kens about what to use from nature to cure people. She's lived in nature a guid part of her life. In the Scottish Highlands."

"But ye said ye are outcasts and canna go back until ye are redeemed."

"I dinna care."

"Gavin, I dinna want ye to be punished again. Nay, I canna let ye do this."

Gavin could tell by her words, her tone, and her expression that she had already given up. He couldn't let her. She was too strong of a woman to just stop trying. It was up to him now to help her. She had done all she could do.

"I will go back to the dungeon if I have to, it doesna matter," he told her, once again looking directly into her sad, green eyes. "I am takin' yer faither to the castle, and I dinna want to hear another word about it."

"Thank ye," she said, biting her lip so she wouldn't cry.

"The wagon is ready," announced Nash, walking in with a bottle of whisky in his hand. "What should I do with this? Graeme seems like he's unconscious."

"North, help me get him in the wagon," said Gavin, snatching the bottle from Nash.

"I thought that was for the sick man," said Nash.

"Nay, it's for Davita." Gavin handed it to her.

"Me?" She took it, looking very confused.

"I want to see ye smilin' and relaxed when I return, and this will help ye. We have a lot of shoes to repair and construct, and if ye're so worried, ye are never goin' to be able to teach me a thing."

IT WASN'T LONG before Gavin drove the wagon up to the gates of Hermitage Castle, and took it right inside the courtyard without even stopping at the gatehouse. Cam sat on the bench next to him and the twins were in the back, holding on to Graeme.

"What's this?" One of the guards rushed over to them as soon as they passed under the open portcullis. "I thought ye four are outcasts. What are ye doin' back here?" the man asked them.

"We've got an injured man that needs help," said Gavin, stopping the cart and jumping off.

"We've been instructed by our chieftain, no' to let ye return until he tells us ye can," said another of the MacKeefes.

"I dinna care." Gavin didn't even look at them when he spoke.

"Nash, find the healer, fast," he instructed.

"Ian willna like this," said the guard.

"Where is Storm?" asked Gavin, knowing Storm would stick up for them.

"He and Callum went back to the Highlands," the man informed them. Gavin was happy that at least Callum wasn't there because the old man would certainly have given them trouble.

"Go back to your posts," came a feminine voice from behind them. "Let them pass." It was Ian's wife, Lady Clarista. She walked up with Lady Wren, Storm MacKeefe's wife, at her side. Both the women were English and nobles, married to the Scots.

"What's wrong?" Wren hurried forward to see for herself as Cam and North picked up Graeme to carry him inside.

"This is Davita's faither from the town," Gavin explained. "He's been injured and is close to death. Lady Wren, we need ye. Ye ken a lot about herbs. Can ye help to save him?"

"I will do my best," said Wren. "I'll also call for the help of the clan's healer. Take him inside to the solar, quickly."

"Ian will no' like this," said one of the guards again.

"You just leave Ian to me," said Clarista. "We will not look the other way when our help is needed. Gavin, you did the right thing by bringing him here."

"Men, after you take him to the solar, go to the kitchen and wait for us there," said Wren. "Get yourselves something to eat. But stay there instead of wandering around the castle. I will send a messenger for you as soon as we know more."

THREE HOURS LATER, Gavin was feeling as happy as a pig in mud, sitting in the kitchen, having had his fill of food to eat, and heather ale to drink. His belly was full of haggis and pheasant, sweetmeats, and even cock-a-leekie soup. He moaned and sat back on the chair, rubbing his stomach. Once again, he hadn't been able to stop once he started eating and drinking, because it all tasted so satisfying to him.

"Are ye finally done eatin' all the food in the kitchen?" griped the cook. She was a plump woman who looked like she ate more than all of them put together.

"Gavin never gets full," said Nash.

"Aye, he is a glutton," agreed North.

"Nay, that's no' true," said Gavin, feeling so full that he couldn't eat another bite. "I think I have finally had my fill." Unfortunately, he was already starting to feel sick because he ate and drank so much.

"Ye should have stopped eatin' two hours ago like the rest of us." Cam sat on a bench polishing his sword with a cloth.

"I'm surprised Ian agreed to let us stay in the kitchen," said Nash with a chuckle. "I figured he'd have us wait in the bowels of the castle instead."

"Aye," agreed Cam. "If it wasna for Ladies Wren and Clarista, I'm sure he would have locked us in the dungeon to wait."

"Gavin?" A young MacKeefe boy who Gavin recognized as the castle's messenger approached. Gavin pushed up to his feet.

"Is there any word on Graeme yet?" he asked the boy anxiously, almost afraid to hear what he had to say.

"Lady Wren would like to see all of ye in the great hall, anon."

"Uh oh," said Nash. "This doesna sound guid."

They all followed the boy to the great hall to find Lady Wren talking with Ian. Ian was with Clarista, nodding slowly as Wren spoke. Then he and his wife headed away without even saying a word to Gavin and his friends. Wren came over to see them.

"Lady Wren," said Gavin, feeling very nervous. The last thing he wanted was to have to go back to town and tell Davita that her father had died. She would blame herself for his death for the rest of her life. "Is Graeme . . . is he . . . is he any better?" he asked, not wanting to say dead.

"It is a good thing you brought him in when you did," said Wren. "He was burning up with fever and the infection was traveling through him fast."

"Will he live?" asked North.

"I believe so," Wren answered, and Gavin let out a deep sigh. "However, it will take a long time for his bones to heal. His arm, as well as his ankle are broken."

"That's guid news," said Nash with a smile. Gavin threw him a dirty look. "What? I meant guid news about no' dyin'," explained Nash with his palms in the air.

Wren smiled. "I know what you meant, Nash. I also want to say that whoever sewed him up did a wonderful job. The stitches were so tiny and precise that it won't leave bad scars at all."

"That was his daughter, Davita," said Gavin, beaming with pride. "She is a cordwainer's daughter so she kens how to sew."

"I'm sorry to have to ask you to leave, but you boys better get going," said Wren. "Ian was wondering how many shoes you've fixed and if Callum's boots are finished yet. I told him, I didn't know."

"Nothin' is finished, or even started yet," Gavin admitted. "But I'm goin' to learn to make shoes as soon as we return."

"Good," said Wren with a nod. "Because the faster you complete your mission and are redeemed, the faster the rest of your friends can get their punishments as well."

"Och, I can wait," grumbled Nash.

"I'm in no hurry," added Cam.

"I dinna mind stayin' in town. For now," added North.

"Let's get goin'," said Gavin. "I want to hurry home to tell Davita and her siblin's the guid news about her faither."

"Home?" asked Nash as the men headed away.

"I mean, back to the cordwainer's shop," Gavin corrected himself. Even so, his little slip-up must have been because he was somehow already starting to think of Davita's place as his home, too.

CHAPTER NINE

DAVITA PACED BACK and forth inside the shop, continually checking out the window for Gavin and his friends. Not having been able to focus on her work, she had finally given up. Now, she anxiously waited for news on her father. She'd made a meal for her siblings earlier, and Aila and Archy were cleaning up the kitchen.

She looked out the window again, but instead of seeing Gavin, she saw Clyde outside his cobbler's shop. He was talking with a tall, lean boy about Aila's age that Davita had seen before. She recognized him as Clyde's nephew whose father was also a cobbler from a nearby town. If she remembered correctly, Ethan was his apprentice. When Clyde looked her way, she quickly stepped out of view, hoping he hadn't seen her. She didn't want him coming to the shop today asking if her father or the other men were there. If so, he'd be sure to tell the guild that she was alone, and she would have even more problems.

"Davita, the dishes are washed," said Aila, drying her hands on a towel, coming out to join her. "Are they back yet?"

"Nay," Davita answered, peeking out the window at Clyde again. "Where is Archy?"

"He said there was somethin' he had to do in the garden."

"In the garden?" she asked, glancing at her sister. "I canna ever get him to work in the garden or pull a single weed. I wonder what all that is about."

"I'm no' sure," she commented. "What are ye lookin' at?" Aila leaned forward and followed her gaze. A smile quicky spread across the girl's face.

"Sister? Why are ye smilin' at that horrible man, Clyde?" asked Davita.

"I'm no'," she said, putting down the towel and pressing her one hand against the window. She waved with the other.

"Nay! Dinna do that." Davita pulled Aila's arm down. "I dinna want Clyde comin' here while Gavin is gone. Bid the devil, why are ye wavin' at him? What is the matter with ye?"

"I'm no' wavin' at Clyde, Sister," Aila said, frowning at Davita. "I'm wavin' at Ethan."

"Ethan? Oh, ye mean the boy," said Davita, peeking back out the window.

"Aye. He is the handsome nephew of Clyde. He arrived a few days ago to be Clyde's new apprentice."

"New apprentice?" Curious, Davita walked closer to the window and stretched her neck to take a better look at the boy that her sister thought was so handsome. Davita vaguely remembered meeting him once or twice years ago, but he seemed so much younger at the time. Now, he almost looked like a full-grown man. Aila liked all the boys, but at least this one was more her age. That made Davita happy. However, the fact that Ethan was related to Clyde truly concerned her. "Clyde already has an apprentice, Aila. Why in heaven's name would he want another?"

"Ethan told me that his uncle is expectin' the business to pick up immensely verra soon. He came to live with Clyde now, since his faither just passed away. Didna ye ken?"

"I guess no'."

"Well, he will be workin' at the cobbler's shop now since Clyde is goin' to need more help."

"I am sorry about his faither. But what Clyde really means is that he intends on stealin' all of our business if he can. And he's goin' to use Ethan to help him do it. Well, that will never happen, because I willna allow him to steal our customers."

"They're comin', they're comin'," yelled Archy, running in from the back door. "I saw the wagon from the garden." He skidded to a stop next to them, and when he did, something fell out of his trews and clattered to the ground.

Davita bent down and picked up a metal spatula, holding it in front of her face to peruse it. "Archy, this is no' ours," she said, turning it over and over. "Where did ye get it?"

"I – I found it." He used one foot to scratch his opposite leg, looking the other way.

"Look at me," she demanded and, finally, he did. "Did ye steal this? From the baker, perhaps?" She waved the spatula under his nose.

"Give it back. I need it, Sister." He tried to take it from her, but she held it away from him.

"Ye stole it, didna ye? Well, ye are goin' to return it right away. Do ye understand?"

"I canna."

"Why no'?"

"Because, I told ye, I need it."

"Ye dinna cook, Archy. Therefore, what would ye ever need a spatula for?"

"It's no' for cookin'." Archy was being very vague and this made Davita even more suspicious of his actions.

"Then what is it for?" asked Aila.

"It's for . . . catchin' flies."

"That's the most ridiculous thing I've ever heard." Davita let out a deep sigh, turning and putting the spatula down on the table. The wagon pulled up outside with Gavin and his friends and stopped.

"I dinna see Da with them," said Aila, peering out the open window. "The wagon looks empty in the back."

"I dinna see a coffin either." Archy jumped up, trying to see over them.

"I suppose we should find out what happened," said Davita,

her stomach clenching. She was afraid to hear the truth. Hopefully, her father wasn't dead.

"I'm goin' out there." Archy started to run to the door, but Davita grabbed his arm to stop him. "Let go. I want to find out about Da," whined the boy.

"We all do," said Davita. "But we'll wait inside."

"I want to go say hello to Ethan when we're done." Aila started for the door next, but Davita stopped her as well.

"We will wait here. Do ye hear me? I dinna want Clyde or anyone else in town hearin' us talk about our faither and his condition."

"What difference does it make?" asked Aila.

"Aye, if he died, they're all goin' to find out anyway," added Archy.

"Haud yer wheesht! Both of ye, and just be patient." Davita stood there with one hand on each of her siblings, waiting for the men to walk in. She, too, wanted to run out there and find out what had happened, but part of her was also frightened that the news might be bad. Her heart pounded against her ribs as Gavin entered first, followed by his friends.

"Gavin?" she asked, her fingers slackening on her grips, releasing her siblings. She felt now as if she were going to swoon. "How is Faither?" she asked with a shaky voice, holding her breath while she waited for him to answer.

The second it took for him to respond seemed like eternity to her. Then she heard the words she'd been longing for as Gavin smiled and answered.

"He's goin' to live," he announced, getting a hoot from Archy, and a sigh of relief from Aila.

"Thank God," she said, her lips trembling as she released her breath. She was no longer able to hold back the tears of happiness as she dove into Gavin's embrace. Hugging him to her, she buried her face against his chest. His arms closed around her, pulling her closer. When he spoke again, his deep voice rumbled against her cheek.

"Lady Wren was able to bring down the fever and stop the infection, too."

"I'm so happy Da isna goin' to die," said Aila.

"Me, too!" shouted Archy, throwing his arms around Gavin's waist from the side, and giving him a hug as well.

It took Gavin by surprise when Davita threw herself into his arms and hugged him right in front of everyone. However, it surprised him even more when Archy did the same. He half-expected Aila to do so, too. Instead, the girl was clinging to Cam's arm and Cam did nothing to push her away.

"Lady Wren said it was a guid thing we brought him to the castle when we did," Nash told them, sitting down and stretching out his long legs. "If no', he probably would have died for sure."

"Nash, I'm tellin' the story," Gavin grumbled. Nash often spoke without thinking, and sometimes the things he said were a little insensitive to others.

"Did they really say he would have died?" asked Davita with a sniff, pulling away and looking at Gavin with tears dripping down her cheeks. "So, I really did almost kill him?"

"That's no' what Lady Wren said." Gavin patted Archy on the head and then had to pry the boy's fingers from his plaid. "What she did say was that whoever stitched him up did an excellent job."

"She did?" Davita wiped away a tear with her sleeve and grinned slightly.

"Aye, I heard it, too," agreed North. "She also said he will have to stay there awhile since his arm is broken now as well as his ankle. It must have happened when he fell in the dark."

"Oh, nay. That was my fault," said Davita, once again taking the blame.

"Now listen. All of ye." Gavin turned to include everyone in the room. "What happened to Graeme is no one's fault."

"It is the fault of the men who tried to kill him," said Archy.

"What's done is done. I think we should all focus on the fact that yer faither is in guid hands and will be cared for at the castle until he is able to come back here."

"Thank ye, Gavin, for takin' him there." Davita flashed him a smile and looked up at him with wet eyes. "Ye saved his life."

Nash cleared his throat. "We all were a part of this."

"Thank ye all," said Aila. She smiled at Cam and he seemed pleased that she was paying so much attention to him. Gavin wasn't sure the girl wasn't going to kiss his friend before this was over.

"Well, we can all relax now, and I can get to work." Gavin walked over and slapped Cam on the back. "I'm sure ye boys will be able to find somethin' to do while I learn how to make shoes."

"I can help keep them busy," said Aila, only making matters worse.

"Aila, ye have chores to do," Davita reminded her. "Now that faither is gone, we are all goin' to have to work twice as hard."

Aila scowled at her. "There isna anythin' to be done right now."

"The floor needs sweepin', and the garden needs to be weeded," Davita told her.

"I'll take care of the garden," Archy offered eagerly, and Gavin knew why. The boy didn't want his sisters to find his toad house and make him get rid of Hamish. "Oh, I almost forgot." Archy ran over and picked up the spatula, and took off at a run to the back door.

"Ye need to return that!" shouted Davita, but the lad was already gone.

"What does he need that for?" asked Cam.

"For swattin' flies," said Aila with a shrug. "I think my little brathair must eat them."

"Speakin' of that, I'll bet ye men are hungry," said Davita. "I made a double batch of gruel to make sure we'd have enough to go around this time. The leftovers are in the kitchen. It's been sittin' there for a while, so it might have thickened a little. I'm sure it should be fine though. Tonight, I'm goin' to have Aila help me make a kettle full of cabbage soup."

"Gruel?" asked Cam, making a face. "I've got to stable the horse. No time to eat." He headed for the door.

"I'll help rub it down," added North, hurrying after him. "Dinna bother savin' any for me. I'm no' hungry."

"No thanks, I dinna like gruel," said Nash, being too honest as usual. "Besides, we're full from all the pheasant, haggis, and sweetmeats we ate at the castle." He stretched and yawned, closing his eyes, leaning back on the chair. "I think I'll take a nap."

"Ye ate at the castle?" asked Davita, sounding severely disappointed. "Oh, I'm sure none of ye will want any of our simple food then. I'm sorry, but gruel is one of the only things we can afford right now. I wish I could offer ye somethin' better."

"I told ye no' to make so much of it," said Aila, opening the door, preparing to leave. "Highlanders dinna want gruel, they want real food, like haggis." She turned and headed away.

"I was only tryin' to do somethin' nice to thank all of ye," said Davita, looking so sad that it sent a pain shooting through Gavin's heart. "I suppose I can give it to the butcher's pigs as slop since no one wants it. At least that way, it willna be wasted."

"Nonsense," said Gavin, wanting her to feel better, and to know that she was appreciated. "It will no' go to waste. We might have eaten, but Nash and I will have some of yer gruel. Sounds guid, doesna it, Nash?"

"What?" Nash's eyes popped open and he about fell off the chair. "Now, Gavin . . ."

"Davita worked hard to make it for us and we wouldna want to disappoint her. *Would we?*" He put emphasis on his last two words, so Nash wouldn't even try to leave like the others.

"But Gavin –"

"Now, Nash, I ken how much ye like to eat since ye and the others ate all my pottage without even offerin' any to me. Mayhap I should let ye eat all the leftover gruel by yerself, since it would only be fair. What do ye think?"

"Nay," he spat, getting up off the chair. "I insist on sharin' it with ye this time, guid friend." Nash looked like he wanted to kill Gavin, and this made Gavin chuckle inwardly. He only wished now that he had stopped Cam and North from leaving. He was already so full that he wasn't sure how much gruel he could possibly eat before he became ill.

CHAPTER TEN

"WE WILL START with repairin' shoes, since that is easier than constructin' a new pair," said Davita, setting up everything they would need on the worktable. "It's no' that hard to fix the stitchin' when it becomes loose, but it never should have weakened to begin with, if the job was done properly."

She looked over her shoulder at Gavin, but he didn't seem to be paying any attention to what she was telling him. Instead, he had his hand on his stomach, and he was staring at the floor. His mouth turned downward into a frown.

"Gavin? Are ye listenin' to me?" she asked.

"Aye," he answered, looking bewildered.

"Ye dinna seem like ye are. It is verra important that ye pay close attention to my every word. Learnin' the art of cordwainin' is no' simple."

"I was just wonderin' if with everythin' that happened today . . . with yer faither and all, I mean . . . if mayhap . . . we should start on the morrow instead."

"On the morrow? Nay! We are so far behind schedule that it'll be a miracle if I ever get caught up."

"I was just thinkin' that perhaps it would be better no' to start now . . . so late in the day."

She let out a sigh. If he hadn't taken so long eating the gruel, they would have had a pair of shoes repaired by now. Still, after having heard how hungry he was when he missed out on the pottage, she didn't want to hurry him or deprive him of something he enjoyed so much, such as eating.

"Well," she said. "I suppose I could start preparin' the cabbage soup for supper now, since it does take a while to cook. It's too bad my da isna here. It is his favorite."

Gavin's eyes opened wide at hearing this. "Nay! Nay, we're guid," he blurted out, holding up his hand and moving closer. He didn't look at all comfortable and she couldn't imagine why. "Let's make shoes. That is more important than cookin' or eatin'."

"I'm glad to hear ye say that." She smiled and nodded at him, thinking that mayhap he was learning how to change, after all. "Well, the first thing we'll want to do is to don our leather aprons." She tied an apron around her that had a bib covering her chest. It was long, and went all the way down past her knees. She picked up a second apron, and handed it to him. "Here ye are, Gavin. It is my da's but will be yer apron now until ye leave."

"No thanks. I dinna need it."

"Ye really should wear it. Workin' with the tools and leather, yer clothes can get damaged or punctured. Besides, sometimes I need to use tallow on the leather to smooth it or make it supple. If I do that, chances are, things will get messy from the animal fat. Here, let me help ye." She slipped the top apron loop over his head, and then put her arms around him, tying the apron around the back of him, with her chest purposely pressed up against his. She liked being close to him, and was hoping he'd try to kiss her again. Now that she wasn't as worried about her father, she thought she might even enjoy Gavin's presence more. She also wanted to sleep in Gavin's arms again. Last night, she'd felt so safe pressed up against him with his arm around her that she'd had a restful sleep. She felt well protected, even though they were sleeping outdoors.

"I've got it," he said, gently pushing her away from him and tying the apron himself. That disappointed her, but she tried not to show it.

"How much do ye ken about shoes?" she asked, tightening the strings of her apron.

"What's there to ken?" Gavin shrugged. "Ye wear them on yer feet and they protect ye when ye walk." He smiled and held up his foot to show her.

"Is that really yer extent of knowledge?" She started feeling doomed again. This man didn't know a leather-strap pair of boots from wooden pattens. "I think we'll need to start at the verra beginnin'. But honestly, it takes years and years to learn the craft. Does Laird MacKeefe really expect ye to make a pair of shoes? This is a jest, right?"

"Callum just wants a new pair of boots, and is tryin' to torture me to get them." Gavin plopped down on a chair and stretched out his legs and moaned.

Davita could see what a distraction Gavin was going to prove to be. He would be of little help, or none at all. Why had she made this agreement in the first place? Then she thought of her poor father and knew she had to do anything to help him keep the business. Taking a deep breath, she released it slowly, and decided to try again.

"All right," she said, struggling to remain calm even though she was becoming more and more anxious with every minute that passed. She felt as if they were wasting precious time. She couldn't stop thinking of all the work piling up. "If Callum's boots are the most important thing for yer redemption, then we should get them constructed first. Tell me what kind he wants."

"Cordovan leather boots," he answered, settling himself on the chair, getting comfortable.

"I will have to go to the tanner's to get the leather. Cordovan leather comes from Italy and is verra expensive. We dinna have extra stock just lyin' around."

"I'll pay for it," he said. "Let me ken how much it is when ye return. I'll wait here." His eyes closed and he honestly looked as if he were about to take a nap.

"What style of boots were they?" she asked, waking him up

with her question.

His eyes opened and he looked up in the air as if he were thinking. "No' too fancy," he answered.

"What color?" she asked next.

"Black," he answered quickly. Then he scratched his head and his eyes went up to the ceiling again. "Or mayhap they were brown. I canna remember."

"Long or short?" she asked, trying to get a general idea of what they looked like.

"I think they were . . . short. Nay. Mayhap they were taller. Och, what does it really matter?"

"It matters!" she exclaimed, losing her patience with the man. For something as important as his redemption, she thought he'd take this a little more seriously. "I need to ken the length and style so I have an idea how much leather to buy."

"Just get extra leather, and then ye'll have enough," was his doitit answer.

"Gavin, ye are no' takin' this seriously."

"Sorry," he said, shaking his head, and slapping himself on the cheek. "I'm just so tired that I canna focus. What did ye ask me again?"

"Callum's boots," she said, feeling frustrated. This conversation wasn't helping her at all.

"What about them?"

"Did they have buckles or laces?"

GAVIN COULDN'T REMEMBER a thing about Callum's bloody boots, and neither did he really care. "Laces," he said, just guessing, wanting her to stop asking questions.

"Guid. Now we're gettin' somewhere. So, were they front or side laced?"

"Does it matter?"

"To Callum it will."

"He's old and probably canna reach around to the side, so make them front laced."

"Are ye sure they werena drawstring?"

"Aye. Nay. Davita, I dinna ken. I just need a pair of Cordovan boots to replace the ones I ruined."

"I canna possibly make them without knowledge of their length and size. Were they ankle boots or calf boots, or all the way up to his knees?"

"Arrrgh, I dinna ken, I told ye. Do ye want me to go to the Highlands and ask him?"

"Didna ye see them?"

"From the floor, aye, but my vision was blurred at the time. Besides, they looked different after I retched on them. I canna be sure of anythin'."

"Mayhap yer friends saw them," she suggested. "Why dinna ye go find them and ask?" It sounded like she was trying to get rid of him and, honestly, he was glad. He had such a bellyache after eating all that cold, thick, tasteless gruel, that all he wanted to do was to hide away somewhere and take a nap.

"Ye're right. It's important. I'll find my friends and ask them if they remember anythin' about Callum's boots." He shot up off the chair and hurried to the door.

"Be sure no' to tarry," she called after him. "I'll have cabbage soup ready in a few hours. I hope ye and yer friends like onions. I have lots of them from my garden and need to use them up before they go bad."

The pain in his belly got worse just thinking about eating cabbage and onions right now. He hightailed it out of there, spying his friends over by the stable. Archy was with them.

"There ye are, Gavin," said Cam, getting down on one knee. As Gavin approached, he could see his friends were playing cards and dice. They were making bets for money with a few men that he'd noticed drinking in the tavern last night.

"Want to get in on the game?" asked North, blowing on his hand and shaking dice in his fist. Nash sat silently over to the side with his hand covering his stomach.

"Nay. I dinna gamble and ye ken it." All Gavin wanted was a

nap.

"I want to play," said Archy, sounding way too enthusiastic.

"Nay, ye're just a lad," said Cam. "This is a game for men only."

"Besides, ye dinna have any money," added North, throwing the dice and cheering when they landed, making him a winner. "Pay up," he told the other two men with an outstretched arm.

Gavin's eyes opened wide when he saw Archy pickpocket one of the men's money pouches. No one else noticed.

"I do, too, have money," Archy told them. Gavin realized he was about to hold up the pouch right in front of the man he'd stolen it from. Not a good idea.

"Archy, ye're just a lad," said Gavin, picking him up under one arm, making the boy laugh. "Ye need to play with the children instead of the men." He snatched the pouch of coins from the boy and quietly tossed it to the ground at his feet.

"Pay up, men," North said again, holding out his hand.

"Wait. Where's my coin pouch?" asked the man that Archy had stolen from. He tapped his side and looked around. "I've been robbed."

"Is this it?" asked Gavin, reaching down and picking up the pouch, handing it to him. "Ye must have dropped it. Ye need to be more careful."

"Aye, I guess so. Thank ye," said the man, plucking a coin out and handing it to North.

"Ready for another hand of cards?" asked Cam.

"I'm out," said the other man, leaving.

"That was all the money I had to feed my family." The first man threw down the empty pouch and stood up.

"Then why were ye gamblin'?" asked Gavin, placing Archy down on the ground.

"I was hopin' to win some money to be able to buy more food for my youngins to eat."

"Dinna ye have a job?" asked Gavin.

"No' any longer. I worked for the butcher, but business has

been slow lately, and he had to let me go."

"If ye'd stop drinkin' at the tavern, my friend, mayhap yer young ones wouldna have to go hungry." Gavin waited for the man to deny it, but instead he nodded.

"I ken ye are right, and I am ashamed of my actions," he agreed. "But yesterday, I only had a drink because if I didna, I was goin' to take my own life."

Nash's head popped up at that, and Gavin's friends didn't say a word.

"Give him back his money," Gavin told North. "Give him everythin' he lost."

North did as told, and Cam handed him some coins, too.

"I dinna ken how to thank ye," said the man, sounding ever so grateful. Gavin wondered if this action might have just kept the man from killing himself, after all.

"What is yer name?" asked Gavin.

"I'm Bram," he answered.

"Well, Bram, go home to yer wife and children. From now on, stay out of the tavern. If it's work ye need, come by the cordwainer's shop in a few hours. There is so much to do, I'm sure Davita could use yer help."

"Thank ye, Gavin," said the man, his face lighting up with a wide smile. "Thank ye, so much."

"Ye ken who I am? How?" asked Gavin, surprised to hear his name springing from the man's lips.

"Aye, ye and all the MacKeefes are highly respected in town."

"Gavin, are ye sure Davita will want to hire him?" asked Cam in a low voice.

"I dinna think she has money to pay him," said North.

"Will ye work for food for yer family instead of pay, for now?" asked Gavin.

"Aye. Any morsel ye can spare would be appreciated," answered the man with a renewed sense of hope.

Gavin rubbed his belly and looked back at the cordwainer's shop across the street. "I ken where ye can get some cabbage soup later, and I would be more than willin' to give ye my share."

"See ye later," said Archy as soon as the man left. He started away, but Gavin cleared his throat and the boy slowly turned around. "Aye?" he asked sheepishly.

"That was a close one, lad. Ye almost got caught stealin'."

"But I didna, so what does it matter?" He turned to go but, this time, Gavin reached out and clamped his hand over the boy's shoulder. "What?" Archy looked up at him nervously.

"Yer stealin' is no' a guid thing and has to stop."

"I didna hurt anyone," the lad protested.

"Ye are hurtin' yer sisters and riskin' yer faither's reputation in town with every pocket ye pick."

"I only take things that others dinna need anyway."

"Do ye really think that man didna need his money? Ye heard what he had to say. His family is starvin' and thanks to ye, they almost went hungry tonight. Yer action might have even caused him to take his own life."

"Sorry," said Archy, looking like he meant it. "The man has his coins back now, and ye even offered him some of our supper. So, now, we'll go hungry instead."

"Aye, why did ye have to say that?" asked North.

"I'm willin' to give up my share to feed them," said Gavin.

"Me, too." Nash moaned from the shadows.

"No more stealin' or I'm goin' to tell Davita yer toad is livin' in her garden." Gavin was blackmailing him, but he had to do something to make the boy realize there would be consequences for his actions if he didn't change.

"Please, dinna do that. I like Hamish. He is part of the family now."

"Then do ye promise to stop stealin'?" Gavin lifted a brow, waiting for the boy's answer.

Archy made a face and looked at the ground, kicking at the dirt. "Aye. I promise."

"Then go and help Davita in any way ye can."

"Are ye comin' back to the shop now, too?" asked the boy.

"No' yet, but soon. Now go." Archy started away, walking slowly, watching the men over his shoulder.

"That was a noble thing for ye to do," said North once the boy left. "I mean, offerin' the man yer share of food and all."

"Aye," agreed Cam. "We ken how ye like to eat, and that surprises me as well."

"I dinna want any cabbage soup," said Nash from behind them. "I feel sick from eatin' all that gruel."

North and Cam laughed.

"Glad we didna stick around," said North. "It sounds like Davita is skilled at makin' shoes, but no' with makin' meals."

"I have to admit, it didna sit well with me, either," Gavin told them, rubbing his belly.

"So that's why ye offered Bram the soup," said Cam with a chuckle. "Ye didna want to have to eat it yerself."

"I didna want to disappoint Davita," said Gavin. "After all, she's givin' up much to cook for us and I want her to ken she's appreciated."

"Then go tell her that," North challenged him.

"Mayhap after a short nap, I will. I'm goin' to find an empty stall and get some rest." Gavin headed to the barn. "Och," he said, snapping his fingers and turning on his heel. "Do any of ye remember what kind of boots Callum had?"

"Cordovan leather," said Nash.

"I ken that. But Davita asked me if they were short or tall."

"Short," said North.

"Tall," replied Cam at the same time.

"Thanks, that helps a lot." Gavin said in a sarcastic tone. "Did the boots have buckles or laces?"

"Aye," said Nash, getting a roll of the eyes from Gavin this time.

"She also wants to ken if they laced up the side or the front," said Gavin.

"What does it matter?" asked Cam. "A pair of boots is a pair of boots."

"My thoughts exactly," agreed Gavin.

"Ye should remember, since ye saw them close up from down on the floor when ye retched on them," North remarked.

"Dinna say the word retched, or I might do it again right now." Gavin headed into the barn, trying to forget about boots or food for a while.

"Next time, dinna be so gluttonous, and mayhap ye willna feel so ill," he heard Cam say as he left his friends behind him. Gavin was starting to think that by the time this punishment was over, he might never want to eat again.

❖◦◇◦❖

CHAPTER ELEVEN

"**I** CANNA IMAGINE what is takin' them so long." Davita looked out the open window, watching for Gavin and his friends. The shop was a simple wooden two-story building with the walls constructed of wattle and daub. The floor was wood as well. Glass was expensive and rare and only the nobles or churches really had it. So the window was just a large, open hole in the wall. At night, the shutters were closed and latched to keep out intruders as well as the cold.

"I'm sure they willna miss a meal," said Aila, lighting a few candles since it was already starting to get dark.

"Gavin and Nash dinna like yer cookin'," Archy blurted out, setting the table in the kitchen.

"What did ye say?" That took Davita by surprise. She spun around, knocking a few pairs of shoes off the worktable in her haste as she hurried to the kitchen. She'd managed to repair a half-dozen pairs of shoes today, but had spent too much precious time making the meal for Gavin and his friends. The last thing she wanted to hear now was that they didn't like her cooking after she'd given up so much to do it. "Archy, ye are just sayin' that."

"Nay! It's true. They were talkin' about it at the livery earlier. They thought I left, but I hid behind a barrel and listened."

"Ye were there spyin' on them?" She crossed her arms over her chest and tapped her foot on the ground. She wasn't happy with her brother's actions.

"Nay, I wasna spyin'."

"Then what were ye doin'?" asked Aila, coming to join them.

"I was there just . . . watchin' them gamble."

"Archy!" Davita's jaw dropped and her hands fell to her sides. "I canna believe ye were hangin' around men when they were gamblin'. That is a bad influence on ye."

"Sorry, Sister."

The bells above the door jangled, taking her attention. "Ye're finally here, I see," she called out, thinking it was Gavin and his friends. "The food is gettin' cold." She hurried out to the shop part of the building to meet them.

"Excuse me?" A thin man old enough to be her father stood just inside the doorway, wringing his hat in his hands. His feet were bare, and his clothes, ragged. She recognized him as the man who helped the butcher.

"Bram? What are ye doin' here?" she asked. "I didna order anythin' from the butcher lately."

"Nay, Davita, and I'm sorry to disturb ye," he said, sounding very nervous. "Gavin told me if I came by the shop ye'd have work for me, since the butcher had to let me go."

"Gavin told ye that, did he?" Her fury with the Highlander was growing. "I'm sorry, Bram, but my faither is ill and I dinna have any money to pay for yer help."

"Bram said I could work for food. For my family. To feed them." He looked so sad and forlorn, how could she turn him away?

"Well, I suppose the front walkway could use sweepin'. But that is about all for tonight."

"I'll do it." He ran to find a broom and went back outside, eager to work. She felt sorry for the man. No one should have to go hungry, especially not children.

Laughter filled the air as Gavin, Cam, and North, entered the building, making a lot of noise.

"It's about time ye showed up." Davita crossed her arms over her chest and tapped her toe on the ground. She scolded them much the same way she did with her nine-year-old brother. "Ye were expected back here a half-hour ago. I have been keepin' the soup warm."

"We're sorry," said North.

"Aye, time got away from us," added Cam.

"Go on, then." She waved her arm toward the kitchen. "The soup is in the kettle. Help yerselves. I made a double batch tonight, so there is plenty for everyone."

North and Cam quickly headed for the kitchen, but Gavin didn't move.

"Where is Nash?" asked Davita, her gaze going to the window once more. The sound of the broom on the wooden walkway filled the air as Bram busied himself with the unimportant work. If only Gavin were as eager to work as this man was, she might have actually gotten more done concerning shoes.

"Nash . . . he . . . made some new friends and will be spendin' time with them tonight," Gavin told her. He shifted from one leg to the other, and seemed uncomfortable. Davita had never seen the Highlander act this way before. "Nash said no' to save any cabbage soup for him."

"Why no'?" she asked, still angry to have learned that Gavin and Nash didn't like her cooking. She'd tried so hard to please them. Now, she wondered if he'd come clean and be honest with her, or if he'd lie to hide the truth.

"I mean – he'll be eatin' with his friends. So he willna be hungry . . . later, I mean. For cabbage soup."

THERE WAS NO mistaking the perturbed look on Davita's face. Gavin was starting to wish that he had stayed in the stable along with Nash now. Nash hadn't made any new friends to eat with. He just couldn't stomach any more of Davita's meals, after that nasty gruel. His only hope of not having to eat it was to stay there until the meal was over.

"Gavin, Bram is here to work for me but I canna pay him," Davita told him.

"Aye. He is in a bad way, and I sent him over. His family is hungry, so I told him he can work for food."

"Ye did, did ye?" If Gavin wasn't mistaken, Davita was giving him the death stare. One of her eyes squinted half-closed, and her teeth were clenched tightly together. He swore he saw her jaw twitch. Or was it just a vein throbbing at the side of her neck? He shifted back and forth, then looked down and fussed with his weapon belt so he didn't have to see her glaring at him.

"I'll give up some of my soup," he told her. "To make sure there's enough to feed Bram and his family." When he glanced back up at Davita, she had her hands balled up in fists, and resting on her hips now. He felt a shiver go up his spine. This couldn't be good. "I just want to help the poor man and his family, ye realize," he added, his throat feeling so dry that he started to cough. Damn it, he needed a good swig of Mountain Magic right now. Too bad he couldn't have it.

"There's no need to give up your share of the food," she said. The corners of her mouth twisted up into some sort of evil grin. Or at least that's the way it looked to him. Suddenly, he had the thought that she might know they didn't want to eat her cooking. God's teeth, he hoped she didn't realize what he was doing.

"W-what do ye mean by that?" he asked, feeling a bead of sweat travel down the side of his face.

"What I mean is, of course, I'll help the man and his family."

"Oh, guid." Relief washed through him, but only for a brief moment. Everything changed once he heard what she had to say next.

"It's just a guid thing I made up a double batch of soup to-night. Now, there will be plenty for everyone. As a matter of fact, since ye like to eat so much, and I feel terrible that ye went hungry the other day, ye can have Nash's share, too. So it'll be a double portion for ye, Gavin. How lucky is that?"

"Aye. Lucky." He swallowed forcefully, his stomach already lurching just from the thought of it. Lucky, she said? Hah! Bad luck was all that was in store for him.

"I ken that makes ye happy." She patted him on the shoulder and smiled. "Let's go eat, shall we?"

Well, mayhap it was just gruel that she couldn't cook well, Gavin tried to convince himself. In her defense, it was cold and thickened. Aye, that was it. Perhaps when it came to cabbage soup, it would taste delicious, with lots of flavor. He could only hope he was wrong thinking it would taste bad.

Well, he wasn't.

As he found out a short time later, she was no better at making soup than she was gruel. Trying his hardest to get down the second bowl of food, Nash's share, Gavin sat at the table with his friends who were eating slowly as well. Davita had gone back to work in the shop, saying there was so much to be done that she wouldn't even be able to sleep tonight. She had to get caught up with all the work.

Bram had left with food for his family earlier, happier than ever. Archy and Aila, Gavin figured, must have gotten used to their sister's cooking through the years. Somehow, it didn't seem to bother them. The siblings finished their food long ago and left, to go somewhere out on the town.

"Gavin, as soon as ye're finished, come here and I will teach ye about shoes. There is so much ye need to learn," called out Davita from the other room.

Gavin groaned, not wanting to eat anything more, and not caring a bit about shoes at the moment. "Aye," he answered, pushing the soup around with his spoon.

"Now I see why Nash didna show up," whispered Cam, making a face. "This doesna taste verra guid at all."

"I agree." North threw down his spoon on the table. "Let's go to the tavern and get some real food. This tastes like someone washed their dirty hose in it."

"Nay," said Gavin, as they both stood up. "If either of ye leave before yer bowls are empty, ye'll insult Davita. She made this for us out of the kindness of her heart, when she didna have the time to do it. We dinna want to hurt her feelin's or disappoint her in any way."

"Well, I suppose we can dump it in the garden." North picked up his half-eaten bowl of food.

"Nay, she'll find it," said Gavin.

"Then we'll take it to Bram. Mayhap his family will eat it," suggested Cam.

"Stop it," Gavin commanded. "Ye two are only thinkin' of yerselves. If Bram tells her what ye did, it'll make Davita sad . . . or mayhap angry." He shivered slightly, remembering her evil death stare.

"Ye're right," agreed Cam, walking over and dumping the rest of his soup into Gavin's already nearly full bowl. It splashed up, getting on Gavin's leine. "Ye eat it then."

"Careful," said Gavin, dabbing at the wet spot with a cloth.

"Have mine, too." North did the same. Then he held up his bowl and smiled. "It's empty."

"Now wait a minute," said Gavin, looking at his bowl of soup that was threatening to run over the rim. "Ye are no' goin' to leave me with all this to eat. Ye canna do that."

"Yes, we are and yes we can, because we just did." Cam walked out of the kitchen with North. Both of them were laughing.

"Gavin?"

Gavin's head whipped around to see Davita standing in the doorway. "Are ye still eatin'? We have a lot of work to do before bedtime. Ye'd better hurry up."

"Blethers, Davita, I dinna think I can work anymore tonight." His eyes went back to the bowl.

"Why no'?" She walked over and collected the empty bowls from the table. "And what is takin' ye so long to eat? Everyone else is already finished, and it doesna even look like ye've started yet."

"Well . . . I . . . I . . ."

DAVITA TURNED AWAY with the dirty dishes, smiling wickedly to herself. She'd been standing in the doorway and heard the whole thing. Gavin's friends didn't like her food any more than he did. It hurt her feelings, and made her angry. Yet, at the same time, when they dumped their soup into Gavin's bowl, she'd almost laughed aloud. Part of her wanted him to suffer. At least a little. Then again, she felt sorry for him at the same time.

She turned around and his eyes met hers. They were filled with desperation. Then he slowly picked up his spoon, and started to eat. By the look on his face, she wasn't sure he wouldn't retch.

"All right, ye've suffered enough, I guess," she said, walking over and taking the spoon from him, placing it down on the table.

"Davita? I dinna understand." He looked down at the spoon and then back up at her.

"I ken that ye and yer friends dinna like my cookin', Gavin."

"Och, now that's no' true," he said, forcing a smile as he swiped his hand through the air.

"Archy overheard ye at the stable and told me everythin'." She crossed her arms over her chest.

"Oh. I see." He suddenly became lost for words.

"Why couldna ye just tell me that ye dinna like my cookin'?"

"I'm sorry," he apologized. "I didna want to hurt yer feelin's." He slowly stood up from the table, towering over her.

"The truth, I could have handled," she told him. "However, lyin' to me, and givin' my food away to half the town really hurts."

"It wasna half the town. Just Bram and his family."

"For now," she said. "I'm sure by tomorrow ye would have found a few more needy families, too."

"Forgive me, lass," he said, laying his large hands on her shoulders. He bent over to look into her eyes. "Yer happiness means the world to me. The last thing I wanted to do was to disappoint ye. Especially after all ye've been through lately."

When he looked like he was going to kiss her, she backed away. She wasn't sure if she wanted anything going on between them right now. "We've wasted enough time talkin' about this. There are shoes to repair and make, and we need to get busy." She hurried out into the shop area, with Gavin on her heels.

"Davita, I am tryin' to apologize."

She sat down, holding back the tears, reaching for a pair of shoes. His hands shot out and cupped her hand in his. She bit her lip, and her eyes closed.

"I dinna want to think about food, or even shoes anymore tonight," he told her.

"I dinna have a choice," she answered, letting out a deep sigh. "Without my faither here, everythin' lies on my shoulders. I am all alone in this, and I dinna ken if I can do it."

"That's where ye're wrong." He helped her to her feet and turned her toward him. "Look at me, lass." He lifted her chin until she stared directly into his mesmerizing blue eyes. "I promise that I will help ye, in any way I can."

"Gavin, ye dinna ken how to construct or repair shoes, and we both ken it would take ye years to learn the skill."

"Then let me help with what I do ken."

"What do ye mean?"

"I will be the one to cook the meals from now on, and that alone will save ye time to work on the business."

"I suppose," she said, not sounding that thrilled with the idea. "After all, yer food tastes better than mine."

"Sweetheart, I have been cookin' for my clan in the Highlands ever since I was a child. I enjoy it, so let me do it. I will also help ye with Archy and Aila, and take that burden away from ye as well."

"Ye will?" She looked up at him, and he gently wiped a tear from her cheek. His sincere, kind smile made her feel better already.

"Now that yer faither is in guid hands, ye dinna have to worry about his health. With me and my friends here, we will fill in whenever and wherever we can to make certain that yer family is taken care of. I willna let ye lose the business."

"Oh, that is verra generous of ye to offer, but I dinna ken what to say."

"Ye need to stop tryin' to do everythin' yerself, lass. Start askin' for help when ye need it. Archy and Aila would probably no' get into so much mischief if ye relied on them more, too."

"Do ye really think so?" Davita asked him, never having thought of this.

"I ken so. Now, no more workin' tonight," he told her. "Ye and I are goin' for a little ride." He pulled her toward the door, stopping when he spied the bottle of whisky that she'd been hiding from her father. "I think we'll take this along." He snatched up the bottle.

"Gavin, nay," she told him.

"It's no' for me, lass. It's for ye, because ye need to relax."

"Where are we goin'?" she asked, allowing him to pull her along with him out the door.

"We're goin' to take my horse to a secluded spot I ken of, where ye willna be able to work or fuss over anyone. Just relaxin' is all ye'll be able to do."

"Where is it? After all, it is dark out and willna be safe to leave the town now."

He stopped in his tracks and she crashed into him, feeling like she'd hit a brick wall.

"Lass, I am a fully armed Highland warrior," he said, his fingers tapping the hilt of his sword at his waist to prove his point. "Do ye really think I canna protect ye?"

"Nay," she answered with a smile, already starting to feel better. "When I am with ye, Gavin, I feel safe. I ken ye will protect me. I will go with ye, because I ken ye are right about everythin' ye said. Besides, I, too, want to make ye happy."

"If ye truly want to make me happy, then please, do no' cook for me again."

She giggled, feeling pleased that they talked. She realized he didn't mean to insult her, but was trying to make her smile instead. Taking his hand in hers, she started to run, not able to wait to leave all her worries behind. Right now, all she wanted was to spend time alone with the sexy Highlander warrior, Gavin MacKeefe.

◆·◇◇◇·◆

CHAPTER TWELVE

DAVITA SAT IN front of Gavin on the horse as they left town in the darkness. His arms were wrapped protectively around her, and his thighs cradled hers. It was a beautiful, starry night with a warm breeze blowing. She'd always been frightened to leave town at night, because that is when bandits roamed freely, and dangerous animals hunted.

Tonight, she was not scared at all. With Gavin at her side, she knew no harm would ever come to her.

"We're here," he said, stopping near a creek, and dismounting. He held up his arms to help her down, and she willingly accepted. With her hands on his shoulders, he closed his fingers around her waist, lifting her from the steed. Slowly, he slid her body down his, until her feet touched the ground. She wasn't sure if he lingered with the action on purpose or not, but she found it very sensuous.

"Thank ye," she said shyly, looking up at him and wetting her lips. He was staring at her mouth and it made her wonder if he was going to kiss her. He'd almost done so in the kitchen, but she'd pushed him away. Now, she regretted her action.

"I'll tie up the horse," he said, clearing his throat and stepping away from her. Disappointment filled her that he hadn't kissed her again. As he took care of the horse, she went over to the travel bag that he'd removed and placed on the ground. Her nimble fingers quickly searched inside the bag until she found what she was looking for. Grasping the neck of the bottle, she pulled out the whisky. Normally, Davita didn't drink to get drunk, but tonight she felt like she needed this more than anything. Her emotions were heightened being around Gavin, and she wasn't sure just how to act now that they were alone.

Uncorking the bottle, she held up the whisky, taking a quick draw. It burned on the way down and she coughed slightly.

"Ye need to drink slowly, unless ye're used to it." He took the whisky from her, and she saw the want in his eyes as he stared intently at the golden liquid inside the bottle.

"Perhaps it wasna a guid idea to bring this along. It is too temptin' for ye." She took the bottle back.

"Nay, I'm fine." He reached up and ran a hand through his long hair. "Let's go sit down by the water."

"All right," she agreed, taking his hand, still holding the whisky in the other. Together, they walked like lovers down to the river.

They sat down on a large, flat rock, staring out at the moonlight shining down on the ripples in the water. The slight breeze drifted past her face, bringing with it the scent of wildflowers. Frogs croaked in a nighttime chorus and glowworms lit up, trying to attract mates.

"This is beautiful," she said, starting to feel very relaxed. Gavin's arm slipped around her waist and she liked it. He'd removed his weapon belt before sitting down, and now he pulled her closer to him.

"Aye, lass. I agree. Beautiful."

When she looked up at him, she saw him staring down at her instead of out at the water. She giggled and took another sip of whisky, corking up the bottle. "Ooo, I think I've had enough of this. I am startin' to feel dizzy."

"I'll make sure ye dinna fall." Gavin pulled her onto his lap.

"What are ye doin'?" she asked, giggling again as she wrapped her arms around his neck to keep from losing balance.

"I'm protectin' ye, lass. That's what ye wanted, right?"

"Aye, but I dinna think I need protectin' from the glowworms and frogs."

His mouth covered hers, and her eyes closed as they shared a sensuous kiss.

"Mmm," he mumbled, his lips vibrating against hers.

"Ye like the kiss?" she whispered, gently brushing back his long hair.

"That, and the taste of the whisky on yer lips."

She hit him playfully on the shoulder, but wasn't angry with him at all. "Is that all ye can think of at a romantic time like this?"

"Nay, but if ye dinna mind, can I taste it again?"

"My pleasure." She touched her lips to his again and, this time, his tongue shot out and into her mouth, surprising her completely. Since she was so relaxed, she returned the gesture. Her tongue dueled with his in a lustful manner. It was intimate and alluring and made her heart beat faster. Then he moaned again, this time closing his lips over her tongue. When he pulled away slowly and released her tongue, it caused a popping sound.

"I have never done anythin' like that before," she admitted, feeling suddenly very naughty.

"Ye like that, lass?"

"It makes my heart beat faster."

"Really? Let me see." He placed his palm over her chest, and kissed her again in the same manner. She felt her body almost going limp in his embrace.

"Do ye feel how fast it is beatin'?" she asked him, hearing the breathiness of her own voice.

"I'm no' sure. I dinna think I can feel it through all these clothes." With that, he reached out and untied her bodice, looking deeply into her eyes as he slowly slid his fingers down her neck, stroking her skin. Dipping even lower, the tips of his fingers brushed against the tops of her breasts.

"Oh!" she gasped, surprised, excited, and aroused. She arched her back, and his whole hand disappeared under her clothes with his next stroke. Then she felt him palm her breast, making her even more randy. "That feels guid," she said, feeling very relaxed from the whisky.

He kissed her gently, and then pulled back just a bit to talk to her. "If ye think that feels guid, lass, wait until ye feel this!" His thumb grazed over her nipple, causing her to suck in a breath. She felt a tingle of excitement climb her spine. And then he rolled her nipple between his fingers until she became taut.

"Och, Gavin MacKeefe, ye really ken how to excite a lass." Her chest heaved, making the swells of her breasts almost seem to glow in the moonlight.

"If it's excitement ye want . . ." This time, he lowered his mouth to her bodice and ran his tongue slowly over the skin at the base of her neck.

"Gavin? What are ye goin' to do next?" she asked, thinking that she knew where this was going.

"Just relax, lass. I promise ye will like it." He used one hand to brush back the cloth, and then he lowered his mouth to her, taking her nipple in between his lips. A few flicks of his tongue had her squirming on his lap in delight. And when he started suckling at her like a babe, she couldn't help but moan in ecstasy.

"Ooooo, Gavin. I like that. Ye are right, it does excite me." Her hands gripped at his hair. She found herself pushing his face closer to her.

Before she knew what was happening, he'd pulled her bodice down completely, exposing both of her breasts. Moonlight lit up her pale mounds and when she looked at herself, she could see both her nipples were standing up straight and hard like little soldiers. The one he'd suckled was glistening wet.

"I feel so . . . naughty," she told him, licking her lips, breathing heavily. If this was wrong, she didn't care. She wanted . . . she needed more!

"Naughty is nothin' to be ashamed of when it is dealin' with makin' love."

"Makin' love," she repeated. The thought of it actually happening suddenly made her feel frightened. "I have never been with a man before in that manner."

"There is nothin' to it, and nothin' to be afraid of, I assure ye." He kissed her passionately, his hands sliding down her back, rounding her butt cheeks, squeezing gently. And when she felt the poking of something from under his plaid, she jumped up, and turned to face him.

"Gavin, what was that?" She knew what it was, but just wasn't sure what to say to him right now. She'd aroused him, and he'd done the same to her. Davita liked the foreplay, but was reluctant to continue since she barely knew this man and was still a virgin.

A hungry, dark and dangerous look filled his eyes that told her he wanted so much more than just a little foreplay. This time, it wasn't only whisky he longed for, and the thought excited, but yet scared her, too.

"That's my want for ye," he said, gently taking her hand and pulling her back toward him.

"Y-ye want me?" she asked, feeling foolish for questioning him about it since his erection spoke louder than words.

"Aye, lass. And yer actions tell me that ye want me, too."

"They do?"

"Our bodies are callin' out to each other. What is more natural?" he asked.

Her eyes traveled down to the tented plaid at his waist again. It looked so big . . . so hard . . . so inviting. "Look for yerself, if ye dinna believe me." When he pulled up his plaid to expose himself, she saw how engorged he really was. The sight was so fascinating and exciting to her that she couldn't look away.

"Ye are no' wearin' undergarments," she gasped.

"Nay. Highlanders usually dinna bother with them."

"Ye are . . . so . . . big," she said, her tongue flicking out to lick her top lip. Her breathing deepened and she felt a stirring in her core. Suddenly, she felt so hot . . . and so ready to experience something such as this for the very first time. Even though she was frightened, she found herself growing more and more excited, just looking at his beautiful manly weapon of love.

"Come, lass." He guided her to him, straddling her legs on each side of his as he pulled her back atop his lap. Now she was now pressed up against his erection and could feel it clearly. He was ready to make love with her, but her cautious nature rose to the surface. Mayhap she wasn't ready for this yet, after all.

"I – I am scared, Gavin," she admitted.

"Davita, I promise I will no' hurt ye."

"I'm no' sure I am ready for this."

"I can help ye get ready." He took one hand, sliding it up under her skirt, getting closer and closer to her most private part.

"This is too fast. I canna do it," she told him when he reached for the ties on her braies. She could hear the panic in her own voice. His hand stilled when he heard her words. Then he slowly pulled back to look into her eyes.

"Blethers, lass, ye really are no' ready for this, are ye?"

"I – I'm sorry, Gavin," she said, shaking her head. "I ken how much ye want it."

"I only want it if ye do," he assured her. "However, now I can see that will no' be tonight, after all."

She heard the disappointment in his voice. This was not at all how she wanted it to play out in the end. "I want it, too, I really do," she told him. "But I . . . I guess I am just no' sure what to do."

"Come here," he said, taking her bottom in his hands and pulling her up against his hardened form. "Press up against me and let down yer guard. Ye can pleasure yerself without me even enterin' ye."

"Are ye sure?" she asked, feeling confused.

"Try it."

He pulled her legs around him tightly, and his erection pressed up against her womanhood, enabling her to feel him bringing her to life.

"Rub up against me. Do it," he whispered, suckling her breast, and fondling the other at the same time, stimulating her in the most delicious way.

She did as he instructed, still feeling lightheaded from the whisky she'd drank. Before long, an odd feeling throbbed between her thighs. She was sure she felt a wetness gathering there. Aye, her body was coming to life.

"Oooooh, I see what ye mean," she said, gyrating her hips against him, because every time she rubbed up against his hardened form, it excited her more and more. With that, as well as his mouth on her breasts and his hands fondling her bottom end, her excitement grew so intense that she heard herself cooing and moaning in the moonlight. Her own sounds of being pleasured made her feel excited in the naughtiest, but also the most delightful way. "Oh, Gavin, this feels so . . . freein'."

GAVIN HELD BACK, even though he wanted nothing more than to pump into Davita until he exploded, making her scream out even louder. He wanted her so bad right now that it was driving him mad.

Still, she had said she wasn't ready to take the plunge, so to speak, so he tried to respect her wishes. The essence of her kiss still lingered on his lips, and the slight flavor of whisky on his tongue only made him feel like he was going mad. He wasn't sure how much longer he could continue this foreplay. He wanted Davita to experience her release. By the sound of it, she just had. But before he could even say anything about it, the sound of hoofbeats in the night made his hands still.

"Gavin?" she asked. "Is somethin' the matter?"

"Shhh," he said, with his finger against her lips. Still in a playful mood, she sucked his finger into her mouth, making him groan. The feel of her hot, wet enclosure only made him envision another part of him in another part of her. Bid the devil, if this wasn't hell, he didn't know what was. The worst part about it was that he was so close to experiencing heaven. "Someone is comin'," he told her.

"Gavin? Gavin, are ye here?" he heard a voice call out that

unfortunately sounded a lot like Nash.

"God's toes, no' now," he grumbled, getting up and putting Davita's feet on the ground. "Get yerself back together, lass. Quickly," he told her.

"Gavin? Davita? Are ye out here?" called out Nash, getting closer.

"Nash, what the hell do ye want?" shouted Gavin, trying to don his weapon belt, but having trouble since he was still fully erect under his plaid.

"Ah, there ye are." Nash rode up and stopped before them, looking at them oddly. "Did I interrupt somethin'?"

"If ye have to ask, then ye are stupider than I thought," snapped Gavin. He looked over at Davita and, thankfully, she was fully covered. "I'll ask ye again, Nash, why are ye botherin' me?"

"I'm sorry, but I saw the horse was gone. Then Archy said he saw ye leavin' with his sister."

"Spit it out! What was so important that ye had to hunt me down instead of waitin' until I returned?"

"It's Aila," he said.

"Aila?" Davita turned around quickly to face him. "Has somethin' happened to my sister?"

"We dinna ken," he told them. "No one has seen her for hours. Archy said she didna come home. It seems she is missin'."

"Nay! Gavin, we have to find her," cried Davita. "Where should we look? Oh, God, I hope nothin' has happened to her. I never should have left town so late at night." Davita kept going on and on, and Gavin had to shut her up so he could think straight.

"Hush, lass," he told her, noticing her eyes becoming glassy in the moonlight. Hell, he hoped she wasn't going to cry, because he couldn't handle that right now. He was still trying to forget that he was sexually excited. "We will find her, I promise. Where was she last seen?" Gavin asked Nash.

"Well, Archy said he saw her talking to . . . Ethan, did he say?"

"That's the cobbler's nephew," Davita told them.

"Then that's probably where she is. Did ye check the cobbler's shop?" asked Gavin.

"We did, but Clyde and Gregor said they hadn't seen Ethan for hours either. Actually, Clyde is furious and makin' all kinds of threats against Davita and her shop. That's why I decided to come and try to find ye. I think trouble is brewin'."

"Trouble is brewin' here, too," mumbled Gavin, wishing Nash could have waited a little longer before he thought to interrupt them. "Davita, ride with Nash back to town," he said, spying the bottle of whisky in the moonlight, not trusting himself alone with it. "And take this with ye." He handed her the bottle.

"I dinna understand," said Davita, looking and sounding so innocent and let down. "Why canna I ride back to town with ye?"

"Ye'll be safe with Nash," he told her. "I just have somethin' to take care of, and I'll be right behind ye."

"Well, all right," she said, mounting Nash's horse. "Please, dinna tarry. We need to find my sister quickly. I am so worried about her."

"I'll be quick," he grumbled, watching them ride away. Then he took off for a plunge in the creek, needing to cool down after his time alone with Davita.

❖◆◇◆❖

CHAPTER THIRTEEN

"**H**AS ANYONE FOUND her? Does anyone ken where my sister is?" Davita jumped off Nash's horse even before he could help her dismount. She ran to the street where a crowd was gathering. People held torches, and Clyde was there with his apprentice, Gregor. Clyde's wife died years ago, and he didn't have any children. Mayhap that is why he seemed so upset about his missing nephew.

"If I find anyone here has harmed my nephew, yer heads are goin' to roll," yelled Clyde. Anger blazed from his eyes.

"Clyde, please just calm down." Davita was still relaxed from the whisky as well as from her intimate time with Gavin. If not, she wouldn't have been the one telling anyone to calm down.

"Ye dinna care." Clyde walked forward and sniffed the air near her. "Ye smell like whisky. Mayhap ye have the same problem as yer old man. Ye're both drunkards."

"Say another word and I'll pull yer tongue right out of yer head." Gavin dismounted, having overheard the conversation. He came over to join them with his hand on the hilt of his sword.

Cam and North were already there as well. Nash tied up the horses and came over to join the group.

"Gavin, why is yer plaid wet?" asked North, looking down at Gavin's clothes.

Davita felt suddenly embarrassed. Now she knew why he'd stayed behind.

"I took a dip in the creek, dinna worry about it," spat Gavin. "Now, everyone. The important thing is that we find Aila and . . . what is the lad's name?" He looked over to Davita, but Clyde answered for her.

"My nephew's name is Ethan. Ye Highlanders better no' have had anythin' to do with his disappearance," warned Clyde.

"Please, remember that my sister is missin', too," Davita reminded him, trying to keep the man from causing trouble.

"We'll need some lanterns, and to check everywhere," said Gavin. "Look for signs of struggle."

"Struggle?" This truly worried Davita. "I hope they are no' injured."

"Aila would scratch a man's eyes out before she'd let him take her," said Archy, pushing to the front of the crowd. "That is, unless she liked them, and then she'd kiss them instead."

"Archy, please haud yer wheesht," said Davita, not wanting to think that any man had accosted her sister.

"Did anyone check the upstairs rooms in the tavern?" asked Gavin.

"The whores' rooms?" gasped Davita. "Gavin, please."

"I'm sorry, Davita, but we canna leave any stone uncovered."

"Ye're right," she said, feeling frightened as well as angry. If her sister wandered off on her own, there would be hell to pay. "I'll get more lanterns."

Davita hurried back into her house, lighting a candle near the door. She almost screamed when she saw all the shoes strewn about, but then remembered she had knocked them down earlier and never picked them back up. Making her way to her father's bedroom for lanterns, she held the lit candle high to light the way. She stopped at the door, her hand wavering in the air. Was that feminine giggling coming from inside the room? She was sure it was.

Throwing open the door, she was shocked to find her sister, Aila, rolling around atop the pallet kissing the cobbler's nephew.

"Aila!" screamed Davita, causing her sister to look up at the door.

"Davita! I thought ye were no' home," said Aila, scooting off the pallet and putting her clothes back into place.

"Well, ye were wrong. I am ashamed of ye," said Davita with a scowl. "Ye, too, Ethan. Half the town is lookin' for ye both, thinkin' ye've been kidnapped."

"Nay, we're fine." Ethan jumped up and smoothed down his hair. "We didna mean to cause trouble."

"Ethan, go on, leave. Yer uncle is waitin' outside. Tell the others that I found Aila. No search is necessary."

"Aye." The boy hurried for the door, but stopped and looked back. "Guidnight, Aila."

"Guidnight, Ethan." Aila beamed, smiling from ear to ear.

As Ethan left, Gavin came in, stopping just outside the bedroom. "Is everythin' all right?" he asked, hesitant to enter.

"I suppose so." Davita paced back and forth. "Come in, Gavin." Davita figured mayhap he could help her, since she had no idea what to do in this situation. He was hesitant to enter, but finally stepped inside the room.

"What were ye doin' in here?" asked Davita.

"I'd think ye two would ken more than anyone, since ye were doin' it, too," replied Aila.

"What does that mean?" she snapped.

"Everyone saw ye two ride out of here snuggled up together atop the horse," Aila retorted. "That's what gave me the idea."

"I doubt it, but continue," said Davita.

"I like Ethan. We were just kissin'," she said. "I canna say the same for ye, though." She perused Gavin's wet plaid, causing him to hold his wrist, covering the sight of his groin with his hands.

"I think mayhap I should leave," said Gavin.

"Nay. Stay," ordered Davita. "Aila, with Faither gone for now, Gavin will be in charge with me until Da is healed and returns."

"Him?" Aila blinked her eyes. "He's a Highlander who is here as an outcast and tryin' to redeem himself. That is like puttin' the wolf in charge of the sheep."

"It is no'," spat Davita. "Gavin is a mature man, a guid protector, and verra guid at –" She looked over at him and could tell he was extremely uncomfortable. "Verra guid at cookin'," she added. "Now, I dinna want to see ye with Ethan, or flirtin' with any of the men again. Do ye understand?" Davita put her hands on her hips for emphasis.

"So ye and the Highlander can kiss and get randy but I canna?" asked Aila, getting angry. "I half-expect ye two already coupled."

"Now, that is none of yer business," Davita answered, not wanting to tell her sister a single thing about what happened between her and Gavin.

"I am six and ten years of age now, Sister. I am old enough to make love or to even get married if I want to." Aila stuck her chin in the air defiantly.

"Nay, ye're no'. And from now on, ye will report to me and tell me where ye are goin', and when ye are comin' home. Also, whom ye'll be with. Now go to bed!" Davita stormed from the room, and Gavin followed. The sound of Aila stomping up the stairs and slamming the bedroom door echoed through the house. Davita was so upset that she didn't know what to do.

Archy ran into the house with something in his hands.

"Brathair, what do ye have there?" asked Davita, thinking he had stolen something again.

"Nothin'," said Archy, putting his hands behind his back. His eyes roamed over to Gavin.

"Let me see." She held out her hand, and Archy looked over to Gavin once again.

"I'll handle this, Davita. Why dinna ye sit down and relax." Gavin put his arm around Archy's shoulders and they headed toward the kitchen.

"It's time for ye to go to bed, too," Davita shouted after them.

"I will, sweetheart. Thank ye for remindin' me," Gavin called out, mocking her, and making her even angrier.

ONCE IN THE kitchen and out of earshot, Gavin spoke in a low voice to Archy. "Ye have yer toad in yer hands, dinna ye?" he asked.

"I didna want Hamish to get trampled with everyone lookin' for Aila," said the boy. "I only wanted to protect him."

"Archy, what are ye doin'?" called out Davita from the workshop.

"My sister is goin' to make me get rid of Hamish. Can ye talk to her, please?" Gavin saw the fear in Archy's eyes. He really did seem to care for the toad.

"I will, but tonight is no' the right time to do it. She is verra upset with Aila, and I think ye should go to bed and no' anger her further."

"She's no' our mathair, but she keeps actin' like it. Aila and I dinna like it one bit. We dinna have to listen to her."

"I think it's best if ye did for now, lad." Gavin reached out and ruffled the boy's hair. "Davita is the closest thing ye have to a mathair, like it or no'. With yer faither gone, she is doin' the best she can to hold this family together. She has a lot on her shoulders. Ye need to help her since ye are the man of the house now with yer faither away."

"I am? Och, I guess I am," said Archy, his frown turning into a smile.

"Now, give me Hamish and I'll put him to bed. In the mornin', I am sure things will all be better."

Gavin took the toad from the boy and stepped out into the garden, bending down to put it under the bowl that served as its home. "Guidnight, Hamish. Do yerself a favor. If ye every get yerself a lassie, move to a garden far away from here. Go someplace where there isna so much trouble."

"Gavin? Who are ye talkin' to?"

Gavin turned around to see Davita pulling a blanket around her shoulders and padding over to him with bare feet.

"No one, lass," he told her, wanting this day to be over. Now that he'd entered Davita's life, he'd taken on her problems as his own. Without a little Mountain Magic to help out, everything seemed so much harder.

"Yer friends decided to sleep in the barn tonight. I think they heard me yellin' at Aila, and are afraid to come inside," Davita told him.

"I dinna blame them," he mumbled under his breath, but she heard him.

"Gavin? Do ye think I was too tough on her?" She walked over and reached out, holding on to his arm.

"She is no' a child anymore, lass. But I think this conversation should wait until the mornin'."

"I suppose a solid night's sleep would do us all some guid. Are ye comin' inside?"

"No' yet," he said, sitting down on the ground, looking up at the sky. "I'm goin' to stay out here and just watch the stars for a while."

"Do ye want me to stay with ye?" she asked.

"Nay," he answered, seeing the disappointed look on her face. "Please understand that I am usually a loner. I am no' used to dealin' with all the problems that face a family such as this one."

"I understand, Gavin. It is a lot for anyone to take. Thank ye, though, for helpin' me get through it. I'll leave ye alone so ye can find some peace of mind."

She left the garden, and Gavin flopped down on his back, looking up at the sky. Tonight had been exhilarating and disappointing all at the same time. He had told Davita he'd help her with her problems, and he would. However, he had no idea that he'd be put into situations that had him starting to feel as distraught as she'd been lately.

As he watched the stars twinkling above him, he started wishing for food, whisky, and to make love with Davita. He thought on what he normally did when he was feeling like this. Usually, he'd find a whore to help him out when he was feeling lustful. But now that he'd spent intimate time with Davita and tasted her kisses, he didn't want a whore. All he wanted was her.

Davita, in some ways, was full of experience – like when it came to making shoes. However, when it came to making love, he realized she was innocent . . . and he was far from it. Did he really want to be the one to take that innocence from her? He was only going to be here a short while, and then he'd be headed back to the Highlands. Was it right to take a girl's virginity, and then leave her stranded with just the memory as he never even looked back? Or would he?

In the past, he wouldn't have been struggling with a decision such as this. Now, part of him didn't ever want to leave Davita. He almost felt like he was starting to be part of her family, no matter how flawed or broken it was. It didn't matter. He oddly liked the feeling of belonging. Then again, he was a warrior and always on the move. She, on the other hand, was going to stay in this little town making shoes until the day she died.

They were so different from each other, and did not belong together. He knew that. However, an aching in his heart kept him from admitting that he was no good for her. He should let her go. What Davita needed was a successful merchant to marry and with whom she could bear many children of her own. She would make a terrific mother someday. She cared so much for everyone who meant anything to her. Davita needed to stay here to care for her father and siblings. Her future life was here, while his was back in the Highlands.

Or was it?

Suddenly, he didn't know what to think anymore.

DAVITA TRIED TO sleep, but she just couldn't. With so much on her mind, she kept tossing and turning. Everyone seemed angry with her, and rightly so. She supposed she shouldn't have been so hard on her siblings, but it was her job to protect them. With her father gone for now, it was up to her to make sure things ran smoothly.

She slept in her father's room, and left the door open. Her sister's crying could be heard from upstairs. Archy probably had the pillow over his head, because he never liked hearing his sisters crying.

Davita got up to close the door, feeling frustrated and confused. Then she looked out at the workshop with all the shoes, feeling overwhelmed once again.

Tonight started out as the first night where she actually was able to forget her troubles for a short time. With the help of a little whisky, she had even been able to relax. Thinking back on the intimate time she'd spent with Gavin, her heart warmed. She liked being with him, and she loved the way he made her feel. But like the day Gavin missed out on the food, she felt that, once again, he missed out on what he truly desired.

Should she have made love with him? Everything was moving so fast. Even so, now she found herself wishing she could have thrown her cares aside and lived just for the day, not worrying about tomorrow. She hadn't. She'd been scared and unsure of herself when she should have just trusted in Gavin.

Feeling bad about leaving him hot and aroused, she quietly made her way out into the garden to find him sound asleep. He had one arm thrown over his face, and was lying on his back.

He'd fallen asleep looking at the stars again. Mayhap he'd been thinking about his own family. She wanted more than anything to lie down next to him and spend the night in his arms. Then again, if she did that, she'd only be tempting him. Besides, she didn't want Aila to see her sleeping with Gavin after what had just happened.

Davita had never been with a man, but now she felt as if the only man she ever wanted was Gavin. Crazy thoughts flitted through her head. What if he was her husband? She felt safe with him, and he seemed to care not only about her, but also Archy and Aila. Aye, she could see he'd make a good husband someday, as well as make a good father. He could even cook! That made her smile. She envisioned him cooking a meal for their three children, while she made shoes to sell in the other room.

Nay, it was crazy to even think this. Gavin was a Highland warrior. Even if they did marry, he'd want to go back to the Highlands where he belonged. That was his home. She could never leave her father, and especially not Archy and Aila. They needed her. She wouldn't abandon them. Her home was here in town, not in the Highlands. Nay, a union between her and Gavin would never work. It broke her heart, but she needed to be real. Gavin MacKeefe was a Highland warrior, and didn't belong with a simple cordwainer's daughter.

She took the blanket from around her shoulders and placed it over him since his plaid was wet from the creek and she didn't want him to catch cold.

"Guidnight, Gavin," she whispered, throwing him a kiss.

Then she looked up to the sky, feeling a new type of loneliness deep inside. When the time came for Gavin to leave her, she didn't know what she was going to do. Ever since he'd come into her life, things seemed different. Her head spun with everything that had happened lately. All she'd been doing was trying to take care of others. But without even realizing it, she'd lost her heart to a man she'd just met. Never had she ever felt this way about anyone before.

Looking at him lying there on the earth once more, she realized she didn't have the right to even try to change him. Nothing made sense anymore. Everything seemed to confuse her since Gavin had walked through her door.

"Who am I?" she whispered, her lip trembling, as she realized, she didn't really know.

Davita turned around and ran back to the house. She would spend the night in the workshop, quietly stitching shoes, trying to get caught up with the orders. There was no way in the world she'd ever be able to sleep now with all these thoughts filling her head.

CHAPTER FOURTEEN

"SO, YE'RE REALLY goin' to cook for us from now on?" asked Archy the next morning, watching as Gavin stirred the kettle hanging over the fire. He'd woken up early to find a blanket covering him that he remembered seeing Davita with last night. When he'd entered the house, he found her asleep at the worktable, with the lantern flickering, almost out of oil. That's when he'd put the blanket around her shoulders and headed back to the kitchen to see what he could find to cook up for all of them to eat.

"Aye, I'm really goin' to cook. For now," Gavin told Archy, chopping up some onions he'd found, and adding it to a pot of cooked oats.

"When will it be ready?" asked Archy anxiously.

"The Skirlie needs just a little more cookin'. Then I'm goin' to add some fried eggs to the top. Is there somewhere I can buy eggs?" he asked.

"I can get all the eggs ye want from the tavern. I get them there all the time."

"Really?" Gavin tasted the Skirlie off the wooden spoon and added a little more salt and a handful of chopped herbs.

"The proprietor has chickens he keeps out back," Archy informed him.

"How much does he charge for the eggs?"

"I dinna ken." The boy was suddenly silent.

"I thought ye said ye get them there all the time."

"Did I? I didna mean to say that."

That told Gavin all he needed to know. "Ye usually steal the eggs, am I right?"

Archy didn't say a word.

"Lad, dinna lie to me. Do ye steal the eggs, or no'?"

"Aye," he finally admitted, playing with a cup on the table, not looking at Gavin when he answered. "But Keithen doesna ken it. He thinks the wolves steal them, since I usually do it at night."

"Archy, this is no' guid, and has to stop."

"It's only eggs," the lad answered with a shrug of his shoulders. "What does it really matter?"

"Here," said Gavin, handing the boy a few coins from his pouch. "Go purchase two dozen eggs if he has them."

"That many?" The boy's eyes lit up. "How many are ye goin' to cook for the meal?"

"All of them. While ye're there, tell the man that ye'll come back later and clean his chicken coop for free."

"What? Nay! Why would I do that? It is a filthy, nasty job."

"Mayhap it is, but it's goin' to be the start of ye payin' the man back for all the eggs ye've stolen from him in the past. Whether he kens it or no'."

"Ye are no' goin' to tell him, are ye, Gavin?" Archy looked suddenly scared.

"Only if ye refuse to work off what ye stole. This will be the start of it, and our little secret."

"Fine," he said with his head down, getting off the bench and shuffling out of the room.

"Go fast," Gavin called after him. "Hurry, but at the same time be careful no' to drop any of the eggs."

"Gavin? What's goin' on?" Davita stood in the doorway to the kitchen, the blanket wrapped around her shoulders. Her hair was mussed, and sticking out in all directions. She'd fallen asleep in her clothes and they were wrinkled and disheveled.

"I'm sorry if we woke ye, Davita, but since ye're up, the food will be ready soon."

"Mmmm, somethin' smells guid." She walked over and lifted the lid, peeking into the kettle hanging over the fire. "What is it?"

"I made Skirlie with onions. As soon as Archy returns with the eggs, I'll fry them up and put them on top."

"Eggs?" Her eyes widened and she put the cover back on the pot. "Oh, Gavin, nay. Archy is goin' to steal them, I'm sure of it. He's been doin' it for a long time now."

"No' anymore, he willna." Gavin lifted the lid and stirred the oats with a long wooden spoon. "I gave him money to purchase them. Plus, he's goin' to clean out Keithen's chicken coop for free later." He put the lid back on, and laid down the spoon.

"He is?" She giggled. "I'm no' even goin' to ask how ye got him to do that."

"The garden is all weeded, and here's the kale ye requested." Bram came in the back door with greens gripped in his fist.

"Perfect," said Gavin, taking the kale, chopping it with a cleaver on a wooden board.

"Bram? Ye're here early," said Davita. "Were ye . . . weedin' my garden?"

"Aye, Davita. Gavin came and got me out of bed but I dinna mind. I'm happy to help. Losh me, somethin' smells guid in here." The man stretched his neck, looking over to the kettle.

"I'll be sendin' some Skirlie for ye and yer family as well," Gavin told him, throwing a handful of kale into the pot and stirring it some more.

DAVITA WATCHED WITH wide eyes, thinking this was all a dream. Gavin had things running so smoothly that it seemed as if all her problems had disappeared overnight. He had managed to take care of everything, and she'd slept through it all.

"We're back," came a voice from behind her.

Davita turned around to see Aila walking into the shop carrying a pail. The cobbler's nephew, Ethan, balanced a large metal tray in his arms with loaves of freshly baked brown bread atop it.

The bread was hot and steaming, and looked like it had just been taken out of the oven. The aroma filled the air, making Davita's mouth water.

"Fresh baked bread, too?" asked Bram, looking so excited. "My, this will be a sumptuous meal. I canna wait to take it to my family."

"Aila?" Davita scowled at her sister. "What did I say about being with Ethan?"

"I told her to ask Ethan to help her carry the bread and fresh milk from the baker's," said Gavin.

"Gavin, we need to talk about this," she said under her breath, not liking that he went behind her back and changed her orders without even asking her. Especially since it was where Aila was concerned.

"Just put the things on the table, then go across the street to the tavern and help Archy carry the eggs," Gavin instructed Aila and Ethan.

"The tavern?" Davita glared at Gavin now. The last thing she wanted was Aila going into the tavern, and he knew it. What was he thinking?

"Bram, can ye go to the livery and tell my friends that the meal is about ready?" Gavin asked the man who was still standing there.

"Of course. I'll go right away." Bram left through the back door.

Once everyone was gone, Gavin turned back to Davita. "Sit down," he said, pulling out a chair for her.

"I dinna want to sit!" She was becoming very angry with him now. "I want to ken why ye are sendin' my siblin's to the tavern, and tellin' Aila she can be with Ethan, when I forbade it?"

"All right, stand if ye insist." He turned back, opening up a cupboard and pulling out a cast iron pan to cook the eggs, along with a jar of lard. "I am no' tryin' to go behind yer back, but I thought it was important."

"Important? To send them exactly where we are tryin' to

keep them from goin'? I dinna understand."

"Lass, Aila and Ethan are workin' together. I am keepin' them busy. The more ye try to keep them apart, the more they will sneak behind yer back to be together. Do ye see what I mean?"

"Ethan is the nephew of the cobbler," she protested. "My enemy, in case ye've forgotten."

"Did ye ever hear the sayin' keep yer friends close and yer enemies closer?"

"Nay, I did no', and it makes no sense at all."

"Well, at least this way, ye ken where she is and who she is with. Would ye rather have Aila with those drunkards at the tavern?"

"Well, nay. Of course, I wouldna."

"Ethan is her age, and they already have eyes for each other," he pointed out to her. "If they see we approve of them bein' together, they willna have to sneak around behind our backs to see each other."

"But Gavin, I dinna approve! And I dinna like that ye are sendin' Archy to the tavern either. Especially so early in the mornin'."

"He's goin' for eggs, no' whisky, I assure ye, if that's what ye're worried about. I think ye are actin' ridiculous, Davita. Trust yer siblin's a little more, and mayhap they will show ye respect in return."

Gavin picked up a loaf of bread and ripped off a chunk, popping it into his mouth. "Mmmm. Taste this." When she opened her mouth to protest, he stuck a piece of brown bread into it. Her taste buds exploded with the flavor. The bread was not only delicious, but also warm and fresh.

"This is really guid," she told him, swallowing and licking her lips to savor the flavor.

"I made the bread early this mornin' with ingredients I found in yer cupboard. Then I sent Aila to the baker's with it so they could bake it in their ovens. I think it would be even better with a little honey on it. What do ye think?" He opened up the cupboards until he found some honey, dribbling the golden, sticky liquid over the top of the bread. Then he handed her another piece to try it.

"I can see already that ye are a better cook than I'll ever be," she said, taking the honey-coated bread from him, sticking it eagerly into her mouth. "Mmmm, this is really a treat."

"A man who likes to eat, has spent lots of time makin' food as well," he told her. "So ye see, I have had plenty of practice."

The bells over the front door jangled and lots of voices could be heard as a group of people entered the workshop.

"Please, work with me," he said in a low voice. "Yer siblin's deserve a chance to prove themselves, and I beg ye to give it to them."

"I'm no' sure."

"Do ye trust me, Davita? Because if ye'll give me a chance, I am sure I can help solve all yer problems."

"All right," she said with a slight nod. "I do trust ye, Gavin."

"Here are the eggs," said Archy, holding a dozen in his tunic, using it like a basket.

"I've got the rest." Ethan walked up with eggs stacked up, carrying them in his tunic, as well.

"Somethin' smells guid," said Cam, following them into the room with his friends right behind him. Bram brought up the rear.

"Bram said ye were cookin'? No' Davita?" asked Nash, still sounding worried that he might have to eat some of her food.

"Gavin is cookin', no' me," Davita assured Nash. "We've made a deal. From now on, he is goin' to cook, and I am just goin' to make and fix shoes."

"That's the best news I've heard all mornin'," said Nash, looking totally relieved. "Let's eat!"

Gavin quickly fried up some eggs, then sent Bram away with enough food to feed his family, and even a little extra. Next, he started scooping out Skirlie into wooden bowls. Archy used his stolen spatula to help drop two eggs at a time on top of each portion.

"Two eggs?" gasped Aila. "I dinna even ken if I'll be able to eat all that."

"If no', I will," said Archy. "I've already worked up a powerful hunger this mornin'."

"Well, I suppose I should be goin' now," said Ethan, sounding like he didn't really want to leave. He and Aila stood together at the back of the room.

Gavin caught Davita's eye and shot a glance over at Ethan. Davita scrunched her nose and shook her head, knowing exactly what he wanted her to do. Gavin raised an eyebrow and, once again, jerked his head toward Ethan.

Davita let out a big sigh, and decided she'd better do it. After all, she'd told Gavin she trusted him, so she needed to prove it, she supposed.

"Ethan," she called out, as the boy turned to leave. "Why dinna ye stay for somethin' to eat?"

"Really?" He sounded so excited that Davita decided it had been the right thing to do, after all. Aila's face lit up in a big smile. "Are ye sure there is enough for me, too?" he asked, trying to be polite.

"If no', ye can have some of mine," Gavin told him, flashing a big smile at Davita that showed his straight, white teeth. She knew he was reminding her of the past meals in a joking manner.

"Aye, we'd love to have ye stay," said Davita, getting a nod of approval from Gavin.

Breakfast went smoothly, and even though Davita had initially fought it, she could see now that Gavin's decisions had been the right ones. The food was delicious, and there was happy, carefree talking and laughter around the table instead of crying or arguments. Davita couldn't remember hearing laughter at a meal in a long time now.

"I can stay and help clean up," Ethan offered, when the meal was finished.

"Nay, ye'd best get back to yer uncle's shop," said Gavin. "If ye are trainin' to be an apprentice, it is important ye dinna show up late for work."

"Aye, that's right," he said, getting up in a hurry. "Plus, I dinna want to anger my uncle after last night. I'll see ye later, Aila."

Aila looked up and her cheeks blushed. "I'll be lookin' forward to it, Ethan," she said, sounding so sweet that Davita had a hard time believing this was her sister.

"Well, that was guid. Thanks," said Nash, pushing up off the bench.

"I think I'll go see what Violet and Red are doin'," announced Cam.

"I'll come with ye." North got up as well.

"No one eats for free," said Gavin, stopping his friends in their tracks.

Cam looked back over his shoulder at Gavin. "What does that mean?"

"Aila and Archy, do ye ken anythin' about makin' or repairin' shoes?" asked Gavin.

"Da always said I was guid at stitchin'," said Aila. "Even though Davita never lets me do it."

"I used to help him draw the patterns, and sweep up the leather clippin's after he cut out the pieces," Archy answered.

"Guid. Then ye two shall join me today to help Davita in the shop."

"All right. We're leavin'." North led the way, with Cam and Nash pushing to get past him. Gavin cleared his throat loudly, stopping them once again.

"I'm no' finished yet," Gavin told them. "It seems since Aila and Archy will be workin' in the shop today, that leaves ye three to clean up the mess from breakfast."

"Us? Now, come on," complained Cam. "We're warriors, no' scullery maids."

"If ye three are goin' to be eatin' here, or even sleepin' here once in a while, ye're goin' to have to pull yer weight, and that's all there is to it," Gavin warned them. "Now hurry up and get washin' the dishes. And when ye're done, I'll need ye to go fishin'. I'm goin' to make up some Cullen Skink for supper."

"Och, I havena had a guid fish stew in a while," mumbled North, suddenly seeming interested. "All right, I'll help."

"I have had a taste for cock-a-leekie soup, the kind that Lady Wren makes," said Nash. "Were ye thinkin' of makin' that anytime soon?" He tilted his head in question and looked over at Gavin.

"We'll see," Gavin answered. "It depends on how much cooperation I get around here."

The men all headed back into the kitchen in single file, listing off one food after another that they wanted to eat.

Gavin chuckled. "I think they're missin' the niceties of Hermitage Castle, just a wee bit."

"I'm impressed," said Davita, reaching up and giving him a peck on the mouth. "Are ye ready now to help me with the shoes?"

He stopped laughing. "We did say that I'd cook and ye'd make the shoes, right?" he asked her.

"Aye, but I can see now that it isna goin' to work."

"What do ye mean?"

"Part of my deal with Laird MacKeefe was that I would teach ye how to make shoes, so ye can help me construct a new pair of boots for Callum, and therefore be redeemed."

"Now, Davita, ye said yerself it would take years for me to learn the trade. I'm sure that Storm didna really mean I had to do the work. Canna I just watch ye?"

"If my siblin's are goin' to help repair and make shoes, then so will ye," she said with an outstretched arm. "After all, if they can do it, then a smart man like ye should be able to learn as well. Nay?"

She saw Gavin look up at Aila and Archy who were both giggling under their breaths.

"He canna do it," whispered Archy.

"It'll be a disaster," said Aila.

"Mayhap ye can just sweep the floor," suggested the little boy.

"Or perhaps take our laundry down to the river to wash it," said Aila, giggling even more. "What do ye think, Sister?"

Davita looked over at Gavin, feeling sorry for him. He'd worked so hard cooking and organizing, and bringing this family back together. He even got three rugged Highlanders to wash her dishes. She didn't have it in her heart to send him to the river for anything unless it was to finish what they'd started there earlier.

"I think Gavin will make a fine apprentice and be a fast learner," she said to her siblings. "Now, get to work."

"Davita," said Gavin, putting his hand on her arm. The warmth that transferred between them felt nice. He leaned over and whispered into her ear. "Please. We both ken I am no' goin' to be able to do this." His breath tickled her ear, and it took all her control not to reach up and kiss him right now. She didn't want to do that in front of her siblings. Especially not after she'd made such a big stink about Aila kissing Ethan.

"Do ye trust me?" she asked.

"Well I . . . I mean . . ."

She was the one to raise a brow now. "Well? Do ye?"

"Of course, I do," he said. "Ye ken that."

"Then put on an apron, Apprentice, because ye've got a lot of work to do."

⬥◦◇◦⬥

CHAPTER FIFTEEN

"H MMM, WHERE TO start?" Davita tapped her index finger against her lips, looking around the workroom as Gavin donned his leather apron.

"Teach him the types of shoes," suggested Archy. "That's easy."

"All right," she said, collecting up a bunch of shoes and boots and dropping them onto the table. "We've tried talkin' about types of boots before, but mayhap this time will be easier since they are no' Callum's."

"I'm ready this time," said Gavin, rubbing his hands together, willing to learn.

"Ye've got yer ankle boots, yer button-front boots, buckle-front boots, drawstring, and ridin' boots," she said, quickly lining up the boots on the table. "Of course, there are a lot more, like the front and side-laced boots, and thigh-high fold-over boots, but we'll just start with these."

"Boots. Right," said Gavin with a nod. "I've got it." He was concentrating, looking at every boot, trying to take it all in. Even so, he probably wouldn't remember much of what she was telling him in the end. Still, he had to try.

"Then there are the shoes." Davita plopped down one shoe after another, and rattled the types off so quickly, it made Gavin's head spin. He wondered if she was trying to purposely trip him up, just for the fun of it. "There are peaked shoes, ankle strap, side strap, basic long-toed, toggle-latchet ankle shoes, front laced, front tied and, of course, just the general commoner's shoe." She looked up at him and smiled proudly. "Understand?"

She may as well have been speaking a foreign tongue to him, because the information swarmed around in his head, buzzing like a bee in a hive. Still, he didn't want to seem weak or stupid. After all, if her siblings who were very young could understand all this, then so could he. "Aye. Got it," he said, nodding, and faking a smile. He hadn't the slightest idea of what she'd just said, but didn't want her to know it.

"Guid. So, hand me the toggle-latchet shoe, please." She held out her open hand and waited.

Gavin reached out for the shoes, his hand hovering over one, and then another, trying to remember which one was which. The bloody things all looked the same to him. He hadn't the slightest clue which shoe to choose.

"Here it is. Toggle-length," he said, snatching up the closest shoe and handing it to her, just to get this over with.

Her brows dipped and she scowled at him. That was a good clue telling him it wasn't right. "There is no such thing as toggle-length, Gavin."

"Nay?" he asked with a shrug.

"I asked for toggle-latchet, and this is no' it. This is a front-tied shoe. Anyone can see that."

"Even I knew that," said Archy, only making him feel worse.

"Of course. My mistake," said Gavin, choosing another shoe at random and handing it to her. "There ye are."

"Nay. That's a commoner's shoe," she said in a scolding manner. Then she picked up the correct one, showing it to him. "See the toggle? That should have been a giveaway." With one finger she flicked the chunk of rounded wood that reminded him of a misshaped button. "Ye dinna need laces with toggle-latchets. Understand?"

"There are too many shoes," he told her. "Ask me for a boot instead. Those I have memorized completely."

"Do ye, now?" Her eyes narrowed and she looked over at the table. "All right. We'll try an easy one this time. Just give me a front-laced boot, please."

Gavin looked down at the collection of boots staring up at him. He was sure he knew which one to choose this time. It was much easier than the shoes. He picked up the only boot on the table with laces. "Here ye go," he said proudly, handing it to her. There was no way he could get this one wrong. "One front-laced boot, just like ye asked for."

He knew by the giggles from Aila and Archy, that it wasn't correct, even before Davita shook her head. "Nay. This is a drawstring boot," she said, taking it from him. His eyes flashed back to the table and he searched it frantically. His attention went from one boot to another but he just couldn't see another boot with lacing on the table at all.

"Nay, that has to be it," he told her. "The other boots have buckles and buttons, or no laces at all. There is no way that I got it wrong."

"Gavin, there isna a front-laced boot on the table. However, I did mention it to ye. I was just tryin' to see if ye were really payin' attention."

"That's no' fair. Ye tricked me!" he spat, listening to Aila and Archy laughing louder. "I dinna like bein' the brunt of an ill jest."

"I'm sorry, I suppose that wasna fair," she agreed, sitting down, pulling a toolbox over toward her. "Mayhap we should go over some of the tools we'll be usin' instead."

Gavin spied the knives in the box, and this took his interest. "Aye, that's better. I ken a lot about weapons and blades, so this'll be easy."

"We'll see," she said, sounding stuffy. She gingerly plucked a few tools from the box and spread them out in front of her on the worktable. "This is an awl, used to punch holes through the leather before pushing the needle through. The small hammer is needed to put nails and tacks into the soles of the shoes."

"And this is a knife." Gavin picked up one of the knives, inspecting it.

"Aye, it's a carvin' knife. I use it to trim the inseam while the shoe is still on the last."

"The last what?" he asked, getting more giggles from her siblings.

"This is a shoe last," said Archy, walking over with what looked like a wooden foot in his hands. "Even I ken that!"

"The turnshoes are put on it to work," explained Davita. She grabbed a long, wooden stick and held it up. "This turn stick is used to flip the shoe right side out after it is removed from the last."

"Aye. Turnshoes," he said, his mind becoming boggled with all there was to know. "Och, I get it. Ye turn the shoes inside out to work on them and that is how they get their name."

"That's right," said Davita.

"What's this?" he asked, picking up a long leather strap.

"That's used to hold a shoe on yer lap when ye're workin' on it," said Aila, getting up off her stool and taking it from him to demonstrate. She sat back down and put the strap under her foot. Then she brought both ends of the strap up on both sides of her knee and fastened it over a shoe that was resting there. "See?" said Aila, showing her free hands. "Now the shoe stays in one place while I work on it, and it willna slip off my knee."

"I can think of better things to do with that strap," mumbled Gavin, thinking how silly it seemed. Then he spied something that took his interest. "Now that is my kind of weapon." Putting down the knife, he picked up what looked like a small ax blade mounted on a wooden grip, having a curved handle. "Heavy," he said, weighing it in his hand. "It must be made of iron."

"It is," said Davita. "It is called a Half Moon Knife and it is used to trench, or cut out the leather, after I've drawn a pattern."

The bells above the door jangled, and Nash walked in with a fishing pole in his hand. "Gavin, we're takin' the wagon down to the river to fish. Are ye comin' with us?"

Gavin looked over to his friend, wanting more than anything

to go fishing instead of learning things that would do him no good at all in life. Still, he'd made a deal, and this was part of his punishment. He didn't have a choice but to stay.

"Nay," he said sadly, placing the knife back down on the table. "I am needed here."

DAVITA SAW THE longing in Gavin's eyes, and her heart went out to him. Anyone could see he had no interest in cordwaining. He didn't belong here, trapped in this dark little room, tinkering away on shoes all day. Gavin was a Highlander and she knew he had adventure running through his blood. By the rood, the man loved the outdoors and she was sure he longed for physical activity. He even slept out under the stars. In nature is where he belonged, and needed to be.

A customer walked in, and Davita jumped up to wait on him. "I'll be right with ye," she said, looking over at Gavin. "Why dinna ye go fishin' today," she whispered. "This is a lot to learn, and it can become overwhelmin'. Honestly, it'll take ye years to understand it."

"Nay. I'm supposed to stay here and help ye repair the shoes, as well as construct a pair of boots for Callum."

"I think we should just start out with ye watchin' me work for a few days first. After all, seein' is the best way to learn and understand it. Excuse me, please." She left to assist the customer, leaving Nash and Gavin standing there.

"WELL, ARE YE stayin' or goin' with us?" asked Nash. "Cam is in a big hurry to leave since he promised Violet he'd spend time with her later when she got off work."

Gavin looked back at Davita who was inspecting a pair of shoes the man brought in. She was smart and talented, and more than he could ever ask for in a lass. He knew she was telling him to go join his friends because he would probably just be in the way if he stayed there. She did have Archy and Aila helping her, so he supposed he wasn't really needed, after all.

His eyes remained fixed on Davita's face as she small talked and laughed with the customer. He got lost in the lass' smile, thinking of what little intimate time they'd spent together. Her kisses were like honeyed mead, and her squeals of delight when she'd found her release reminded him of –

"Gavin! Are ye goin' to answer me or stand here all day starin' at Davita?" asked Nash, snapping his fingers in Gavin's face.

"He likes my sister," said Archy, causing Aila to look up from her work. Aila's eyes opened wide and her gaze ran down Gavin's chest, stopping at his waist. He knew why. Gavin was getting hard just thinking about Davita, and Aila noticed. When Aila gasped and covered her mouth, giggling once again, he figured it was time to leave.

"Let's go," he said, leading the way out the door. "I think I need a wee bit of fresh air."

"I think ye need a whore," mumbled Nash. "Either that, or bed the lass already, because this is gettin' embarrassin' to be around ye when ye're like this."

Gavin realized his friend was right, but he could never lay with a whore now. Not when Davita was the only lass he wanted to warm his bed.

⟫⟫⟫⟨⟨⟨

"WHY SO GLUM, Gavin?" Cam asked, stabbing a hook through a worm as they sat at the riverbank fishing.

"Aye, ye are quiet today," added Nash, flipping his line into the water, holding on to the long stick that served as his pole.

"I've just been thinkin', that's all," said Gavin.

"About Davita." North nodded, tossing his line into the wa- ter. "Ye have the look of a man who is about to do somethin' stupid, Gavin. Ye'd better think hard before ye do anythin' ye might regret."

"What do ye mean?" asked Gavin.

"He's talkin' about ye possibly beddin' the lass." Nash got a nibble on his line, and held on with two hands. "Ah, I'm goin' to catch the first fish today."

"I didna bed her, if that's what ye're referrin' to," said Gavin. Part of him wished that he had.

"Why no'?" asked Cam, who Gavin knew would never understand his reasoning. When Cam wanted a lassie – which was quite often – he got her. Easy as that. No regrets afterwards either. Not where Cam was concerned.

"Well, for one thing, she is a virgin," Gavin explained.

"Ah, no experience." Cam nodded, throwing his line out into the water, still sitting on a rock since he was too lazy to actually stand up to fish. "Those kinds of lassies are no' nearly as fun as ones who ken a few tricks." He leaned back, sticking the end of the makeshift pole in the dirt so he wouldn't have to hold it. Then he crossed his arms behind his head and closed his eyes, lifting his face to the sun. "What ye need is a whore who kens how to please a man. No' a frightened, inexperienced lass. She'll never satisfy yer needs."

"Why would ye say that?" Gavin suddenly felt defensive. "Davita is quite pleasin', I assure ye."

"Gavin, ye were no' sated by her and everyone kens it. Damn, it got away," spat Nash, losing the fish, and throwing his pole to the ground in frustration.

"It got away because ye have to actually stand in the water, no' on the shore," Nash's brother told him. North walked right into the water, not bothering to remove his shoes. He didn't stop until he was waist high in the river.

"I could have been sated verra easily." Gavin's' manly pride was getting in the way. "I didna want to bed her. That's why I stopped."

"Aye, like I said, those virgins are no fun." Cam opened one eye to talk to him, but quickly closed it again.

"That's no' the reason," said Gavin. "I didna do it, because I didna want to hurt her."

"Whores like it rough," Cam answered, having a one-track mind.

"Haud yer wheesht, Cam!" Angry, Gavin jumped up, throwing his pole to the ground. "Davita is kind and smart, and bonnie. She is everythin' I've ever wanted in a lass. Dinna ever call her a whore."

"I didna," said Cam in his defense. "I was speakin' about lassies like Red and Violet."

"What do ye mean she's everythin' ye've ever wanted?" asked North, turning his head and making a face at Gavin. "God's eyes, dinna tell me ye are already fallin' in love with the lass."

"Ye just met her," said Cam. "What are ye thinkin'?"

"Are ye really? Are ye fallin' in love with Davita?" asked Nash, being the nosy busybody he always was.

"I – I didna say that." Gavin started to pace. "I only said she was everythin' I've always wanted in a lass."

"She's the daughter of a cordwainer," Cam reminded him, pushing up to his elbows this time.

"So what?" he asked. "I'm no' bothered by that fact."

"That means she'll never leave the town she lives in," said North. "Ye do realize that, dinna ye?"

"We belong in the Highlands," Nash told him before Gavin could even answer. "Ye are comin' back with us to the clan when yer sentence is over, right?"

Gavin didn't say anything because, honestly, he didn't know what to do or what to think right now. He was here to redeem himself, and he never expected to be having feelings for Davita. They were strong ones, too, like never before. He cared for her, and he also cared about her family. The problem was that he was also devoted to the MacKeefe Clan who had been his family since the day he lost his own.

"Aye, of course, I am goin' back to the Highlands with ye," Gavin answered with a smile. "After all, I'm a MacKeefe now. I would never abandon my family."

"Guid," said Cam, seeming satisfied with Gavin's answer, laying back again on the rock. "I'd hate to think ye'd give up bein' a warrior, just to settle down and be content as the husband of a cordwainer's daughter. Ye'd have to give up fightin' and instead be makin' shoes the rest of yer life."

"Nay. I wouldna want that," admitted Gavin, terrified by the idea.

"Me, neither," said North. "Just the thought of it makes me shiver."

"Hah! He's no shoemaker. He's really just a cook," said Nash, never thinking before opening his mouth. "Gavin, ye may as well trade in that plaid for an apron."

"And no' a leather one," laughed North. "One that a kitchen maid would wear."

"Stop it," said Gavin, knowing his friends meant no harm, but were just having fun. Still, he didn't like it. "If ye three want Cullen Skink tonight, then ye'd better get yer arses in gear and start catchin' some fish or it's goin' to be a pretty thin stew."

"Ye want fish? I'll get ye one. After all, I'm better at fishin' than any of ye," bragged Nash like normal, even if it wasn't true. "Just watch this. I'll catch one this time." Nash threw his baited hook back out into the water but nothing happened.

"Blethers, Brathair," spat North. "I'll show ye how to catch somethin' to eat. I want somethin' bigger and better than just the wee fish ye'll catch. Watch this." North threw down his pole, diving under the water. His feet kicked above the surface, splashing about wildly. Then he emerged, holding on to a lamprey with two hands, lifting it high for them to see. "Let's see any of ye catch a lamprey." Then he looked at the eel-like creature and laughed. "Ye, my friend, will be part of a stew tonight, and I canna wait to eat ye." When he turned back to smile proudly at his friends, the lamprey slipped in his grip. "Och, bid the devil, help!" cried North.

Gavin looked over to see the lamprey's disc-like mouth stuck on North's neck. The parasitic fish couldn't bite, but attached itself to hosts, and sucked, much like a leech.

Cam and Nash bent over laughing, but did nothing to help North who was still holding on to the fish, running out of the water and to the shore in a panic.

"Och, dry yer eyes ye big bairn," said Gavin, walking over and taking hold of the lamprey. It was lodged on to North tightly, but Gavin used two hands and yanked hard. With a popping sound, the suction was broken, and Gavin threw it to the ground.

"That hurt," said North, rubbing his neck. "Am I bleedin'?"

"Bid the devil, mayhap we have all been here too long and need to get back to battlin' in the Highlands," said Gavin. "Since when did a little blood ever bother any of us?"

"Ye never should have taunted the thing by tellin' it that ye were goin' to cook it in a stew," Nash told his brother.

"Pick it up, Nash," said North, nodding to the lamprey squirming around on the ground.

"Nope." Nash picked up his pole and looked the other way. "I'm busy fishin'."

"Cam?" asked North.

"I'm sleepin'. Leave me alone." Cam made sure to keep his eyes closed.

"Losh me!" Gavin walked over to the lamprey, unsheathed his sword and lopped the thing's head off in one jerk. Then he picked up its body and tossed it into the basket they'd brought with them to hold the fish they caught. "And ye three are teasin' me about wearin' a kitchen apron? Mayhap what ye all need is a guid lass like Davita to make ye act like men again."

"Guid idea," said Cam, sounding interested. "I havena had a virgin in a while now."

"Haud yer wheesht," spat Gavin, now realizing he should have chosen his words more carefully. The last thing he wanted was for any of his friends to think they could make a move on Davita. She was his woman. "If any of ye even think of touchin' her, ye're goin' to have to answer to me. And I promise ye, heads will roll," growled Gavin, turning and walking back to the wagon, hearing his friends mumble from behind him.

"Och, aye, he's smitten with the lass all right," said Nash.

"Aye. He's got it bad," agreed North, rubbing his sore neck. "Even so, I dinna think he'd really do anythin' to us if we touched Davita. Do ye?"

"Ye'd better watch out, North," said Cam with a chuckle from his rock. "After all, ye just almost lost yer neck to a fish. Ye dinna want to lose yer head to Gavin as well."

— ◆◇◆ —

CHAPTER SIXTEEN

"GAVIN'S BACK!" ARCHY ran across the room, bolting out the front door of the shop to greet Gavin and his friends. They'd finally returned after a full day of fishing.

"I'll be back later." Aila jumped up as well, following her brother out the door. Davita had a feeling the girl would end up over at the cobbler's since she hadn't seen Ethan all day.

"Wait!" cried Davita, putting down the shoes she'd been making, letting out a sigh when her siblings kept going. "Oh, well, they did help me," she spoke to herself. "I never expected them to stay this long."

"Davita, look at all the fish they caught!" Archy came back into the building, holding up a string of fish. It was long, nearly touching the ground. Plus it looked heavy. Archy could barely carry it with two hands.

"Those are just mine," Gavin told him with a chuckle. "I have plenty of haddock now to make a killer batch of Cullen Skink for supper."

"Blethers, ye caught a lot," said Davita, coming to join them. "We'll have extra now to dry and smoke to use throughout the winter. I'll bet ye could feed half the town with all the fish ye boys brought back."

"We like to do our part, helpin' out," said Gavin, flashing her a handsome smile and then leaning over and giving her a quick peck on the mouth.

"I just saw ye two kiss," said Archy looking over his shoulder at them.

"Never mind, Brathair," Davita warned him.

Gavin looked so happy and refreshed now, having gone out to fish with his friends. His skin was tanned from the sun, and his cheeks were rosy. Davita felt happy for him, but had missed him dearly today. She wished she had been with them at the river instead of being cooped up in the shop fixing shoes, just trying to get caught up with all the work.

"Archy, give me that," said Gavin, taking the string of fish back from the boy. "Go on out and see what my friends caught."

"Did they get haddock, too?" asked Archy excitedly.

"Aye, and more. North reached into the river and pulled out a lamprey."

"With his bare hands?" Archy's eyes opened wide in astonishment.

"Yup."

"Really? I want to see it!"

"No' me," said Davita, shivering slightly, not wanting to see the eel-like creature that only reminded her of a giant worm.

"Ask North to show ye where the lamprey latched on to his neck, too." Gavin grinned. "The danged thing almost sucked the life out of him." Just thinking of what happened seemed to amuse Gavin, and he chuckled. The sound of the deep rumble in his chest filled Davita's heart. She liked having a man around here. A man besides her father, that is. Having Gavin living here, somehow made her home seem more . . . complete.

"I want to tell all my friends about the lamprey," shouted Archy, running out the door.

"How was yer day today, lass?" Gavin seemed so relaxed that Davita wasn't even sure he was the same person.

"No' as guid as yers, I believe. Ye seem happy, Gavin."

"Why wouldna I be?" he asked with a shrug. "It was a guid day of fishin', and my friends and I shared some laughs and a fun time."

"So, it sounds perfect then."

"Nearly perfect," he answered, making her curious as to what he meant. "Ye ken what would have made it even better?"

"What's that?" Davita looked up at him shyly from the corners of her eyes, hoping he was going to say her. She longed to have him tell her that he missed her as much as she missed him. Hope filled her that he would tell her he wanted to be spending time with her and not just with his friends.

"Well, a little Mountain Magic would have helped." He smacked his lips together when he said it.

"Is that all?" she asked, feeling confused, fishing for a compliment. Unfortunately, she wasn't as skilled at fishing as he was.

"Nay. I ken it's silly but . . ."

"Aye?" Her heart beat faster as she waited for his answer. His eyes settled on her mouth, and she could only hope he was thinking about kissing her again. Mayhap, this time, it would be a passionate kiss, and not just a quick peck. "What were ye goin' to say, Gavin?"

"I was just goin' to say that –" Just then, one of the fish lurched and flipped around, scaring her and making her jump.

"Sorry, lass. I'll take these out back to clean them. Then I'll start makin' supper. I'm sure ye are starvin' after workin' so hard all day." He turned and walked away, leaving her standing there alone, feeling disheartened. Mayhap he didn't have the same feelings for her as she did for him, after all.

She went back to her work, feeling sad and lonely.

"Get used to it, Davita. This is yer life now," she told herself, knowing that as soon as Gavin's redemption was complete, he'd go back to the Highlands and she'd never see him again.

"LOOK HOW FAT Hamish is gettin'," said Archy, holding up his toad as Gavin cleaned the fish out in the back garden. "I've been givin' him lots of flies to eat."

"That's nice," said Gavin, not really paying much attention to the boy. He lopped off the heads of a few fish, not able to get his mind off Davita.

His friends were right. He was a Highlander and didn't belong here, in town. Davita made a living here. She had a business and a family. He and she were so different, and really didn't belong together. He agreed with it. But if so, why did it feel like a stab to his heart realizing he would have to leave her soon?

"Are ye goin' to marry my sister?" asked the boy, snapping Gavin out of his wallowing misery. It shocked him, since he never expected the boy to say that.

"What did ye say?" He turned and looked over his shoulder, thinking mayhap he'd misheard him.

"I said are ye goin' to marry Davita?" He held the toad up to his face, made some ribbiting sounds, and smiled at it.

"Now, why would ye even ask such a thing? Did Davita say somethin' to ye about it?"

"Nay. All she thinks about is makin' and repairin' shoes, if ye havena noticed."

"I did," he said with a sigh, turning back and continuing to clean the fish.

"What's goin' to happen to me if my faither dies?"

"Now, wait a minute. Stop right there." Gavin put down the knife and turned around. "Yer faither is no' goin' to die, Archy. So, just get that idea out of yer head right now. Besides, ye always have yer sisters to care for ye, so dinna worry."

"But I want someone like ye for a faither," continued the boy. "Mine doesna pay any attention to me at all. All he does is drink, ever since my mathair died."

"I wouldna be a guid faither to anyone," said Gavin, honestly believing this. He turned and busied himself with the fish.

"Gavin, ye're fun and fair, and do excitin' things. Ye're a Highland warrior! I want to be a warrior someday and use my sword to kill people, too."

"Haud yer wheesht!" Gavin spun around, putting his hands on his waist. "Ye dinna ken what ye're sayin', lad. Now listen carefully. I am no' yer faither, and I am no' goin' to marry yer sister either. I am needed back in the Highlands. It is where I belong. I will be leavin' to rejoin the MacKeefe Clan as soon as my sentence is over."

Archy lowered the toad, and his smile disappeared. "Oh," he said, sounding so sad that Gavin regretted saying all those things now. Archy put the toad back under the bowl that served as its house, and took off at a run.

"Archy, come back here!" Gavin called out, but the boy kept on going. "Lad, I didna mean to upset ye."

"What's the matter?" Davita walked out, looking curious as to why he was shouting. "Where is Archy? Is everythin' all right?"

"Aye. Everythin' is fine." Gavin continued to gut the fish.

"I thought I heard shoutin'."

"There is nothin' to worry about, lass. I just . . . I think the sight of me guttin' fish just scared him, that's all."

"Scared him? Archy likes to fish and he's even baited the hook for me and Aila, and gutted and cleaned fish himself. He's no' scared of them."

"Well, mayhap somethin' else scared him then. I dinna ken. I am no' a mind reader."

"All right," she said, not sounding at all like she believed him about anything, but also not pushing him to know more.

DAVITA WAS SURE she'd heard Gavin and Archy saying something about marriage when she walked up, but Gavin didn't mention it at all. He was trying to make her believe that Archy ran off because he was afraid of gutted fish. That was the most ridiculous thing she'd ever heard. Archy wasn't afraid of much, and certainly not of fish.

She could tell there was something bothering Gavin, but he wasn't going to tell her. Even though she wanted to pump him for more information, something told her to just let it go for now.

His protective walls were up around him, and there was no use trying to get him to lower them because it wasn't going to work. Not now. She would wait until the right moment, and then she would try to ask him about it again.

"I was thinkin' that we could make a visit to the tanner's shop tomorrow, and pick up some Cordovan leather to make a pair of boots for Callum." She decided changing the subject was the best thing to do.

"Aye, that will be fine." He used a scraper to de-scale the fish, working like a madman, not even glancing at her once. Scales flew through the air in all directions.

"I'm sure ye're in a hurry to get the boots made, so yer sentence can be over."

"I'm sure."

The silence between them was deafening, and she didn't like it. "I can teach ye more about constructin' boots tomorrow, and ye can start helpin' me, as well, if ye'd like."

"Look, Davita." He put down the knife and finally turned to face her. "We both ken that I'll never be able to do it, so stop pretendin' that I can. Makin' boots and shoes is yer talent, lass, no' mine. What I'm guid at, is fightin' and bein' a warrior. I'll just watch and assist ye any way I can, but dinna expect me to do more."

Davita couldn't understand why he'd been so eager to learn and help her before, but now it didn't seem like he even wanted to do it at all.

"Did I do or say somethin' to anger ye, Gavin?" she bravely asked, needing to know. "Because if so, I am sorry."

"Nay, it's no' ye." He kept his head down and turned back to the fish.

"Is it Archy? Or perhaps Aila? I hope they are no' causin' ye trouble. If they are, I will do somethin' to punish them."

"Nay!" He spun around, seeming startled. "Dinna punish yer siblin's or ye'll just push them further away. Get to ken them better instead. Talk to them and ask questions. Find out what they are thinkin'. After all, Davita, they are yer family. Ye should be happy just to have them with ye."

"I am happy to have them," she told him. "I never said I wasna. And it's odd to hear ye say to get to ken them, because that is what I'm tryin' to do with ye. I am tryin' to talk to ye to find out what ye're thinkin', and ye willna cooperate at all."

Gavin let out a sigh, and scooped the cleaned fish into a bowl. "I'm sorry, Davita. I just have a lot on my mind, and I'm no' sure what to do, that's all."

"Tell me about it, and I can help ye."

"Nay." He shook his head sadly. "Excuse me, lass." He picked up the bowl and started for the house. "Everyone is expectin' me to make Cullen Skink, and I need to get it cookin'. They are all countin' on me."

"Aye. Everyone is countin' on ye more than ye ken," she said in a soft voice, watching him walk away. She was the one counting on him the most to be there for her. Davita needed Gavin more than ever, to help her make it through these hard times. But after this conversation, she was starting to wonder if mayhap she'd put too much faith in the rugged Highlander, after all.

◆◦◇◦◆

CHAPTER SEVENTEEN

"**E**GADS, THE STENCH!" Gavin dismounted once they got to the tanner's shop the next morning, reaching up to help Davita from the horse as well.

"Gavin!" she gasped, looking at him oddly.

"No' ye, lass. I am talkin' about the odor around this place."

She smiled and allowed him to help her down. "I ken ye are," she said with a giggle. "I was just havin' fun."

"What is that smell?" he asked her curiously.

"The tannin' pits are far on the outskirts of town for a reason," she explained. "Urine and dung are used in the tannin' process."

"Ye have got to be jestin'."

"Nay, no' at all. There are many things used to no' only remove animal hair, but to soften the leather and preserve it when it comes to tawin' and tannin' hides."

"Well, now I ken what stinks."

"It could be the animal brains they soak the hides in that ye're smellin'. They do that before they smoke the hides." She pointed to skins sewn together, shaped like a tent. There was a fire burning, and the skins were immersed in smoke.

"Losh me! I hope the leather we're gettin' for Callum's boots doesna smell like piss! He's already sore that I retched on his boots."

"It takes months, and sometimes up to a year to prepare

169

leather, before it is ready to be made into a pair of shoes," she told him, walking into the work area. Gavin followed. There were pits filled with liquid built right into the ground. Long slats held stretched skins, dipping them into the liquid below them. "The skins have to be cleaned and soaked, and sometimes salted. It is all necessary to keep them soft and to stop them from deterioratin'."

"I guess there is a lot I dinna ken about this trade. What is he doin'?" asked Gavin as they passed by a man using a long, dull blade to scrape the skin.

"He is scuddin' – removin' the hair and fat from a hide. The animal fat is used in tallow soap."

Gavin shook his head, glad he didn't have to do this kind of work. "And I thought a battlefield was a nasty place to be," he mumbled, seeing the skins and waste and mess everywhere. The smell was assaulting his senses, and he couldn't wait to leave. "Let's get the Cordovan leather and go," he told her.

"All right. I hope it is ready. My faither ordered it months ago." Davita walked into a small shop, and a man behind a counter looked up.

"Davita. How is yer faither?" asked the man, drying his hands on a cloth.

"He is at the castle, healin', thanks to Gavin," Davita answered. "Tomas, this is Gavin. He is a Highlander and has been sent by Laird MacKeefe from Hermitage Castle to help me until my faither returns."

"Aye. Nice to meet ye," said the man, holding out his hand.

Gavin was reluctant to shake it since it was stained and dirty. Still, he didn't want to be rude, so he did it anyway.

"Is the Cordovan leather ready yet?" Davita asked the tanner.

"Aye. I dyed it black as well. Let me get it for ye." He walked away to get the leather and Davita looked over at Gavin.

"I hope Callum's boots were black, since that is the color he dyed the leather."

"I canna remember, but I'm sure it'll be fine."

"I'm surprised Callum even had such an expensive pair of boots to begin with," remarked Davita. "After all, Cordovan leather is usually reserved for nobles only. How was he able to afford them? My faither only ordered this type of leather because we've been gettin' quite a few requests for it from the nobles over the past year."

"Dinna fool yerself," Gavin told her. "Old Callum makes a fortune on his Mountain Magic. It is sought after by everyone from both sides of the border. He's even had orders from as far away as across the Channel. He makes guid money, and secures some nice trade with it as well. He supports the clan more than any of our other members, with the coin from his special whisky."

"Gavin, Cordovan leather is strong, and while it can get damaged, it can still be repaired. I'm surprised Callum is insistin' on a new pair of boots, instead of just cleanin' them."

"I think he is tryin' to make an example out of me, and doesna even need new boots at all. That's why I'm no' concerned if they look exactly the same as the last ones or no'."

"Here ye are," said Tomas, holding out the leather for her to inspect.

"Aye, this is fine," she said with a smile, running her fingers along it.

Gavin let out a low whistle and ran his hand along the smooth surface as well. "Verra fine," he commented. "And smooth."

When Tomas told her the price, Davita seemed flustered. That told Gavin that she didn't have enough money to pay for it.

"Allow me," he said, digging into his pouch, using what money he had left to pay for something that Callum didn't even really need to begin with. This was a very expensive lesson to learn.

"Ye seem busy here at the tannery," said Gavin, glancing around. He'd seen half a dozen men or so who seemed to have a lot of work to do.

"We are. I'm short on help right now, and orders are takin'

longer to fill than usual," admitted Tomas.

"Well," said Gavin, rubbing the back of his neck with one hand. "I have a man in mind who could use a job to feed his family right now."

"Really?" asked Tomas. "Who? I could use the help."

"His name is Bram," Gavin told him. "He used to work for the butcher, so I'm sure he has experience that will come in handy with this kind of work."

"Aye, I ken him. Thank ye," said Tomas. "I will contact him immediately. This isna the best job to hold, but if he is willin' to do it, I would be more than happy to hire him and pay him well."

"Oh, that would be wonderful!" exclaimed Davita, flashing Gavin a quick smile. "I am sure Bram will be more than willin' to accept the job."

As they turned to leave, they stopped dead in their tracks when Clyde and Gregor entered the building right behind them.

"What are ye two doin' here?" snorted Davita, not at all happy to see the cobbler and his apprentice.

"Davita, I'm sure they are here to buy leather for the shoes, the same as we are," said Gavin under his breath, sounding as if he didn't want trouble.

"They are cobblers," she told them. "Only cordwainers are allowed to buy new leather for shoes. They are supposed to use old leather only."

"Really?" asked Gavin, surprised to hear this. "Why is that?"

"It is in the guild rules," she explained. "Clyde, ye shouldna be here. Besides, ye ken that Tomas canna sell ye new leather for shoes." She looked back at Tomas. He put his head down before he answered.

"I'm sorry, Davita," said Tomas. "But I need to make money just like ye do. A lot of my orders are from over the border and even overseas. It takes long for me to collect my money. I have a family to feed as well."

"If ye are goin' to keep repairin' shoes when ye are no' supposed to, then I'm goin' to use new leather," said Clyde.

"Davita, what is he talkin' about?" asked Gavin, looking confused.

"Accordin' to the guild rules, cordwainers are only supposed to construct new shoes, no' repair them. That is the job of cobblers," Gregor spoke up.

"That's right," agreed Clyde. "Davita's faither has been stealin' our business for a long time now."

"Stealin'?" Davita's eyes shot open wide. "It is no' our fault that yer work is so shoddy that yer customers are comin' to us instead of goin' back to ye when the shoes need repair. Either way, ye are no' supposed to be buyin' and workin' with new leather! That is for the cordwainers only."

"Well, now, I dinna think ye're goin' to report it to the guild," said Clyde, sneering at her. "After all, ye are breakin' the rules as well. Ye wouldna want them to ken that, would ye?"

"I dinna want trouble at my tannery," said Tomas from behind the counter. "Please."

"We're leavin'," Gavin informed him, putting his arm around Davita and escorting her past Clyde and Gregor, heading out the door. Once they were atop the horse and heading back, he spoke. "Is all that true?" he asked. "Is yer faither stealin' Clyde's business?"

"Gavin, Clyde does poor work and his customers are aware of it. If he did his job properly, they wouldna have to come to the cordwainer for repairs at all."

They rode a little and then Gavin spoke again. "Do ye like repairin' shoes or makin' them better?"

"I despise repairin' shoes," she told him, leaning back slightly in his arms atop the horse. "It is tedious and borin'. I like designin' and constructin' new shoes much better. It is more creative and I feel . . . freer, I guess ye could say."

"Then, mayhap ye should talk to Clyde and make an agreement. I mean, since ye are both breakin' the rules and might get thrown out of the guilds if they find out. This could be a guid solution."

"Gavin, there is no talkin' to men like Clyde! Besides, I canna prove it, but I think he and Gregor were the ones who hurt and almost killed my faither."

"Nay," he said. "Ye canna really think they'd try to kill a man over naught but shoes."

"I'm sure ye ken men who would kill for less," she told him, shutting him up completely. He did know a lot of Highlanders who would kill someone if they only looked at them the wrong way. He supposed she had a point.

They got back to the shop to find a piece of parchment folded and tacked to the door.

"Gavin, I hope that isna a note from the guild." Gavin helped Davita to the ground and dug into the travel bag for the new leather as she ran to the door to read the missive.

He walked up, and looked over her shoulder. "Is that from the guild?" he asked.

"Nay," she answered. "It is a missive from one of the nobles, askin' about their shoes. A messenger must have dropped it off. I wonder why Archy and Aila didna greet him?" She entered the building and Gavin followed. "Archy? Aila? Where are ye?" she called out, but they were nowhere to be found.

"Do ye want me to go look for them?" asked Gavin.

"There's no time." She took the Cordovan leather from him and laid it out on her workbench. "They are probably out with friends, and I dinna have time to track them down. I have too much work to do."

"Well, it's understandable, lass. After all, everyone has friends and wants to spend time with them. I'm sure ye have friends, too, that ye'd like to be with."

"I dinna have time for friends. All right, let's start on Callum's boots since they will take a few days to make."

"Davita, if ye need to work on the shoes for the nobles, Callum's boots can wait."

"Nay," she said with a shake of her head, donning her leather apron. "I am sure ye are anxious to be done with yer sentence so ye can go back to the Highlands. We'll make Callum's boots first. It is more important."

"Aye," said Gavin, although he wasn't sure he agreed. Part of him wanted her to work on other shoes first, because that meant he would need to stay here longer. Then again, it wasn't really fair to his friends. They had to wait to receive their sentences until Gavin finished his. He knew Cam, North, and Nash longed to go back to the Highlands. So did he. Who was he to keep them here longer?

"The first thing I need to ken is the size of Callum's feet," she said. "I need to make a pattern."

"I dinna ken. He's a short, little man. Just make them small."

"But if they're too small, then they willna fit him," she protested.

"All right, then make them bigger. He can shove some moss in the toes if they are too long, I suppose."

"Gavin." She looked at him in a scolding manner. "I really need to ken the details."

"Ah, there ye are," said North as Gavin's friends came in through the front door.

"Where were ye this mornin'?" asked Cam. "We came here and the shop was empty."

"We needed to go to the tanner's," said Gavin. "That reminds me, did any of ye see Aila or Archy?"

"I saw Aila with the cobbler's nephew earlier," said Cam. "They were headed out of town and they were carryin' a basket."

"Och, I'm sure they were goin' somewhere private to have a bite to eat," said Davita. "They'll probably be gone all day now. I could really have used Aila's help repairin' shoes. I need to get caught up."

"I saw Archy cleanin' out the chicken coop earlier," said North.

"Again?" Gavin raised a brow. "Are ye sure he wasna stealin' eggs instead?"

"Mayhap," said North, shrugging his shoulders. "I didna ask him."

"Gavin, we're goin' to practice with our weapons down by the river," said Nash. "It's been so long since we've used our blades that we dinna want to get rusty. Will ye come with us?"

Gavin wanted nothing more than to practice his swordfight. They'd been in town for days now and, honestly, he longed for the Highlands and a good spar more than anything. He looked back at Davita, not wanting to leave her here alone. Everyone had deserted her, and she was struggling. He couldn't walk away from her at a time like this.

"I dinna think so," he said. "I am goin' to stay here and help Davita."

"If ye're sure. All right, let's go," Nash told his friends.

"Hold on," said Gavin walking over to his friends and looking down at their feet.

"What's wrong?" asked Cam.

Then Gavin dropped to the floor and studied their feet from a prone position lying on his stomach.

"What in the name of the clootie are ye doin'?" Nash kicked at him. "Stop tryin' to look up my plaid, ye fool."

"I'm no' doin' any such thing." Gavin's eyes went from the feet of one man to the next.

"Bid the devil, Gavin, what is wrong with ye?" grumbled North. "I've never seen ye act this way before."

"No' when I'm sober, anyway," Gavin replied, grabbing on to Nash's foot. "I think yer foot is the closest size to Callum's. Or at least it looks that way, since I was in this position when last I saw Callum's boots."

"Blethers, let go of my foot!" Nash swatted at him, and Gavin jumped up, pulling Nash over to Davita. "Here ye go," he told her. "Nash's feet are the closest size to Callum's. Does that help?"

"It does," she said, laying a parchment on the ground. "Stand on this barefoot," she told Nash.

"Now wait a minute," Nash started to protest, but Gavin

pushed him forward.

"Come on, we dinna have all day," said Gavin. "The lass needs to trace around yer foot to make a pattern for Old Callum's boots."

"Oh, is that all?" Nash removed one shoe and started to remove the other when Davita stopped him.

"I only need one foot. Both boots will be made from the same pattern, flipped over." When she began tracing around Nash's foot, he started laughing. First it was a soft chuckle, and then it ended up being a full-blown bellow.

"He's bluidy ticklish," North told them. "He always was, ever since he was a child. Doesna he sound like a lassie when he laughs?"

"Hurry up," begged Nash, trying to hold back his laughter.

"I'm sorry. Does it tickle too much?" asked Davita.

"Nay," Nash answered. "I want ye to hurry so I can strangle my brathair for his doitit comment."

"He is right, ye ken," remarked Cam. "Ye do giggle like a lass."

"That's it! I'll kill ye both." Nash stepped off the parchment and his friends bolted to the door. Nash bent down and grabbed his shoe, throwing it at his friends. It hit the door with a loud bang as his friends left the building. Then he hurried over and picked up his shoe and ran out the door after them.

"Nash, get back here!" Gavin went to the door and looked out.

"It's all right," Davita told him. "I got what I needed." She measured the size of Nash's foot against a few of the wooden lasts, choosing the one that was closest in size. "I will use this one," she said.

"What can I do to help?" he asked, wanting to be useful.

"Well, just watch and learn for now," she told him. "I am goin' to start with cuttin' out soles for the boots. This will be a different leather, because it is thicker and stiffer," she told him.

Gavin wasn't paying much attention to her words. Instead,

his focus was on Davita's beauty. Her long, light brown hair fell in waves cascading over her shoulders. One end of a stray piece disappeared into her cleavage.

"Sit down," she told him. "Are ye even listenin' to a word I'm sayin'?"

"Aye," he said, sliding up behind her on the stool, wrapping his legs on either side of her, rather than sitting on a chair of his own.

"Gavin!" She scooted forward a little, but he wrapped his arms around her waist next, and pulled her to him until he was rubbing up against her back.

"I heard ye, lass." He gently ran his fingers up and down her arm, hearing her breath hitch as her motions stilled. "Ye were sayin' somethin' about thick and stiff." He felt himself growing harder as he breathed in her flowery essence and kissed her gently behind her ear. Her grip on the cutting knife slackened. "I have somethin' that is thick and stiff as well," he whispered into her ear, letting his tongue flick at her lobe.

Davita's body warmed, and a tingle flitted over her skin every time Gavin trailed his fingers over her arm, or licked her ear. She should have stopped him from distracting her from her work, but she wanted this more than anything. When he repeated the words thick and stiff, she felt his erection pressing up against her back. Then he nibbled at her neck and continued to talk.

"What else?" he asked her.

"Well," she said, licking her lips, trying to concentrate on cutting out the soles. "If they were goin' to be soles for shoes of a noble, then the toe would need to be longer. How long did ye want . . . it?"

"Och, lassie, I think ye should be the one to decide if it's long enough." Every time he spoke, his words sounded more and more sexual to her. Or was it just her own mind that made it sound this way? She wasn't even sure.

"Gavin, I am tryin' to make boots," she whispered, her eyes

closing as he gently blew into her ear next. Her head fell to the side and he started licking her neck. That only made her imagine his mouth on other parts of her as well.

"Go ahead, lass. Dinna let me distract ye." His hand settled on her knee. And when his fingers dipped below her skirt and his hand slowly slid up her bare leg, she felt a throbbing sensation of anticipation between her thighs. Her breathing deepened. She could no longer think about anything but making love with Gavin.

"We shouldna be doin' this," she said in a breathy whisper.

"Why no'?" he asked, one hand sliding up to cup her breast, while his other hand snaked beneath her braies. The next thing she knew, he'd cupped her womanly mound with his large hand, causing a delicious wetness to form.

"Oooh, Gavin," she said, feeling her nipples harden. His fingers caressed her, making magic, and she didn't want him to stop. Then she felt him slide his finger between her womanly folds. She gasped at the intimate action, and then couldn't help but let out a satisfied moan. "Ye dinna ken what ye're doin' to me, Gavin." She opened her legs wider for him, and he somehow managed to rub his thumb up against her nub as he prodded her with one finger, then two, slipping in and out of her slowly, guided by her own liquid passion. "Oh! Oh!" she cried, feeling herself already starting to climb to that place where she now knew she would find release and completion. "Gavin, stop," she begged him, not really meaning it, but those were the words that came out of her mouth.

His fingers stilled. "Really, lass? Are ye sure?" He sounded so disappointed. "I thought ye liked this."

"I do. Too much." When his fingers stilled, she realized that she wanted it to continue. "I enjoy it but, this time, I want ye to enjoy it as well."

"What are ye sayin'?"

"I'm sayin, let's go into the bedroom where we willna be disturbed. Here, anyone can see us from the window. It would be embarrassin' and highly unprofessional if a customer walked in to see us doin' . . . this."

"Losh me! Ye are right. What are we waitin' for?" He jumped up and took her in his arms, sweeping her off of her feet. She squealed with excitement.

"There is no one here, and it seems yer friends and my siblin's will be gone for a while," Davita told him. He nodded, and quickly headed to the bedroom.

Kicking the door open with one foot, Gavin laid her gently on the stuffed sleeping pallet. "Are ye sure about this, Davita?" asked Gavin, his voice taking on an urgent tone. "I mean . . . can we . . . go all the way?" he asked her. "Ye're no' goin' to change yer mind, are ye?"

"I'm sure we can," she said, knowing in her heart that this is really what she wanted. "I mean, only if ye want to do it as well?"

He stood up and closed the door, then walked back to the pallet. He lifted his plaid to show her his stiff manhood. "Does this answer yer question, lassie?"

"Och!" She covered her mouth with her hand. Her eyes stayed fastened to his huge, hardened form. Then she took a deep breath and released it. "Ye really do want to do this, Gavin. I can see that now."

"More than ye'll ever ken."

He was undressed in seconds, and standing above the pallet, naked. His manhood looked straight as an arrow and highly engorged. Curious, she sat up and reached out for him, stopping right before her hand made contact.

"Go ahead. Feel me, love," he told her, taking her hand and guiding it to his swollen member. He closed her fingers around him, sucking in a breath as she gently squeezed. Then she rubbed her fingers up and down his shaft.

"It's like silk over steel," she said in amazement. Next, her fingers rubbed over his tip, and his hand shot out to stop her.

"All right, that's enough. Ye do that once more, and I'm goin' to be finished before ye even begin. Ye need to remove some of these clothes, lass."

"Why dinna ye help me?" she asked, feeling lustful and playful.

"With pleasure." He was so randy that when he undressed her, he was not gentle, and neither did she care. He pulled her skirt off, and then fumbled with the ties on her undergarment, sliding the braies down her legs. Then he straddled her atop the pallet, reaching over to unlace the ties of her bodice . . . but with his teeth. The action was arousing.

She giggled, and when he looked up at her, she stopped. He had the look of a hungry wolf in his eyes, and it affected her in a way that she never thought it would. It made her feel randy and anxious. She needed him. Davita wanted to feel Gavin inside her, right now. "Hurry, Gavin," she begged him. "I canna wait much longer to make love with ye."

He turned into an animal then, reaching out and ripping open her bodice. The sound of the cloth tearing made this experience even more exciting to her. Her breasts spilled out into his hands. When his face came closer, she arched her back, taking his head in both hands, pulling him even closer.

"Taste me, please," she begged him, until she felt her nipple between his lips. "More," she pleaded, pulling his head up against her. He suckled at her, long and hard, causing the heat from her breast to travel all the way down to her groin. She liked this! Gavin awakened a part of her, bringing her sexual side to life in a way she'd never experienced before. Then she felt the light scrape of his teeth against her taut nipple as he released her. Bringing his head upward, he reached out and kissed her on the lips. His tongue slid into her mouth and, at the same time, she felt the tip of his hardened manhood brushing against her groin.

His body covered hers, but he held himself up with one elbow so as not to crush her.

"I am so hot, I think I will explode," she whispered, letting her tongue slip into his ear since her cheek was against his.

"I ken that I will if ye dinna stop that." He rolled onto his back, pulling her on top of him.

"Gavin? What are ye doin'?" she asked.

"I want ye on top," he told her.

"Nay." The thought frightened her of being the aggressor. This was all new to her, and she wasn't even sure what to do. "I canna. Ye need to be on top. That is proper."

"Who is to say what is proper and what is no' when it comes to lovemakin'?" he asked her.

"But I dinna ken what to do."

"Then I'll instruct ye. Dinna worry." He reached up and cupped her cheek in his hand. She leaned in to him, feeling nervous. "Spread ye legs, lassie. Open for me, and I will do the rest from down here."

She did as he asked her, straddling him, opening herself, pressing up against his hot, hard form.

"I'm ready," she said, closing her eyes, her body stiffening. "I hope I dinna do this wrong and disappoint ye."

"Ye could never disappoint me, Davita. Still, I dinna want yer first time to be like this."

"What?" Her eyes snapped open and she looked down at him. The ends of her hair pooled atop the curly, short, crisp hairs on his chest. "Please dinna tell me that we are goin' to stop now."

"Nay," he said with a low chuckle, reaching up and brushing her hair behind her ear. "We are goin' to make love, but I am goin' to prepare ye first."

"Oh, like a tanner prepares a hide before tannin'?" she asked.

"Nay. Nothin' like that! Ye see, yer hide is already covered with the softest skin I've ever felt." He squeezed her bottom gently, then very slowly, ran his fingers over her cheeks, and up her spine.

"Mmm, that feels enticin'," she said, starting to calm now.

"Did ye ken that every part of ye can feel sensuous, if ye ken how?"

"I dinna understand."

"Close yer eyes," he told her, and she did.

"Now dinna open them until I tell ye to."

"Why? What are ye goin' to do?"

"I want ye to just feel. That's it. Can ye do that?"

"I – I guess so," she said, feeling his fingers gently rubbing her skin, then gliding over her back. His hand came close to the side of her breast, and then she felt his wet mouth on her taut nipple. Next, she felt him blowing on it. It felt cool and exciting since it was wet.

"Do ye like that, lass?" he asked her.

"I – I do," she admitted. Her tongue shot out and wet her lips.

"Then ye will like this, too." She felt his hands on her waist, lifting her slightly.

"Gavin?" she asked.

"Shhhh. Just relax. And feel."

He slid down and licked her navel. His tongue swirled in a circle as his fingers gently slid up her sides.

"Oh!" She gasped and jerked. "What are ye doin'?"

"Keep yer eyes closed," he told her, his voice sounding muffled. That's when she realized exactly where he was headed next. His face moved closer to her most private spot, and she felt his tongue flick out again in one fast lick. It sent a bolt of lightning through her.

"Gavin!" She opened her eyes and sat up, only putting her in a worse position, since now she was sitting on his chest with her legs spread and his face was right there. "I dinna think I'm ready for this kind of lovemakin'."

"Why no'?" he asked with a smile, licking his lips with a hungry look in his eyes like he wanted to eat her. It frightened her. This was all too much.

She quickly got off of him and flipped over onto her back, letting out a breath and closing her eyes. "I think for my first time, I'd like to do it the normal way. I would also like to be on the bottom."

"I'm sorry if I scared ye, lass. I suppose that should wait until a different time, once ye are more experienced. Ye are right." He flipped onto his side, using his hand instead. He played with her womanly folds and she was relaxed again in no time.

"Mmmmm, I like that," she told him.

"I can see." He held up his hand and rubbed his fingers together, testing her wetness. "I think ye're ready now, lass." Crawling atop her still pulsating body, he slowly slid his hardened form into her, and waited. "Am I hurtin' ye, love?" he asked, care showing in his words.

"No' at all," she said, barely able to talk since she'd been trying to regain her breathing. Just the thought of this Highlander being inside her made her want to cry out. It was such a good feeling, and excited her more than she thought it would.

"Just say the word, and I'll stop. I swear. No matter how difficult it will be."

"I am sayin' the word for ye to continue. Now stop all the clishmaclaver, Gavin, because I think I am about to find my release."

That must have been all he needed to hear. He glided in and out, slowly at first. Then, when she gripped his shoulders and wrapped her legs around his waist tighter, he pumped into her deeper and harder. She took him in completely, although it surprised her that she could. It didn't scare her, and neither did it hurt except for a brief moment at the beginning. She was so aroused right now that she relaxed and let go of any and all inhibitions.

She trusted Gavin.

She trusted him completely.

Then his grunting and his breathing became faster and faster. His hips rocked back and forth and they did the dance of love.

"Aaaaah, aye!" he cried out, and she understood that he had found his completion. She reveled in the feeling of it all, and reached a peak of excitement that had her crying out in ecstasy. Then the dance slowed, and he pulled out, lying down next to her, wrapping his arms around her in a protective hold.

"That was nice, Davita." He kissed her gently atop her head.

"It was more than nice, Gavin," she told him, looking over to see his eyes closing. He fell asleep almost instantly with his arms wrapped around her. He still had one leg thrown over her waist as well. She wanted to let him sleep. And as much as she wanted to go to sleep too, she realized that she couldn't. So, instead, she decided to just go back to work. The only problem was, she was trapped beneath him now, and could not move his heavy body off of her to get up.

"Gavin?" she whispered, hearing him snoring. "Gavin?" she asked again, but he was fast asleep.

Davita felt so tired, that she just stopped trying to move. Her eyes closed as well. All that wonderful lovemaking had worn her out. "Mayhap I'll just rest for a minute," she said to herself, snuggling up against Gavin, falling asleep along with him.

$$\bullet\!\cdot\!\circ\!\diamond\!\circ\!\cdot\!\bullet$$

CHAPTER EIGHTEEN

"God's eyes, man, I dinna believe this!" Nash's voice woke up Gavin, and it took him a moment to remember just where he was.

"Either put on some clothes, or get a room above the tavern," said Cam next.

"Och, nay!" screamed Davita, struggling to get up, but she was in Gavin's arms and his leg was over her, stopping her from going anywhere.

"Who's in there?" came Archy's voice next. Nash and Cam stepped together in the doorway, blocking the little boy's view so he couldn't see them.

"No one, lad," said North, stepping up close behind his friends, peering into the room. He grinned from ear to ear.

"Blethers! Do ye three have no manners at all? Turn around," Gavin commanded to his friends. "Here, cover up, lass." He threw Davita's clothes to her.

"Gavin?" She covered herself with one arm, and held up the torn bodice with the other to show him.

"I forgot about that." He handed her a blanket, scooting off the pallet, quickly pulling his leine over his head. The tunic was long and hung down to his knees.

"Is that my sister in there?" Aila ducked under the arms of the men and managed to enter the room. Her jaw dropped when she saw what was going on. "Davita, ye finally did it!"

"Aila, I'm sorry," apologized Davita, gripping the blanket to her chest. The last thing in the world she wanted was for anyone – especially her siblings to see her in this position.

"I'm no' sorry," said the girl. She sounded so proud of Davita, or mayhap relieved in some way.

"What do ye mean by that?" Davita slid off the pallet and walked over to a trunk and flipped it open. She pulled out another dress. "Men, do no' dare turn around. And keep Archy out of here," she instructed, then quickly dropped the blanket and pulled the clothes over her head. By the time she was dressed, Gavin had clothed himself in his plaid as well.

"Now that ye've made love with a man, I can admit that I've done it, too," said Aila. Davita figured this to be true, but had hoped it wasn't. After all, her sister was too young, in her opinion, to be acting like an adult where matters of the heart were concerned.

"Aila, please. We'll discuss this later. In private." Davita didn't want to bring any more attention to the act with everyone standing in the doorway. It was embarrassing enough that she and Gavin had been caught naked and sleeping together. She should have tried harder to wake him up earlier. If so, no one would have known what had transpired between them.

"Let me through!" Archy finally slipped past the men, but Gavin caught him, and turned him back around.

"Everyone out," ordered Gavin.

"But it's supper time," complained Nash.

"It is? Already?" Davita looked over to Gavin, unable to believe they had slept so long.

"That's right," said Gavin, clearing his throat.

"What did ye make to eat?" asked North. "There isna any Cullen Skink cookin' in the kettle in the kitchen."

"Nay, there isna," said Gavin.

"How long have ye two been at it?" asked Cam, raising a brow.

"Haud yer wheesht, Cam," spat Gavin. "There is no food

cookin' because . . . because I thought we'd all . . . have an outin' instead." Gavin nodded his head, as if satisfied with his lame response.

"A what?" North made a sour face, obviously not liking the idea at all.

"We're goin' to get food from the tavern, and eat it right here, in the garden," said Gavin, looking over to Davita and nodding. "Right?"

"Right," she said, going along with him to save face, but not really agreeing with this idea at all. What she wanted was only to get back to work. And also, to stop spending so much money.

"All right. I rather like that idea." Nash smiled, coming into the room and sitting down on the pallet, making himself comfortable. "So, what will we be eatin' at this outin'?"

"Whatever ye three buy and bring back here," grumbled Gavin.

"Us?" asked Cam, his hand slapping against his chest.

"It was yer idea," protested North. "I think ye should pay for it."

"Since it was yer idea to walk in here without knockin', I say ye're goin' to pay," Gavin told them through gritted teeth. Then he pulled Nash up and pushed him to the door. "Hurry now. We'll get things ready in the garden while we wait for ye."

Gavin's friends looked back, scowling at him as they left.

"I'll get the bowls," said Aila. "Can Ethan join us?" she asked, sounding hopeful. "He's right outside, waitin' for me."

"Didna ye already have an outin' with him today?" Davita did not like the fact that her sister was spending so much time with the cobbler's nephew. And to make things worse, it sounded as if Aila had been coupling with him as well. All this could possibly do is make more trouble. Clyde was already fighting with her and she didn't need added problems.

"We did, but I dinna care," said Aila. "Is it all right?"

"I thought Ethan was Clyde's apprentice at the cobbler's shop," said Davita. "It seems to me, he never works."

"It is his day off," stated Aila.

"Oh, lovely," spat Davita, not liking the sound of this at all.

"Ethan told me he was about to become his faither's journeyman when he died. So, ye see, he kens more about the business than his uncle and Gregor put together. Isna that impressive?"

"A journeyman?" gasped Davita. "Aila, he is surely jestin'. Ye ken more than anyone that it takes at least seven years for an apprentice to become a journeyman. Most of the time, the apprentice has to wait until he is one and twenty years of age. Ethan is no' old enough. He is lyin' to ye."

"Nay, Davita. He is no' lyin'. He started as an apprentice when he was twelve, and is now eight and ten years of age. He is old enough, and has plenty of experience."

"Mmmph," she mumbled, still thinking of her sister making love. "So, I see he has experience in more things than just one."

"Can I ask him to stay to eat, Sister? Please. I really like him."

Davita was about to tell her no, but when she looked over at Gavin, he slowly nodded. Then Gavin's words rang in her ears. He had told her to try to get to know her siblings better. She supposed he was right. The more she tried to keep Aila and Ethan apart, the more they would want to be together.

"Go, ask him. It's fine," Gavin answered for her. "Dinna ye agree, Davita?"

"Aye," she said, pushing the word from her mouth. She supposed it didn't matter now. She could see that everything she had been trying to protect her younger sister from was done in vain.

"I'll tell Ethan," said Archy, hurrying ahead of Aila.

"Nay. I will tell him, no' ye," spat Aila running off with her brother to get Ethan.

"Gavin, I'm so embarrassed." Davita felt as if she wanted to cry.

"Whatever for, lass?" He pulled her into his arms and kissed her atop the head. She leaned her cheek against his chest. "Ye are no' regrettin' makin' love with me, are ye?"

"Nay. Of course no'," she answered with a slight smile. "That was wonderful and somethin' I'll never forget. I wanted it as much as ye did. I will never regret it."

"I agree, it was special." He rubbed her back gently. "I'm just sorry now that I didna think to lock the door."

"What's done is done," she said with a sigh, wiping at a stray tear. "I just wanted so badly to be strong, and to be a guid and guiding influence on my siblin's."

"Ye are all that and more," he told her.

"How can ye say that? After what I just did?"

"There is nothin' wrong with two people who care about each other couplin', is there?"

"Nay, but only if they're married." She looked up at him shyly, wondering how he was going to react. She thought she'd test the waters, but no matter what bait she threw out, he wasn't biting.

"That's no' true. People do it all the time. Just like yer sister."

She frowned. This isn't what she wanted to hear right now. She was hoping they would talk about their feelings for each other, or mayhap their future. Instead, he brought up an issue that was a sore spot with her.

"That proves my point exactly," she told him. "My sister shouldna be couplin', and neither should I. All I ended up doin' was makin' things worse."

"Davita, ye are overreactin'. Perhaps ye'd feel better with somethin' to eat."

"Can ye never think of anythin' but food, Gavin? I am talkin' about us. I mean, our relationship together. Now that we've made love, what is goin' to happen between us?"

"What do ye mean? We were just havin' a guid time together. Ye are takin' this much too seriously."

"A guid time? Is that all it was to ye?"

"Nay. Of course, that's no' what I meant." He seemed suddenly irritated and uncomfortable.

"Then what did ye mean, Gavin? I'd like to ken."

He shifted from foot to foot and looked at the ground. Finally, he spoke. "I dinna ken what ye want me to say, Davita."

"All I want is an honest answer from ye. About what is goin' to happen to us. Usually, when people care for each other and then they couple, they end up gettin' married."

Gavin shrugged his shoulders, making her want to hit him. Still, he didn't answer her question at all. A typical man, she thought. All any man ever wanted was to get a girl in bed to suffice his lust. Then he left the girl, never to see her again. Well, mayhap that is exactly what should happen between them, after all, even though it felt like a dagger sticking in her heart.

"I . . . I . . ." If he was trying to say something to her, he wasn't doing a very good job at it.

Who was she fooling? Gavin needed to go back to the Highlands, and she needed to forget all about what just happened. It would be the best for all concerned.

"I will finish constructin' Callum's boots in a day or two," she told him. "Then ye are free to go. I will be sure to send a missive to Laird MacKeefe sayin' ye kept yer end of the bargain. Then ye will be accepted back into yer clan, and ye can travel back to the Highlands where ye belong."

"A day or two," he repeated, nodding, not doing anything to object. That irritated her even more.

"Ye dinna have to bother bringin' my faither back from the castle," she continued. "I will go myself to collect him once he is healed enough to return home."

"Davita. Is this what ye really want?" he asked, as she headed to the door.

"Is it what ye want?" she asked, turning to look at him once more. When he stayed silent and didn't answer, she bit her lip and nodded slightly. "I thought so. Dinna save any food for me, I am no' hungry."

"It would do ye guid to take a break," he called after her. "Ye've been workin' so hard."

"I did take a break, and look where that got us," she snapped.

"It's over now," she told him. "My only concern is gettin' the boots made so ye can leave."

GAVIN LEFT THE cordwainer's shop, still shaking his head, not knowing what had just happened. He met his friends coming across the street with food.

"We got chicken, Gavin. Unless ye'd rather have fish, we can get that, too." Nash was already gnawing on a chicken leg as he walked.

"I'm no' hungry. I dinna want anythin'," Gavin told them. "I'm goin' to take a ride down to the river and practice with my weapons since I missed out on doin' so before."

"I think I would have rather been doin' what ye were instead of practicin' swordplay," Cam tried to jest with him, but Gavin didn't even respond. He was too upset to speak.

"What's the matter with ye, Gavin?" asked North. "Ye're always hungry."

"There are some problems that no' even food can cure," said Gavin, heading away.

"Wait up," called out Cam, handing the food to his friends and running to catch up with Gavin. "If ye're havin' a problem with Davita, mayhap I can help," he offered. "After all, we all ken that I'm a lot better with these kinds of things than ye are, where women are concerned."

"I dinna want to talk about it." Gavin continued to walk, not stopping until he got to the horse in the stables.

"Och, the lovemakin' was no guid. I understand," said Cam. "Well, sometimes these are the breaks, I guess."

"Nay, that's no' it at all." Gavin prepared to saddle the horse.

"Then what is it, my friend?" asked Cam, sitting down on a pile of hay. "I've never seen ye so upset."

"It seems since we made love, now Davita thinks we should

marry."

"Ah, I see." Cam made a sucking sound with his mouth and shook his head. "Gavin, this is why ye should have stuck to the whores. They never bring up the idea of gettin' married. The only thing they expect in return is their pay. It's a lot easier than dealin' with a lass who wants to trap ye for the rest of yer life."

"Davita is no' a whore, Cam." Gavin threw a blanket on the horse, followed by a saddle. "Honestly, if I were ever goin' to settle down and get married, it would be with someone like Davita."

"Dinna be daft, Gavin! If ye marry, ye should either do it for an alliance with another clan, or stick to marryin' someone from our own clan. Why would ye even consider marryin' the daughter of the town's cordwainer? Ye'd be trapped in this little place, suckin' in the stench of piss-covered leather the rest of yer life."

"I didna say I was goin' to marry her, did I?"

"Well, ye are actin' like a lovesick knave, and I dinna like it. Gavin, wake up! Ye belong in the Highlands with a sword in yer hand, no' sittin' in a dark room bent over a worktable."

"I ken," he said, fastening the strap. "It's just that somethin' about leavin' Davita behind doesna sit right with me."

"Then bring her to the Highlands with us. I'm sure our chieftains wouldna mind havin' her there. They've allowed us, as well as many others, to join the clan."

"Nay. She'd never come. Especially if we arena married. Davita feels as if she has to take care of everyone, and will stay here protectin' her faither's business for the rest of her life. It's all she kens."

"Then I guess we're back to whores," said Cam with a shrug. "Like I said, it would have been a lot easier."

"I willna be back tonight," Gavin informed him, climbing atop the horse.

"Runnin' away from yer troubles?" asked Cam. "That's so no' like ye, Gavin. I'm no' sure I even ken who ye are anymore."

"I just need time to think. Please, dinna tell Davita where I am. I want to be alone. I dinna want to be disturbed. Do ye hear me?"

"Whatever ye say." Cam got up and headed to the door of the livery. "Dinna think we're goin' to save any food for ye, if ye do decide to return tonight after all."

"I willna," he said, feeling like if he didn't get away from everyone and everything, he was going to go mad. Gavin rode out of the stable, not bothering to look back. His stomach was empty, but his heart was full. He agreed with his good friend, Cam. Something was happening and he was changing ever since he'd met Davita. Hell, he didn't know who he was anymore either. Hopefully, a night alone in nature would help him to clear his head and find the answers. If not, he had no idea what he was going to do.

⬥◦◇◦⬥

CHAPTER NINETEEN

"HAS ANYONE SEEN Gavin?" asked Davita, hours later, coming out into the garden to find Gavin's friends, her sister and Ethan, and Archy, sitting around talking, not doing much of anything else.

"Nay. He didna even show up to eat," said Archy, sounding very disappointed.

"He's no' comin' back tonight," Cam relayed the information.

"He's no'?" That surprised as well as worried Davita. She'd lost herself in her work, but now wondered if she should have had tried harder to have a heart-to-heart conversation with Gavin about their intimate time together. She hoped she hadn't scared him away. "Where is he?" she asked.

"He asked me no' to tell anyone. Sorry." Cam shrugged, as if it didn't matter to him.

"Well, when will he be back?" she asked. "In the mornin'?"

"I'm no' sure," said Cam, yawning. "Perhaps."

"It would be nice to ken," she continued.

"I wouldna worry about it, lass," Cam told her. "Gavin will return when he's guid and ready to do it."

"Well, I hope it is sooner rather than later," she said, worried but angry at the same time. "He is supposed to be helpin' me make the boots. Or at least learnin' by watchin'."

"Gavin is no' interested in shoes," said Nash blowing air from his mouth.

"Nay," added North. "He even goes barefoot a lot. Shoes mean naught to him."

"Well, they do mean somethin' to me. I am tryin' to save our cordwainin' business, but no one else seems to care. I could use help," she told them. "Who is goin' to help me since Gavin disappeared?"

"I've got to get these dishes back to the tavern," said Nash, collecting up the dirty bowls.

"I really should help him." North jumped up, too.

"Dinna look at me," said Cam. "I've got Red waitin' for me, and she is no' a patient lassie."

"Aila?" Davita's eyes sought out her sister's.

"Davita, mayhap later. Right now, I'm goin' to walk back to the cobbler's shop with Ethan." She got up, pulling Ethan with her, and took off at a run.

The only person left now was her brother, but Davita knew he'd be of little help. "Archy? How about ye?" she asked, desperate for any help she could possibly get.

"I've got to feed Hamish," said Archy, looking the other direction.

"Hamish?" The name sounded familiar, but she couldn't remember why. "Who is he? Bram has a job at the tanner's now, if ye mean one of his children. He will be able to feed them all by himself."

"Nay, no' Bram. Hamish is my toad." He held up a toad in two hands and it only infuriated Davita to see it.

"I thought I told ye to get rid of that thing. Why do ye still have it?"

"Gavin helped me make a toad house and said I could keep Hamish if he stayed in the garden."

"He did, did he?" Her hands went to her hips. It seemed Gavin was doing things behind her back and she didn't like that. Especially when it had to do with her family. "Well, Gavin is no' here, and he had no right tellin' ye that. He is no' part of this family. Now get rid of it, please."

"Nay!" Archy said stubbornly. "Gavin said I could keep it."

"I told ye, he is no' part of our family."

"Well, I wish he was. I dinna want to be a part of this family if Hamish canna stay."

That surprised her, since she never expected her little brother to say something like this. He'd been changing lately, and she wasn't sure it was for the better. What he needed was a father to discipline him. Then again, her father was no shining example of how to act.

"Dinna talk that way, and stop bein' a fool, Archy," she scolded him. "Ye are a lad. Ye have no money, and nowhere else to go. Now get rid of the toad and come help me in the shop."

She went back into the house, feeling tired and drained. What had started off as a wonderful, exhilarating afternoon with Gavin, had ended in disaster. She looked out the open window, wrapping her arms around herself when she felt a slight chill from the night breeze. It was dark outside now. Everything seemed different. This was the time when her worries consumed her mind and kept her from sleeping. When Gavin was there, her worries seemed to disappear. Without him, she felt so lonely. Mayhap she had relied on him too much for her own happiness. Or mayhap, it hadn't been enough.

"Where are ye, Gavin?" she whispered, looking up at the stars. How she wished she were with him right now, looking at these same stars, wrapped safely in his arms. Why did he leave? Was it because she had mentioned marriage? She was a fool for saying anything about it to him at all. She could see that now. It should have been clear to her that men like Gavin were independent and loners. They would run at just hearing the word marriage. Nay, Gavin wasn't the marrying kind. It was stupid of her to even think that mayhap they could have had a future together.

Her eyes sought out the boots she was making. Shadows danced on the walls behind her worktable from the flame of the candle that had already burned quite low. Once these boots were finished, Gavin would leave for good. That is, if he was even coming back at all. Her head told her he would return because without the boots, he'd never be redeemed and welcomed back into his clan. Her heart told her he wouldn't, because then he would have to face her and talk about their future. Before, she had pictured a future with Gavin at her side. But now . . . now her future was looking very dark and lonely without him.

GAVIN LAY ON his back at the river with his arms behind his head and his legs stretched out in front of him. The evening breeze smelled sweet from the wildflowers, only reminding him of the scent of Davita's hair. Damn, she was a fine lass. Someday, she would make some man happy as his wife. She was strong, and smart, and cared about others more than she did herself. It wasn't easy to find lassies like her.

He watched the twinkling stars above, thinking about his parents and his siblings. The memories had become fuzzy throughout the years. Lately, he had a hard time even remembering exactly what his family had looked like. The last time he saw them was when he was only a young child.

Gavin seemed to question every choice he made now. Being around Davita and her family somehow filled a void in his heart for the family he'd loved and lost. It was a good feeling. However, he had another family with the MacKeefes. They had taken him in at his time of greatest need. Never would he want to let them down. He couldn't have two families, he decided. He'd known the pain of having no family, and now he knew a new pain of having too many families and not knowing what to do.

"Damn it," he spat, throwing a rock into the water. It landed with a loud splash. The ripples moved outward until they got further apart and finally disappeared. Each man's life touched another's, and the rippling of the water from the rock just proved it.

Now, his life had entwined with Davita's. He'd started to get caught up in her problems, thinking of them as his own. He wanted naught more than to help her. Gavin was fond of Archy. The boy needed a man to look up to, and didn't have a good role model with his father. Aila, on the other hand, was wild, but he was sure she was only looking for someone to love. Davita was another story altogether.

Davita was an amazing woman and, at times, he'd almost felt as if they were already married, even if he'd only known her for a scant amount of time. Something about being around her felt natural and right. It was odd, but he felt that they were meant to be together. He'd never fallen this fast and furious for any woman before. That worried him. Did he truly have feelings for her or was it just some sort of infatuation?

Davita's family meant everything to her, and he liked that. His family had meant everything to him as well. She was devoted to her family and worked harder than anyone he knew. Her only thoughts were to help her father, and to be a good example to Aila and Archy. She was determined to save the family business, and rightly so. These people were not much more than a step above peasants. Her family was far from rich, and didn't seem to have much at all. He supposed that's why the business meant so much to her. It was the lifeline to supporting her family. Years of hard work had made her father a craftsman and part of a guild. Davita was proud of it, and would never let it go.

Gavin couldn't even imagine how hard it must have been for Davita to lose her mother, and then to watch her father drink his life away. Two things Gavin truly understood were loss and drinking. Part of the reason he always drank so much was to chase away the darkness looming in his head. He'd been haunted his entire life by the fact that he'd watched his family being slaughtered, and did nothing to help them. He was only nine at the time, but he was a coward and hated himself for it. He'd hidden behind the bushes, too frightened to move.

If his family hadn't stopped traveling for him to use a bush, would they still be alive today? And if he hadn't been cowering behind the bushes, could he have done something to save them instead? Even if he couldn't have done anything, being just a boy, at least he would have been murdered as well, and then he'd be with his family now. He didn't feel lucky at all to have escaped the blades of the bandits. He didn't deserve it. Nay, instead he felt as if it were a curse. He lived his life always wondering if things could have been different if he had made a different choice. What was the purpose of his life, and why hadn't he died instead of being spared?

He supposed the fear of possibly losing another family some-day is what made him run when he heard Davita mention marriage. Or was it? He froze, his tongue too big for his mouth to speak, when what he wanted to say to her was that he thought he was falling in love. Instead, he stood there like a silent dolt, not able to reveal anything about the way he was feeling. He didn't deserve her. She should be with someone who wouldn't hesitate to marry her. Nay, Gavin didn't deserve to be happy, but she certainly did.

Davita had taken his silence as rejection, and it was under-standable why she did. She probably thought the worst of him right now. Why couldn't he have stayed and cleared things up instead of leaving? He should have pulled her into his arms right then and there, and told her he loved her. Why couldn't he have admitted to her, as well as to himself, that he never wanted to leave her? The shadows of self-doubt lingered in his mind and, this time, he hadn't had any whisky to push them away and dull the pain. Just like that scared little boy so many years ago, all he felt like he wanted to do right now was to hide away.

Gavin's heart ached for the family he once loved and lost. He never wanted to go through that again. But in trying not to relive the past, was he making mistakes regarding his future? His head ached, and he was no longer sure about anything.

The MacKeefes were his adopted family now, and he felt

close to everyone in the clan. But that was different. The MacKeefes were made up of strong, Highland warriors who could fend for themselves. He didn't have to fear for them. Not even for the women and children of the clan. There was always someone with a sword there to protect them.

With Davita and her siblings, it was different. They needed him. He needed them. Or was it just want? Hell, he didn't know the answer to that anymore. All he knew was that he was being pulled in two directions at once, and feeling very torn about it.

Gavin longed to go back to the Highlands and the life he loved. Yet, at the same time, his heart was telling him that he belonged here in town with Davita. Confusion clouded his brain, threatening to drive him mad. Gavin closed his eyes, listening to the sounds of nature and also the sound of his beating heart.

"Give me the strength to do the right thing," he said, drifting off to sleep where life was easier, and his problems didn't threaten to consume him.

CHAPTER TWENTY

DAVITA AWOKE TO a pounding noise, jolting her from her sleep. She picked up her head, opening her eyes, realizing it was morning and she had once again fallen asleep at her worktable. For two days now, she'd worked late into the night, hoping for Gavin's return. She'd managed to finish constructing Callum's boots, but now she wondered if it even mattered. It looked like Gavin wasn't coming back.

"Open up," came a deep growl from outside, even though the door was not locked. She jumped up and opened the door to find Iver, the butcher, standing there with a cleaver in one hand. He looked very angry. Behind him was Grace, the baker's wife, and Keithen, the proprietor of the tavern. None of them were smiling.

"Is somethin' wrong?" she asked, rubbing one sleepy eye, having no idea why they were at her door this early. She yawned, looking up at the sky. The sun had just broken the horizon, and early risers were starting to fill the streets on their way to mass since it was Sunday. The fishmonger drove his wagon filled with fish down the muddy, rutted road, coming up from the river where he had probably been fishing throughout the night. The alewives were gathered in a circle, already gossiping, as the church bells rang out in an attempt to lure people toward the holy walls to pray together.

"I'll say, somethin' is wrong," snapped Iver. "That brathair of yers stole some sausage from me this mornin'. He ran when I tried to stop him."

"What?" she asked, still waking up, and not at all sure she'd heard him correctly. "Archy?"

"Aye," shouted Grace. "He took a loaf of bread off my windowsill that I had sittin' there to cool."

"Nay, I'm sure ye're mistaken," said Davita. "Archy is in bed, sleepin'."

"Nay, he's no'. Because he was already stealin' eggs from my henhouse this mornin'. I saw him out there before it even got light," Keithen told her.

"Nay," she said, unable to believe her ears. "My brathair is here and has been all night. I'll prove it." She walked over to the stairs and called for him. When he didn't come, she ran up to his bedroom, but it was empty.

"Mayhap he slept down here," she said to herself, hurrying to the downstairs room that her father had been using. When she opened the door, her mouth fell open in surprise. Aila was sleeping upon her father's pallet with Ethan. Both of them were naked. She slammed the door and turned around to find not only the butcher, the tavern owner, and the baker's wife, standing inside her house now, but Clyde was also with them.

"Clyde," she squeaked out, not thinking things could get worse, but they certainly did. Her eyes scanned the room for Gavin's friends, hoping for their protection. Unfortunately, there weren't there, and they hadn't been since Gavin had left.

"I ken my nephew is in here," said Clyde. "He didna come home last night. I'm willin' to bet he's with that whore of a sister of yers."

"Haud yer wheesht," she shouted. "All of ye, get out of my house anon." Her arm shot outward and she pointed to the door, but none of them moved at all.

"No' until I see for myself that Ethan is no' here. Now open that door," commanded Clyde.

"Nay," she answered. "This is my home and none of ye have the right to be here."

"Move, I say."

"Ye move. Right out of here. Now." She stood up to the townsfolk all by herself, ready to defend her family, but feeling so alone and helpless.

Clyde pushed her out of the way so hard that she fell to the ground and landed on her bottom.

"Nay! Stop!" she cried out as Clyde pushed the door open to reveal Aila and Ethan who were just finishing dressing.

"I'll tan yer hide, Ethan, for layin' with this whore," screamed Clyde. "That is, right after I teach the bitch a lesson." He gripped a leather strap in his hand that was used by shoemakers.

"Nay, Uncle, I love her. Dinna hurt her." Ethan stood with his arms out, protecting Aila.

"Get out of my way," growled Clyde, stepping into the room.

Davita sprang to her feet, jumping onto Clyde's back, trying to stop him. "Leave my sister alone!" she cried.

Clyde threw Davita to the ground once again. "Mayhap ye're the first whore who needs to be taught a lesson. After all, we all ken ye've been sleepin' with that bluidy Highlander." He raised the leather strap above his head, meaning to whip Davita.

Before he could lower his hand, another hand gripped his wrist so tightly from behind that he cried out in pain.

"Dinna even think of hurtin' my lass or ye'll find yer head layin' on the ground next to yer feet. Do ye understand?"

"Gavin!" Davita's heart swelled when she saw that he had finally returned.

"Dinna hurt me," begged Clyde, trying to break free of Gavin's hold.

"I should kill ye right here, right now, for callin' the lassies whores." Gavin released Clyde's hand and drew his sword. The sound of scraping metal had everyone too frightened to speak. Then he reached down with his free hand and helped Davita to her feet.

"Are ye hurt, lass?" he asked her.

"Nay. I'm so happy ye returned, Gavin."

"I'm sorry," said Clyde. "I didna mean it. It's just that I'm a little on edge lately. I got word a week ago that the cobbler's and cordwainer's head guild masters will be here soon to collect the dues and observe our shops. If they are no' satisfied, we will no longer be members of the guilds."

"What?" gasped Davita. "How come I wasna informed?"

"It's because my uncle intercepted yer missive." Ethan walked out of the bedroom, holding on to Aila's hand. "That's why he called for me to help him. He wants his shop in order when they arrive."

"Ye kent this, and ye didna tell my sister?" asked Aila. "How could ye, Ethan?"

"I'm sorry, Aila. My uncle forbade me to say a word." Ethan shook his head. "I decided last night that I had to tell ye, and that is why I came over here. But then we . . . we got distracted."

"Oh," said Aila, shyly looking up at Ethan. Her cheeks blushed.

"Everyone, out!" commanded Gavin.

"What about the food the boy stole from us?" griped the butcher.

Cam, Nash, and North came running in just then, looking very confused.

"We heard shoutin' and saw a commotion," said Cam, his sword in his grip.

"We came right away to help," added Nash. Each of the men was holding their weapon, ready for battle. Then they noticed Gavin.

"Gavin, ye're back," said North.

"What is goin' on here?" asked Cam.

"Where the hell were ye three?" growled Gavin. "Ye should have been here protectin' Davita and her siblin's in my absence."

"Us?" asked Nash. "Where the hell were ye for the last two days, Gavin?"

"Aye," agreed North. "This is yer punishment, no' ours."

Gavin knew he was going to have to explain his disappearance, but now wasn't the time to do it. "Never mind. Tell me, what would it cost to replace the items that the boy stole?" Gavin asked the merchants.

"Three pence for my bread," called out the woman.

"Same for my eggs," snapped the tavern owner.

"Four for the meat," said the butcher.

Nash let out a low whistle, and Gavin knew it was because the shopkeepers were inflating their prices.

"I dinna ken how many eggs the boy stole, but I could buy a few dozen at that price," said Nash.

"Ye'll all be paid for yer wares." Gavin's hand went to his money pouch, but he had forgotten that it was empty. "Nash, pay them," said Gavin from the side of his mouth.

"What?" Nash's head snapped around. "Why always me?"

"I'll pay ye back," said Gavin in a low voice. "I used all my money at the tanner's, buyin' the Cordovan leather for Callum's boots."

"Fine," spat Nash, digging into his coin pouch.

"Give them each a shillin'," said Gavin.

"A shillin' each?" Nash looked at Gavin as if he thought he'd gone crazy.

"Nay, Gavin. That is way too much money, and ye ken it," argued Nash.

"It'll pay for anythin' else the boy might have stolen," said Gavin. "It'll also pay for his protection, so none of ye come after him again."

"How do we ken the boy willna try to steal from us in the future?" asked Grace.

"I give ye my word he willna," Gavin promised.

"Gavin, we dinna even ken where Archy is," Davita whispered.

"Dinna worry, lass. I will find him. Now, is it a deal?" he asked the merchants.

"If ye'll be responsible for him, I guess so," said the butcher.

The other two also agreed.

"Nash," said Gavin. "A shillin' for each of them. Go on." He nodded toward Nash's coin pouch.

"North and Cam were the ones gamblin', no' me," Nash complained, counting his coins. "They are the ones that have all the money."

"Is that so?" asked Gavin, realizing mayhap he wasn't being fair to Nash after all. "Then each of ye hand over a shillin'," Gavin told his friends. "I think that sounds fair."

"All right," agreed Cam.

"I suppose," said North.

Each of his friends handed over a shilling to one of the shop-keepers, and then sent them on their way.

"As for ye, Clyde," said Gavin. "If ye ever call the lassies whores again, or even think to raise a hand against them, I swear, I will kill ye and no' think twice about it. Do ye understand?" Gavin was angry, and his gruff side came out, but he did nothing to hold it in. His Highland warrior attributes were emerging, and it was a side of him that Davita had yet to see. He hoped it wouldn't frighten her. He only meant to threaten the shop owners so they would stop bothering Davita and her sister. He was there to protect them.

"I just want my nephew, and I'll be leavin'," said Clyde. "I dinna want any more problems."

"Go on, Ethan." Gavin looked over at Ethan and motioned with a jerk of his head. "Go with yer uncle."

Ethan seemed reluctant, but didn't have the nerve to disobey Gavin. No one did when he was this threatening.

"I'll be back, Aila." Ethan gave the girl a quick kiss. "I'm sorry about all this."

"I'll be waitin', Ethan," Aila called after him.

Gavin sheathed his sword, glad he had decided to return after all. For a while there, he'd struggled with his decision but, in the end, he couldn't stay away from Davita, or his friends. It was time for him to face his troubles, even without whisky. He needed to make decisions that would affect him for the rest of his life.

"Thank ye, Gavin," said Davita once they'd all left. She kept her distance. Gavin realized he would have to be the one to break the tension between them. He reached out and pulled her into his arms, kissing her atop the head. She hesitated, but slowly returned the hug.

"Now, will someone tell me what the hell is goin' on around here?" asked Gavin.

"We didna ken anythin' was amiss until we heard and saw the commotion from the stables," said Nash.

"Where's the boy? And why did he leave?" asked Gavin.

"Och, Gavin, I'm afraid that is my fault," admitted Davita. "I told Archy to get rid of his toad two days ago. He was upset about it, and didna speak to me at all. I thought he'd get over it, but I guess no'. Plus, he was upset that ye left and didna return. We all were."

"That was my mistake, and I see clearly now that I should have stayed." Gavin had so much to say, but he needed to find Archy first. The boy could be in danger. "Davita, we will talk later," he said, taking her hands in his and staring into her sad, green eyes. "I promise we will. But right now, my friends and I need to find yer brathair."

"I will go with ye then," she said.

"Nay. It's no' safe. As a matter of fact, I think Nash will stay here to protect ye and Aila until our return."

"Me? I want to hunt for the boy," said Nash. "I'm better at trackin' than any of ye, and ye ken it. I can find him by myself and ye can all stay here."

"Stop the braggin', Brathair, said North. "It's no' appealin'."

"I'll stay with them," offered Cam. Cam was the laziest of Gavin's friends, so it didn't surprise him that he offered. He was also the one who liked the lassies the most. Still, Gavin was sure he could trust him.

"I dinna care who stays. The rest of ye, let's go find the boy."

They were already halfway out the door when Davita

stopped them.

"Gavin?"

"Aye?" He turned around to face her.

"Thank ye for comin' back." Davita flashed him a slight smile, as if she weren't sure if she should or not.

"Lass, ye dinna need to thank me. I'm just glad I got here in time to help ye. Now, I promise ye, I will be back soon. And when I return, I will have yer brathair with me."

Chapter Twenty-One

T IME SEEMED TO stand still as Davita busied herself with work, waiting for Gavin to find Archy.

"I'm frightened for Archy," said Aila, helping to repair shoes as Davita added a few finishing touches to Callum's boots, wanting to do the best job she could so Callum would accept them. "Our little brathair has never been alone before."

"I'm scared, too, Aila," Davita admitted. "However, I have faith in Gavin. He will find and bring our brathair back to us. I ken he will."

"I hope so." Aila continued to stitch. Davita looked over, seeing her sister's fine work. The stitches were smaller and closer together than she usually made them. Davita was impressed.

"Where did ye learn to stich that clean?" she asked. "Ye never did such precise work before."

"I learned it from Ethan," Aila said proudly, breaking the thread and holding up the shoe to inspect it. "Once he is a journeyman, he hopes to get his own shop someday."

"That's nice," said Davita, using a rag to shine the boots.

"As soon as we can, we're goin' to get married!"

Just hearing the word married upset Davita so much that she dropped the boot right atop her foot. "Losh me!" She picked it up and continued to clean it.

"Davita, ye'd better be careful with those Cordovan boots since they are so expensive."

Davita looked over to see Cam leaning back in a chair with his feet up on a bench. He was sleeping. She wanted to talk to someone about Gavin, and figured this would be a good time to confess her feelings to her sister. After all, Aila was feeling the same way about Ethan. Or so it seemed.

"Married?" she asked, trying to sound nonchalant. She glanced once more at Cam, and then over to her sister. "Did Ethan really say he wants to marry ye?"

"Aye. It was his idea."

"It was?"

"Yes. We are in love, Davita. That's what people who are in love do. They get married." Aila let out a sigh, smiling and looking up at the ceiling. She was certainly lovesick. "Plus, Ethan is a wonderful lover."

"Is that so?" Davita didn't really want to talk about coupling, since she was so upset about her own intimate time she'd spent with Gavin. She was about to change the subject when her sister asked a question that she didn't really want to answer.

"Was yer couplin' with Gavin nay guid?" she asked. "Is that why he left ye?"

"Aila!" gasped Davita, so shocked that when she turned quickly, she knocked one of Callum's boots to the ground again. Picking it up, she held it to her chest, wondering just how to answer.

"Sister, what is the matter?" asked Aila. "It's no' like ye to be so clumsy in the workroom."

Davita decided she could no longer concentrate on her work and put down the boot. She glanced once more over at Cam. He was snoring.

"Aila, how did ye ken ye were in love with Ethan? I mean . . . how did it happen so fast?"

"It didna happen that fast. Remember, Ethan has been comin' to help out at his uncle's shop for years now. We have been secret friends for a while. Then again, I knew the first time I saw him that I was goin' to marry him."

"Ye did? I dinna understand. How would ye ken such a thing?"

"Well, just by the way he looked at me. And when he spoke, my heart jumped into my throat just hearin' his voice."

"I see," she said, thinking she felt that way about Gavin.

"When Ethan's hand brushes against mine, I feel a tingle all the up my spine." She sewed while she spoke, smiling down at the shoe she was repairing.

"A tingle? Really?" Davita remembered feeling that same tingle when Gavin touched her.

"Aye, and when he kissed me for the first time, I just about melted on the spot. Lately, when I wake up and realize he is no' with me, I feel sick for a guid part of the day."

"Ye do?" Davita's brows dipped. "Is bein' in love supposed to make ye feel ill?"

"I no' only feel sick sometimes when he is no' with me, but lately I am gainin' weight. I guess bein' around him gives me an appetite. But it doesna matter. Ethan loves me, even if I'm fat. I think I eat more when I'm happy."

"Feelin' sick and gainin' weight?" asked Davita, starting to suspect something but needing to be sure.

"Aye, I even feel a flutter like a butterfly in my stomach just when I think of Ethan."

"Aila," said Davita, dreading this question, but needing to know. "Have ye ever coupled with anyone other than Ethan?"

"Nay, Sister! I ken ye think I'm a whore, like Clyde said, but it is no' true. I've only been with one man, and it has only been Ethan."

"When was the first time? I mean . . . the first time ye . . . did it?"

"Made love?" Aila smiled. "Och, Sister, ye dinna have to be so shy that ye canna even say it. It is a natural thing."

"I guess so. So when did ye and Ethan . . . make . . . love?" God's eyes, this was a hard thing to talk about. But without their mother there, Davita had to step in and play the part.

"I dinna ken exactly. It was a few months ago when he stopped by the shop to see his uncle. We did it in the grass by the river." She put her hand to her mouth and giggled. "Afterwards, we swam naked in the stream."

"A couple of months ago?" This was starting to sound like what Davita suspected. "When was the last time ye had yer courses, Aila?"

"Blethers, I dinna ken. I canna remember. I think it was mayhap a sennight before we made love for the first time."

"And ye dinna think that it's odd that ye havena had it since?" What was the matter with her sister? She was starting to think the girl was daft.

"I didna think much about it, since I liked no' havin' it. I've heard from Red and Violet that they dinna always get their courses either, so I'm sure it's a common thing."

"It may be common for whores who use herbs to control those kinds of things," Davita explained. "But, Sister, it is no' a common thing for lassies like ye and me."

All of a sudden, Aila's face darkened. She looked down and held a hand over her stomach. "Davita, do ye think I'm . . . I'm . . ."

"Pregnant," Davita finished the sentence for her. "Aye, I do, Aila. Ye dinna have to be so shy as no' to say the word. After all, it is only natural that when two people make love, they also end up makin' a bairn."

"Oh," she said quietly. Then she smiled and it didn't seem to bother her at all. "Well, it's a guid thing then that we decided we're already gettin' married. I just hope when his uncle finds out, he doesna kill us. I suppose we'll have to live with him since that is Ethan's home now since his faither died."

"I suppose so," she said, not wanting to hear Clyde's reaction to this!

"So, mayhap ye're with child, too, Davita." Aila picked up another pair of shoes to repair, inspecting them.

"I am no'," she spat. Unconsciously, her hand went to her

stomach. "We've only done it once!"

Aila giggled. "Well, I suppose once is all it takes. Like ye said, it's only natural that when two people couple, they could end up havin' made a bairn. I think it would be great if we had bairns around the same time. Then they can play with each other."

"I'm no' with child, Aila, and I dinna want to hear another word about it," snapped Davita. She got up and walked over to look out the window.

"Dinna ye love Gavin?" asked Aila.

"I . . . I . . . suppose so."

"Does he love ye, too? Because if so, ye two should marry."

"I dinna want to talk about this anymore," she said, hurrying off to the kitchen. Things were happening so fast that it made her head spin. Davita didn't know if Gavin loved her, but she did know by his reaction that he didn't want to marry her.

She sank atop the kitchen bench, looking down and putting her hand on her stomach. She wasn't pregnant. But what if she were? Would she tell him? Would he care? By the time she'd know for sure, Gavin would be long gone and back to the Highlands. He would never know. Davita didn't want to be an unwed mother. She also didn't want Gavin to have to marry her just because she was pregnant either. Her worries just became worse.

"I'm no' pregnant," she said, brushing the thought from her mind, getting up to make something to eat. She was so hungry that it made her feel sick. She stopped in midmotion, thinking of everything Aila had told her and all her symptoms. God's eyes, this was all a big mess.

Davita started missing Gavin, and hoped he'd be back soon with her brother. As soon as he got back and walked in that door, she was going to demand an explanation of why he left when she mentioned the word marriage. Then she was going to tell him how she felt about him, and demand that he tell her his feelings, too.

Sitting down once more, Davita felt extremely tired and

drained. Then again, she thought, if she didn't give him another chance to reject her, she wouldn't have to be hurt like this ever again.

"I THINK WE'D better split up," said Gavin, after searching with his friends for an hour and not even having a clue as to where the boy had gone. "Nash, ye go into the woods. North, stick to the road. I am goin' to ride along the river. If Archy has his toad with him, he might want to keep near the water."

"What if we dinna find him?" asked North.

"We will. We have to," said Gavin. "I will no' give up and neither will I stop until I've found the lad. He needs our protection. I have to do this – for Davita."

"If one of us does find him, we'll need to have some way to contact each other so we'll ken when to stop lookin'," said Nash.

"Whoever finds Archy, bring him back to town," instructed Gavin. "Then ring the bell at the church three times. The sound will be heard far and clear. If ye hear it, head on back immediately."

"Right," said North, kicking his heels into the sides of his horse and heading away. They'd borrowed horses from the stablemaster, knowing without each of them having a horse, it would be nearly impossible to cover much ground. There was no telling how far the boy had gone, or even when he left. If he left early last night, he could have gotten all the way to Hermitage Castle on foot by now.

Gavin traveled quite a way along the riverbank, finally spotting a pile of sticks and a few broken eggshells. He dismounted, looking closer. The boy had tried to start a fire, but it didn't look as if he were successful. He probably hoped to cook the eggs, but now they lay spoiled on the ground atop a pile of dirt.

Gavin traveled further, managing to find skin from the sausage, and even some crumbs of bread. He was on the right path. Archy was leaving a trail. Then he found what he believed to be the boy's footprints and they led back up to the road and directly toward Hermitage Castle.

He rode in that direction, stopping when he spied the castle in the distance. He was told he was an outcast and was not allowed to go there unless he completed his sentence first. Still, he needed to find out if the boy was headed there to see his father.

Gavin was just approaching the castle when he thought he heard someone crying softly from behind a tree. He stopped and turned his horse, heading back to find Archy sitting on the ground with his head down between his knees.

The boy was filthy and barefooted. His clothes were torn and his hair was so dirty, that it was hard to tell what color it was anymore.

"Goin' on a little road trip, lad?" Gavin asked from atop his horse.

Archy looked up and his teary eyes became wide. "Gavin!" He jumped to his feet. "I was runnin' away when I was attacked by two bandits. They stole what little food I had left, as well as the coins I took from the cash box in the shop. Davita is goin' to kill me."

"Egads, no' bandits! Are ye hurt, Archy?" Gavin jumped off the horse, rushing over to the boy, pulling him into his arms.

"Nay. I am small and fast and managed to run away. However, Hamish doesna look so guid." He put his hand in his pocket and pulled out the toad.

"Well, then we need to get him home."

"I was hopin' to see my faither first. I miss him, Gavin."

Gavin stayed silent, looking back at the castle once more. He had been thinking about this a lot the last two nights. There was something he needed to do, but was reluctant to do it. He just wasn't absolutely sure.

"Yer faither is healin', lad. Ye left town and worried yer sisters. The first thing we need to do is to get back to them to let them ken ye arena harmed. It was wrong of ye to just leave like that, without even sayin' a word to anyone."

"It's no different than what ye did," said the boy, making Gavin bite his tongue. "Why did ye leave us, Gavin?"

"Give me yer hand, lad," said Gavin, taking the boy over to the horse and putting him atop it. "I'll tell ye why I left. I suppose I owe ye an explanation, as well as yer sisters. But first, ye tell me the real reason ye ran away, because I dinna think it was all just about a toad." He mounted the horse as well.

"All right," said the boy, hanging his head. He sat in front of Gavin and looked back at him as they rode. "I really ran away because I wanted to find ye."

"What for? I was comin' back. Ye should have just waited."

"I was afraid ye were never goin' to return. That scared me so much that I guess I wasna thinkin' straight."

"Laddie, why did it matter so much to ye if I ever returned?"

"There were two reasons. I left because I ken my sister loves ye, for one. And I really missed ye, too. That's part of the first reason."

"Davita loves me?" He raised a brow. "Did she tell ye that?"

"She didna have to. She had that same look in her eyes as Aila has when she sees Ethan. And everyone kens those two are in love!" The boy rolled his eyes.

"What is the other reason?" Gavin asked, curiously.

"I left because I wanted to ask faither to find ye."

"Archy, ye ken yer da is in no condition to travel."

"I suppose I was hopin' if I went to the castle I'd find ye there, too."

"Well, I wasna there. I just went to the river to think, that's all."

"What were ye thinkin' about? Was it about my sister?"

He chuckled. "I canna fool ye, lad, can I?"

"I told Davita I wished ye were part of our family, and I meant it."

"That's nice of ye, but ye ken I am a MacKeefe. I'm a Highlander, and I live in the mountains, no' in a town. Once the boots are made, I'll be headin' back home."

"Then take me with ye. Please," begged Archy. Gavin's heart about broke when he saw the despair in the little boy's eyes. He started thinking about when he was that young. No lad should have to feel that kind of pain. The pain of losing someone they really cared for. Now, the person that Archy didn't want to lose was him. Gavin had never been in this kind of situation before.

"Archy, ye belong at home. In town. With yer sisters and yer da. With yer family."

"Ye're family now, too, Gavin, and I think ye ken it. How can ye leave us? We need ye."

"Why do ye keep tryin' so hard to make me stay?" Gavin wondered aloud.

"I willna just sit back and watch as my family deserts me," he said. "By that, I mean ye."

The boy's words hit Gavin like a rock. Thoughts flooded his brain of his own childhood, watching as his family was taken away from him, right before his eyes. He didn't stop it then, but mayhap this time he could do something about it, with a different family.

"Ye, lad, are a lot braver than I ever was as a boy."

Just then, Gavin noticed a man lying face down in the road.

"Look! Someone is hurt," said Archy, pointing his finger.

"Or pretendin' like it," mumbled Gavin, searching the area around him for others. It was a wooded area, and although he couldn't see anyone, someone could be hiding, waiting to ambush him.

"Are ye goin' to help him?" asked the boy. "Mayhap the bandits got him, too."

"Stay on the horse, and dinna leave it. Do ye hear me?" He handed the boy the reins.

"All right."

Gavin dismounted, pulling his sword from the sheath, cautiously approaching the man. He kicked at him slightly, but he didn't move.

"He's dead," said the boy.

"I doubt it," Gavin answered. "He wasna here when I came this way earlier lookin' for ye. Also, I didna hear a struggle." He bent down to turn the man over, and when he did, Archy screamed from atop the horse.

"Gavin, behind ye!"

Gavin jumped up and spun around to see a bandit leaping at him from the bushes. He had his blade drawn and aimed right at Gavin's heart. Without even thinking, Gavin lifted the tip of his sword and, before he knew it, he'd killed the man in self-defense. The bandit dropped in a puddle of blood at his feet. That's when he felt the tip of another blade at his back.

"Drop the weapon," the man warned him. "Do it, or I'll kill ye, I swear."

Gavin glanced over to the spot to see the man was no longer lying in the road. Sure enough, just as he thought, it was all a ploy to rob him.

"Kill him, Gavin!" shouted Archy. "Kill him, like ye did the other one."

Gavin didn't like the bloodthirsty sound of Archy wanting to see another man die. This wasn't the life the lad should live. Nay, Gavin couldn't do it. He threw down his sword, and raised his hands in surrender.

"Guid. Now tell the boy to get off the horse and bring it here," the bandit instructed.

"Nay," spat Gavin. "I told him to stay on the horse for his own protection, and that is just what he'll do."

"Do it, or I'll run ye through with my blade."

Gavin felt the pricking of the blade pierce his skin now, and that made him mad. He whirled around, grabbing the man's dagger, kicking him at the same time. The bandit stumbled backwards, but righted himself and started to run. Gavin took off after him, jumping him, and bringing him to the ground hard.

"Archy, there is rope in the travel bag," Gavin called out to the boy. "Bring it to me, quickly, so I can tie him up."

Archy did so, handing Gavin the rope. "That's the bandit that robbed me," said Archy.

"Are ye certain, lad?" This infuriated Gavin even more.

"I am. He and his dead friend did it."

"Ye disgust me, to be hurtin' children," Gavin growled at the attacker, pulling the ropes tightly around the man's wrists. Then he reached into the bandit's tunic and pulled out a bag of coins.

"That's my coin bag with the money I took from the shop," said the boy. "See, it has Faither's maker's mark on it. It's the symbol he puts on all the shoes so everyone kens he made them. Did ye steal from my faither, too?" asked Archy.

The man didn't answer. Gavin picked up his sword and put it to the man's neck.

"Answer the lad, or I'll kill ye like I did yer friend," said Gavin.

"Ye wouldna do that," spat the bandit.

"Want to make a bet? I have the lad back as well as his money," said Gavin. "Since he is alive and well, there is no need for ye." He pushed his blade closer, the tip of it pricking the man's neck.

"All right, I'll tell ye. Dinna kill me," the bandit pleaded.

"Start talkin'," commanded Gavin.

"This is the second time I've seen that maker's mark on a pouch," the man told him. "The last time was when my friend and I robbed a man on the road, but I swear I dinna ken who he was. He put up a damned guid struggle."

"Ye almost killed the lad's faither," growled Gavin. "He's at Hermitage Castle, healin' his wounds."

"Bah, I kent we should have made sure he was dead before we left." The man held no remorse at all in his words.

"I wonder why Graeme didna tell anyone more about what happened that night when he was attacked," Gavin spoke aloud.

"My da was knocked unconscious and said it was night and he didna remember much," said Archy.

"Archy, go check the dead man for yer faither's money

pouch," Gavin told the boy.

Archy ran over and came back with a coin pouch, shaking it proudly. "Yep. It is my da's. And some of the money is still in it."

"I'll hold on to it for now," said Gavin. After securing both moneybags to his waistbelt, Gavin gripped the man by the shoulders, facing him toward Archy. "Look hard, lad," he told the boy. "Is this what ye want to become?"

"Nay!" Archy backed away, wrinkling his nose and shaking his head. "Never."

"Then ye need to promise me that no matter if I am there or no', ye will never steal anythin' again, as long as ye live."

"I promise," said Archy. "I dinna want to end up bein' a bandit."

"This man is goin' to the dungeon, and yer da can testify against him, addin' to ye identifyin' him, too," said Gavin.

"Thank ye, Gavin," said Archy. "If ye hadna found me, I am sure my life would have ended up bein' much different. I want to be just like ye."

"Nay, ye dinna, Son."

"Why no'?" asked Archy as Gavin hauled the man toward the horse. The bandit's hands were tied behind him. He would walk behind the horse on his way to the dungeon.

"I've made a lot of mistakes in my life," Gavin told the boy. "I'm no' sure I can ever redeem myself."

"Isna that why ye came to our town? To redeem yerself? Ye are no' goin' to just give up, are ye?" The boy's eyes lit up with hope. Hope that Gavin once knew but lost and had never recovered.

Gavin thought about it for a moment, and decided it was true. He did have a chance to redeem himself in town. Not only from his demons of the past, but for the ones he'd created in the present as well.

"Get back on the horse, Archy. We are goin' to the castle."

"To take the bandit to the dungeon?" he asked excitedly.

"Aye. But no' just that. We're also goin' to see yer faither."

"Why?" he asked. "I dinna need him to find ye now. Plus, I thought ye said that my faither couldna travel yet."

"There is somethin' I need to do and, this time, I have no doubt that I am makin' the right decision."

❖

CHAPTER TWENTY-TWO

D AVITA FELT SICK with worry, waiting for the men to return. Not able to work, she paced back and forth, watching out the window for Gavin to ride back into town. Her sister wanted to tell Ethan that she was possibly pregnant, so Davita let her go. This was a wasted day, and no more work would be accomplished but she didn't care.

All she cared about was her little brother. So many thoughts kept going through her head. She would never forgive herself if anything happened to Archy. Why hadn't she watched him closer? Why had she insisted he get rid of his toad? Why, why, why. She felt as if this were all her fault. She should have been more understanding. Like Gavin.

"Gavin loves ye, even if he canna admit it."

"What?" She spun around, seeing Cam's eyes open as he watched her from his relaxed position upon the chair. "Why would ye say that?"

"I ken my friend. He's never acted this way over any other lass."

"Well, I wish that were true, but I'm afraid ye are wrong. He only wants me for the boots, and nothin' else." She sadly turned away from him, and crossed her arms over her chest, hugging herself.

"Dinna do this to yerself, lass. If ye want him to stay, just tell the bluidy fool. Sometimes he can be thick-headed and daft."

"I have no idea what ye're talkin' about. Gavin and I are just acquaintances and nothin' more."

"I heard every word between ye and yer sister."

"Y-ye did? Oh." Now she wished she wouldn't have spoken so freely with Gavin's friend in the room.

"Just because a man looks like he's sleepin' doesna necessarily mean he is."

"Well, now that ye ken the truth, tell me. Why do ye think Gavin left me?"

"Gavin is like a brathair to me, but he is no' true family. He's had a lot of demons whisperin' in his head, ever since he was a boy."

"Demons? Does this have somethin' to do with his family? He told me they were killed by bandits."

"Ask him," said Cam, getting off the chair and stretching. "I think he should be the one to tell ye these things, no' me."

"Ye're right," she said. "Just tell me this. Will a man like Gavin ever consider settlin' down someday?"

"If ye're talkin' about marriage, then ye're askin' the wrong man, lass. I like my freedom way too much to ever even consider bein' married."

"Dinna ye want a family someday, Cam?" she asked him.

He laughed. "I am sure I probably have more bastards runnin' around than anyone," he told her. "So I guess ye can say I already do have a family. Well, I'll be over at the tavern havin' a drink if ye need me."

"Pay my regards to Red and Violet," she said, getting a wide smile from the man. She paced for another hour before she finally saw Gavin riding into town with Archy on the horse in front of him.

"Gavin! Archy!" She ran from the shop, reaching up to help her brother from the horse. "Brathair, ye had me so worried. Are ye all right?" she asked. "Let me look at ye." She took his face in two hands, rubbing away the streaks of dirt. Then she pulled her brother to her, kissing him and hugging him hard.

"Stop it, Sister. I canna breathe," complained Archy, causing her to let go.

"Why did ye leave, Archy? Where did ye go? What happened to ye?"

"Slow down," said Gavin, handing the reins of the horse to the stable boy who took it from him.

"Gavin, is that blood on ye?" Davita became suddenly worried.

"I was jumped by bandits," said Archy. "But when they came back, Gavin killed one and put the other in the dungeon of the castle."

"Bandits?" Davita held her hand to her heart. "Archy, ye could have been killed."

"They were the same bandits that robbed and left yer faither for dead," Gavin explained.

"They were?" she asked in surprise. "Are ye sure?"

"The live one admitted it."

"So then, Clyde and Gregor didna do it?"

"It seems no'." Gavin handed her the money pouches. "The maker's mark was yer faither's on both of the bags that the bandits had, so that is even more proof."

"Oh. Thank ye," she said, fingering the pouches, not sure what to say.

"We saw Da," said Archy excitedly.

"Ye did?" She looked up to Gavin in question.

"He's healin' nicely," Gavin told her.

"I thought ye werena welcome there." Davita found it odd that he'd go there now, at a time like this.

"I'm no' welcome. No' really. But there was somethin' I needed to do, and so I went."

"Aye, the bandit needed to be imprisoned," she said, feeling like mayhap he meant something more, but wasn't saying so.

"I'm goin' to put Hamish back in his house and give him a bowl of water," said Archy.

"Ye do that, lad," said Gavin. "Then get cleaned up. I'm goin' to be cookin' supper for us soon." He ruffled the boy's hair. Archy ran off through the back door into the garden, smiling, seeming very happy.

As soon as he left, Davita decided she needed to talk to Gavin.

"Gavin, there are some things we need to –"

He grabbed her, pulling her toward him, kissing her passionately and cutting off her sentence.

"What was that for?" she asked him, pleasantly surprised.

"Does a man need a reason to kiss his lass?"

"Well, I just thought . . . yer lass? Am I really yer lass, Gavin?"

"I hope ye will forgive me for leavin' so abruptly. It was wrong of me."

"Why did ye go?" This was the conversation she'd been waiting to have with him. "Is it because . . . because I mentioned marriage?"

"Losh me!" His eyes opened wide and he bolted to the door.

"Gavin, please come back," she begged him, thinking just the word had scared him off again.

"Come with me, Davita." He held out his hand. "I almost forgot that I need to ring the church bells to let my friends ken they can stop searchin' for Archy."

"Oh, is that all?" Now she felt silly.

They walked at a brisk pace, hand in hand, until they got to St. Michael's Church in the center of town. They went inside and ascended the stairs that led up to the bell tower. Gavin reached out and rang the bell three times. The sound echoed loudly through the streets, and everyone knew that Archy had been found.

"Thank ye for findin' him, Gavin. I was so worried."

"Well, ye need never be worried about him stealin' again. After seein' those bandits and also the dungeon of Hermitage Castle, I think it scared him straight. Archy promised he wouldna do it anymore."

"I hope he keeps that promise. Look at the view from up here," Davita told him, peering out over the entire town. The town wasn't big, but from the bell tower, they could see every street and every shop. It almost seemed magical in a way.

Gavin took Davita in his arms, looking out with her at the sight. His chest was up against her back, and she felt happy and protected. "It's nice, but isna nearly as impressive as the Grampians," he told her.

"I wouldna ken. I've never been to the Highlands," she answered.

"Well, mayhap it is time ye go."

"How could I?" she asked, leaning against him. "My faither and siblin's need me. I canna leave them, Gavin."

His good mood seemed to disappear. "So, ye would never leave here, Davita? No' even if yer faither and siblin's were taken care of?"

"I have responsibilities. Why would I ever want to leave?" Davita looked back at him, wondering if he meant something that he wasn't saying. Could he possibly want her to live with him in the Highlands? Or mayhap even marry him? She was about to approach the question when shouting was heard from down in the street. She looked down to see Clyde chasing someone. Clyde had a knife gripped in his hand.

"God's eyes, he's chasin' Aila and Ethan," she exclaimed. "Gavin, we've got to help them." She took off at a run down the stairs, and he followed.

"Why is he chasin' them with a knife? What is goin' on?" asked Gavin from behind her.

"My sister is pregnant and Clyde must have found out," Davita explained quickly, never stopping as she spoke.

"She's what?" Gavin stopped in his tracks, not sure he'd heard Davita correctly.

"They are in love but Clyde willna accept it." Davita finally stopped and looked back up the stairs at him. "Why are ye just standin' there?" she asked him. "Clyde is goin' to kill them if we dinna stop him."

"Bid the devil," spat Gavin, continuing down the stairs, unsheathing his sword as he walked. All he wanted was a little time alone with Davita, but it seemed like he was never going to get it. He was excited to tell her that he'd asked her father's permission to marry her. He wanted her to know he loved her, but he couldn't even get that out because there was always some sort of excitement.

"Clyde, stop!" cried Davita, running out into the street with her arms outstretched. "Dinna hurt my sister."

"Stand aside, or ye'll be hurt, too," warned Clyde.

"Put the blade down, or ye'll have to deal with me." Gavin lifted his sword to make sure Clyde saw it. People came running to see what all the commotion was about.

"Is that – bluid on yer sword and yer plaid?" asked Clyde, stopping, but still holding on to his knife.

"Aye, so it is." Gavin picked up the end of his plaid and used it to clean his blade. "I still havena had a chance to clean it after I killed the last man just hours ago."

"Ye lie," snarled Clyde, anger still showing in his eyes.

"He killed a bandit and took another one to the dungeon," Archy announced, pushing his way through the crowd, stopping next to Davita.

"Stay back, Archy." Davita reached out and took her brother's hand, pulling him out of possible harm's way.

"Clyde, will ye please leave these two alone?" asked Gavin. "After all, they are in love."

"I canna accept that she is pregnant. They are no' even married," snapped Clyde.

"We're gettin' married, Uncle," Ethan told him. "I was just waitin' until I became a journeyman. Then we were goin' to do it."

"Let them live their own lives," warned Gavin.

"Clyde, mayhap ye should," said his apprentice, Gregor.

"Fine." Clyde lowered his blade. "However, neither of ye will be welcome in my home or my shop ever again."

"Uncle! I need the job," pleaded Ethan.

"Ye should have thought of that before this happened. I willna be embarrassed by either of ye again." He turned and left with Gregor on his heels.

"What are we goin' to do?" cried Aila, holding on to Ethan.

Davita let go of Archy, and threw her arms around her sister. "Ethan can live with us, and I will give him a job," said Davita. "I'm sure my faither would agree. Aila, I will also do all I can to help raise yer bairn."

"Thank ye, Sister." Aila hugged her back.

"I promise ye, we will get married as soon as possible," said Ethan.

"Marriage is a guid thing," said Davita, glancing over at Gavin. "No matter what Clyde or Cam or anyone else might think. Now go back to the house and take Archy with ye. I will meet ye there shortly."

"What did ye mean?" Gavin asked her as soon as the crowd dissipated.

"About what?"

"Ye said marriage was a guid thing, and then ye mentioned Cam's name. Were ye talkin' to him about marriage, lass?"

"Mayhap. I canna remember," she said, pushing her chin up in the air. "Besides, does it really matter? Excuse me, Gavin. I need to go to my family."

Davita walked away, leaving Gavin standing there feeling like he had done something wrong. He was excited and all set to tell her he loved her and that he wanted to marry her. But then she said she needed to go to her family. She didn't think to ask or include him, and that made him wonder if he was wrong about her. Mayhap she didn't want him after all.

He turned to go and bumped into Cam.

"Och, dinna be sneakin' up on me, or I'll take off yer head," bellowed Gavin.

"So, what did she say?" asked Cam.

"Who?"

"Davita. Did ye tell her ye love yer yet?"

"It's none of yer business, Cam. By the way, what were ye doin' talkin' to Davita about marriage?"

"Ask her," was all he said, and turned and walked away.

"I need to think," said Gavin, leaving for the river to bathe and to try to clear his head. Were women always this confusing? Davita was adamant that she'd never move to the Highlands. She said she had responsibilities here and then offered to help raise Aila's baby. That got him wondering. Was he really ready to give up his home and live here with her instead? "I just need to think," he said to himself, once again, wondering about the right thing to do.

✦•◦◇◦•✦

CHAPTER TWENTY-THREE

"JUST MAKE YERSELF comfortable," Davita told Ethan. "This will be yer home from now on."

"Ye are too kind," Ethan told her. "But I willna live here for free. Ye must take rent out of my earnin's."

"I'm sure we can come to some kind of agreement."

Cam walked in, followed by North and Nash.

"Glad the boy was found," said Nash. "We heard the church bells and came right back."

"Where is Gavin? I want to hear what happened." North looked around the small house, but it seemed that, once again, Gavin was missing.

"Aye. Where is he?" asked Davita, feeling suddenly worried.

"He said he would make us supper," Archy told them.

"I think he must have left to think again." Nash made a face when he said it.

"Oh, nay," said Davita. "Why?"

"Were ye talkin' about marriage at all?" asked Cam, making his friends laugh.

"Nay, Gavin would never get married." North swiped his hand through the air, dismissing the silly idea.

"I've had enough of this." Davita put her hands on her hips. "Aila, warm up somethin' fast for supper. Archy will help ye."

"I will, too," offered Ethan.

"Where did Gavin go?" Davita asked Cam. "Tell me."

"All I ken is that last time he went to the river," said Cam. "This time, I am no' sure."

"That's where he is then, and where I'm goin'." Davita stormed to the door.

"By yerself, lass?" asked North. "Can I escort ye? After all, there are bandits out there."

"If a bandit gets anywhere near me in the mood I'm in, he'll be sorry." She walked back to the table, picking up the half-moon knife, her awl, and another cutting knife she used for making shoes.

"Lass, ye are no' really goin' out by yerself," said Nash. "The sun is startin' to set."

"I am goin' to the river to find and talk to Gavin. If anyone so much as interrupts us, ye'll have hell to pay. Understand?" She waved her hands in the air, and the blades whizzed past the men's heads.

"Och, careful with those." Nash jumped back and held up his arm.

North blocked his face and turned in the opposite direction.

"I'm no' goin' to be the one to stop ye," said Cam, backing up with his palms facing her. He plopped down on a chair.

"Have fun," called out North, flashing her a smile.

She stopped in the doorway and turned back. "I need a horse," she told them.

"Take mine. Please," said North. "It is still saddled and tied to the hitchin' post right in front of the shop."

"Thank ye." She picked up a cloth bag with a long strap, placed the tools inside, and left to go find Gavin and settle things between them once and for all.

Riding to the river, Davita looked back over her shoulder, noticing Nash following her. Every time she turned around, he directed his horse behind a tree or bush to hide. She smiled to herself. At least they cared about her. Right now, she wasn't so sure about Gavin.

It was just about night now, but there was enough light left that she could see the bright purple and green colors of the MacKeefe plaid through the trees, and over by the river. When she rode to where she thought Gavin was, she found just his clothes on a rock instead.

"Gavin?" she called out.

At first, she heard nothing. Then, there was the sound of something breaking the surface of the water from the river. She dismounted, tying the reins of her horse to a tree, and hurrying over to the riverbank. She got there just in time to see a flash of bare skin, before Gavin broke the surface again. "Damn, that's cold," she heard him exclaim.

"Gavin? It's me. Davita," she called out, waving to him from the shore.

"Davita? What are ye doin' here?" He stood up, walking out of the water, stark naked. She couldn't help but drink in his manly beauty. Her eyes stopped just below his waist. She chuckled and looked the other way.

"What's so funny, lass?" He wiped the water from his face with his hands, and walked up to greet her.

"I guess that water really is cold," she said, smiling. His hands quickly covered his groin.

"Well, just wait until I kiss ye, and I am sure things will change quickly." Gavin pulled her to him and kissed her, and she almost got lost in the moment until she remembered that Nash was probably watching.

"Nash followed me here," she whispered.

Gavin scowled, then looked out toward the road and shouted. "Leave, Nash. And dinna expect either of us to return until mornin'."

"Aye. Got it," came a voice from the brush. They heard the sound of hoofbeats heading back to town.

"Care for a swim?" Gavin asked her. "I wanted to bathe, but it would be more fun to do it together." He reached out and slid his hand past her breast, and she already felt her nipples going taut.

"No' yet," she said, grabbing his hand. "First, I need ye to put on some clothes because I want to talk to ye without any distractions."

"All right," he said. "I've been wantin' to talk to ye, too, but we always seem to get interrupted." After he'd donned his tunic, he sat on the rock with his knees bent. "What's on yer mind, Davita?"

"I want to ken why every time the word marriage is mentioned, ye seem to bolt. Are ye afraid of commitment, Gavin?"

"Well, I –"

"Cam said somethin' about yer past demons, but I dinna understand it at all."

"It has to –"

"Either ye want to be with me, or ye dinna. Either way, I need to ken."

"Davita, I –"

"Because, I canna keep livin' like this, Gavin. I want to –"

He pulled her atop his lap and kissed her, surprising her in the most delightful way. She felt a tingle travel through her, like the one her sister had mentioned when they talked about knowing if one was in love.

"I thought we were goin' to talk," she said, her tongue shooting out to lick her lips. His essence, his manly essence on her tongue made her heady.

"It was the only way I could shut ye up so I could get a word in edgewise," he told her.

"Oh. Sorry. Go ahead."

"Davita, first of all . . . I mean . . . I love ye. There. I said it."

"Ye do?" She felt tears of happiness welling up in her eyes. "I love ye, too, Gavin."

"I'm sorry it took me so long to tell ye." He let out a deep breath. "Now that I have, I'm glad I did."

She laughed. "It didna take ye long to tell me, Gavin. After all, we've only kent each other for a verra short time."

"True. However, in my mind, it feels like at least years."

"I dinna understand. Is that a guid thing, or is it bad?"

He shifted her body so she sat next to him now. It was a beautiful night, and they were atop a large, flat rock. "I assure ye, it's a guid thing, lass. Look at the stars," he told her, lying back and taking her with him. She snuggled up to him, feeling the ends of his long, wet hair against her face, but she didn't care. "I came here to think, Davita. Bein' in nature helps me to clear my mind. I've had a lot to think about lately, but the most important thing I decided was that I dinna want to lose ye."

"Ye willna lose me, Gavin. I'm no' goin' anywhere."

"Exactly. That worried me, too."

"Ye are makin' no sense at all."

"Oh, hell, I'm no' guid at this." He ran his hand through his wet hair, seeming worried. Then he took her hand in his, turning on his side to look deeply into her eyes. The moonlight reflected in his dark blue orbs, making him look handsome and mysterious. "I'm just goin' to come right out and say it."

"Say what, Gavin? I dinna understand what ye mean."

"Davita, will ye marry me?"

Now it was Davita's turn to be tongue-tied. She'd never expected him to say that! Not even after he'd told her that he loved her. She was so much in shock that she couldn't even speak.

He let out a frustrated breath and shook his head. "I understand." Dropping her hand, he sat up. "I'm a Highlander and ye are the daughter of a cordwainer. I dinna ken what I was thinkin'."

"Gavin," she finally managed to spit out, but he just kept talking.

"I struggled with the decision because, honestly, I didna think I deserved ye. I still dinna."

"Gavin?"

"I feel like I could have . . . should have – done somethin' to help my family instead of bein' so scared when I was a lad. I was a coward, Davita. I hid behind the bushes and watched them die and was too frightened to even try to help them. I was afraid to love again after that, because I never wanted to lose anyone again that I truly loved."

"I will."

"Then I decided, I am a grown-arse Highland warrior, but still actin' like that scared child. I dinna ken what I was still afraid of. I decided it would be worse to lose someone I loved by walkin' away and never tellin' them. That's why I took the risk by askin' ye to marry me."

"I said, yes," she said softly, almost laughing aloud when he never even heard her and kept right on telling his story.

"So, I went and talked to yer faither and asked his blessin' as well as for yer hand in marriage. It did surprise me, but he said yes."

"He did? Ye did?" This surprised her that he would even consider doing such a thing. It meant a lot to her that he wanted her family to accept him before he made things final.

Gavin finally turned and looked at her. "What did ye say, lass?"

"Gavin, did ye really ask my faither for his blessin' and for my hand in marriage?"

"Aye. But what did ye say . . . before that part?"

"I said yes, Gavin. I will marry ye! A thousand times yes, because I have fallen in love with ye, and I dinna want to ever lose ye again."

"Ye will? Really?" His eyes lit up with happiness and his face seemed to glow in the moonlight. "Lass, ye have made me so happy." He hugged her, kissing her atop her head.

"Why didna ye just tell me all this sooner?" she asked curiously.

"It wasna easy for me. Plus, yer life tends to be verra hectic."

"Where will we live, Gavin? I dinna want to leave my family in their time of need."

"I realize that now. I think it would be best if we stayed and lived in town with yer family," he told her. He tried his best to look and sound happy, but she could hear the sadness in his voice. The twinkle in his eyes disappeared.

"Ye really love the Highlands and dinna want to live in town, do ye? Be honest with me."

"All I ken is bein' a warrior, Davita. However, I will learn to sew shoes and like it, if it means ye'll be my wife."

"Ye have made me so verra happy," she told him. "I am the luckiest lass ever."

"I'm happy, too, but could feel luckier." He ran his finger down the side of her cheek. When he touched her lips, she opened her mouth and playfully sucked on it.

"How lucky did ye want to get?" she asked him in a breathy voice. Then she got up and pretended to be leaving. "Och, I forgot everyone is waitin' for supper. We'd better go."

"Dinna even think of it," came his sexy, low warning.

She laughed heartily as he raced after her, scooping her up into his arms.

"That wasna funny, Davita. But this is."

"What is?" He took off at a run for the water and she gripped him tightly, crying out. "Nay, dinna do it. Nay, Gavin, please."

He tossed her into the water and she came up laughing. "Ye are no' kiddin'! The water is cold."

"Let me warm it up for ye, lass. Or should I say, my betrothed?" He stripped off his tunic and stalked toward her. Her eyes dropped to his manhood that was now hard and straight as an arrow. Then he stepped into the water and swam to her, gathering her into his arms. "Have ye ever made love in the water before?"

"We're no' really goin' to – oh!" He picked her up, spreading her legs around his waist, and entering her. She clung to him and threw back her head as he filled her completely. Her excitement grew and she felt herself climbing to heights that she'd never known. "I see stars and, this time, they're no' only the ones in the sky," she told him as he pumped into her, using his hands to help her move her hips back and forth.

They made love in the water and also atop the rock.

"I'd say we've celebrated our betrothal, wouldna ye?" he

asked as they relaxed on the grass atop his plaid, looking up at the stars hours later.

"Mayhap," she said.

"Mayhap? We've done it twice, lassie."

"Well, three has always been my lucky number."

"Then just give me a few minutes to gather myself, love. I promise I will make ye feel lucky all over again."

✦•◦◇◦•✦

CHAPTER TWENTY-FOUR

"D_{AVITA, COME QUICKLY}," shouted Aila the next morning as Davita and Gavin rode back into town. It had been a magical, relaxing night, and something that Davita had needed in her life. She was a betrothed woman now and could barely believe it. Everything was moving so fast. She couldn't wait to tell her sister the news. However, that peace they'd experienced disappeared quickly as soon as they entered the town.

"Aila, I have somethin' to tell ye." Davita was so excited that she dismounted her horse and ran to her sister, leaving Gavin behind. "I had the most amazin' night and somethin' magical happened." She took her sister's hands and looked into her eyes. That's when she knew something was wrong. Aila looked troubled. "What is it, Sister? Has Clyde been botherin' ye again?"

"Nay, it's the guild, Davita. They are at Clyde's shop now and on their way to ours next. Ethan found out that the head guild masters are releasin' anyone who is far behind in their work, or who canna pay the membership fees. Davita, they are goin' to close us down. Faither is goin' to be ruined."

"Nay, that is no' goin' to happen," said Gavin from right behind them.

"She's right, Gavin," Davita admitted sadly. "Now that the money was returned from the bandits, we will have the renewal fee to stay in the guild. However, we dinna have money to buy the supplies we need to finish all the work. The guild will surely hear from Clyde that our orders are all behind schedule. They'll see that I dinna have the proper help either, and that I canna finish the work by myself in a timely fashion."

"Ye willna be alone," said Gavin. "Aila, find my friends and tell them to get to the shop immediately. Make sure Archy and Ethan are there as well."

"Aye," she said, running off to get them.

"Davita, please go to the tavern and tell Keithen to give ye a tray of those small tasty seedcakes, some sweetmeats, and a jug of his heathered ale."

"Gavin, please! This is no time to be thinkin' about yer stomach. We are in trouble and need to figure out what to do about it."

Gavin reached out and ran a loving hand over her hair to smooth it. "That is exactly what I'm doin', sweetheart. Just do what I ask. Trust me."

She hesitated, but when she saw the hurt in Gavin's eyes that she didn't believe in him, she forced a smile and nodded. She needed to give him a chance. Mayhap he truly did have a plan to help. "Of course. I do trust ye, Gavin, even if I dinna understand what ye have in mind. I will do as ye ask, and no' fight ye."

"Guid. Tell Keithen I will be by to pay for the food and drink later."

"Gavin, he might no' agree to that, and I dinna have the coin to give him."

"He will agree. After all, I more than made up for all the eggs yer brathair stole from him. He'll believe I'll pay, dinna worry."

When Davita got back to the shop with the ale and food, she stopped just inside the doorway, unable to believe her eyes. Her jaw dropped open in surprise.

Gavin's friends sat lined up on a wooden bench, each of them repairing a pair of shoes. Aila was instructing them, and Archy was handing them needles, thread, and the tools they needed to use.

"What's this?" she asked with a smile. Gavin came to greet

her, taking the things from her.

"Archy, take all this into the kitchen and put the food on one plate. Get some cups from the cupboard, too. I am goin' to need ye to serve the head guild masters some refreshments when they arrive."

"Aye, Gavin." Archy took the items and headed to the kitchen.

"Gavin? It willna matter if ye give them somethin' to eat. That is no' what they will be inspectin'," Davita tried to explain.

"I understand. But it will help in case they have a sour disposition. Food always helps, believe me."

"Aye, Gavin should ken," North called out from the bench. "After all, he's always in a better mood after he's had food and drink."

"I could use some ale," said Nash, pushing the needle through the leather. "Ouch, that smarts!"

"Ye need to use the thumb guard to protect yerself." Aila handed him a strip of leather.

Nash held it up and made a face. "I have my sword and dagger. That's all the protection I need."

"I'm no' goin' to sew," complained Cam, picking up the small hammer. "Let me pound on somethin' instead."

"That is for placing the tack nails onto the soles of the shoes. No poundin'," explained Aila, running over to Cam to grab the hammer.

"The Cordovan boots are on yer workbench and ready for ye," Gavin told her, escorting her over to the table.

"Gavin, I didna want to tell ye before, but I already finished Callum's boots."

"Ye did?" He looked at her in question, and then over at the boots. "Aye, ye did. They are beautiful, lass. Why didna ye tell me?"

"I'm sorry, but if I told ye, I was afraid ye were goin' to leave, and I didna want to lose ye."

He reached out and kissed her on the cheek, then whispered

into her ear. "Ye will be my wife soon. Ye will never lose me."

She looked up at him and smiled, whispering back to him. "I canna wait to tell everyone."

"Mayhap we should wait until the guild members leave."

"I agree."

"What's all the whisperin' about over there?" griped North, his big hands fumbling with a small lady's shoe.

"They're probably sayin' lustful things they dinna want us to hear," was Cam's answer. Of course, he was always randy, so no one expected him to say anything less.

"Nay. They're probably talkin' about food and ale," said Nash. "Actually, I'm gettin' hungry. When do we eat?"

"We're fixin' shoes now," said Gavin.

"Gavin, ye ken we really dinna have the skills to do this," said Cam. "We're no' goin' to fool anyone."

"They dinna need to ken that," Gavin answered. "Just pretend like ye're workin'. That's all that matters. Ye can stop right after they leave."

"I'm goin' to expect a guid meal when this is done, no' just simple sweetmeats." Nash looked cross-eyed at the thread as he pulled it high over his head, clutching the needle between two fingers.

"What about ye, Gavin?" asked Davita. "What will ye do?"

"I'll be assistin' ye with the new shoe construction," he said, pulling a sheet of leather and some cutting tools over to him on the table. Then he spotted the wooden last that was shaped like a foot. "Och, I like this. It'll look guid here, too." He grabbed the last and brought that over as well.

"Nay. This willna work. We're never goin' to fool them," said Davita, nervously.

"All they need to see is people workin'. We've got to try," Gavin told her.

The bells above the door jangled and Ethan ran in, out of breath. "They're on their way here," he reported. "I'm sad to say my uncle and Gregor are with them. They've told the head guild masters that ye stole all their work and that they were forced to use new leather and to make new shoes. If no', they wouldna have had any work at all."

"That's no' true," protested Davita. "Clyde's customers came to us because yer uncle did a shoddy job repairin' their shoes in the first place."

"Davita, the head guild masters are really angry," Ethan told her, looking as nervous and upset as she felt.

"Oh, Gavin, I'm so scared," said Davita, reaching out to put her hand on his arm. "I canna lose my faither's business."

"Ye willna," he assured her. "Just leave everythin' to me. I will do whatever it takes to make them see that this shop does fine work, and is needed in this town."

The door opened and Clyde stormed in. Two guild members and Gregor followed.

"Welcome," said Gavin, getting up to greet them, sounding much too cheery. "We've been expectin' ye."

"What are ye tryin' to pull here?" growled Clyde, looking over to Gavin's friends. "These men are Highlanders and ken nothin' about shoes. This is naught but a farce."

"What, exactly, are these men doin'?" asked one of the guild masters, walking over to inspect the situation.

Davita was about to speak up, but Gavin took over.

"These men are bein' instructed by Aila, the cordwainer's daughter, how to repair shoes," he told them.

"Where is Graeme?" asked the second guild member, looking around the room.

Davita knew these men well, since they came here once a year to collect dues and inspect the shop. She jumped up to greet them.

"Fergus. Hector, how nice to see ye again," she said to them, forcing herself to smile. Fergus was head master of the cordwainer's guild and Hector of the cobbler's guild. Since the two guilds were similar, they often collected dues and did inspections together. "I'm sorry, but my faither has been injured and is at the castle healin'. He was robbed, beaten, and left for dead."

"Aye, well, that's unfortunate," said Hector, spotting the trunk full of shoes. "What is all this?"

"Those are shoes that they're repairin'," said Gregor. "Shoes that we should be repairin' instead."

"Let me see that." Fergus dug through the trunk, holding up several shoes. "These are the shoes of servants, commoners, and also nobles," he said aloud. "Why are ye takin' this work from the cobblers? Ye ken that the guilds are no' supposed to compete."

"Those shoes are from the castle," said Gavin, before Davita could even answer. "Actually, my friends and I brought them with us. Ye see, it is part of my punishment that all those shoes need to be repaired."

"Punishment?" Hector questioned.

"Aye," said Davita. "When my faither was hurt, I asked Laird MacKeefe to send someone to help me until he is able to return to work."

"And they sent a Highlander," said Clyde, shaking his head. "All Highlanders bluidy ken is how to fight. They have no knowledge at all about shoes."

"That's right," agreed Gavin. "But we are learnin', and Davita and Aila have been guid teachers. For example, look at this fine pair of Cordovan boots Davita has made." Gavin brought the men over to Davita's workbench to see them.

Fergus picked up the boot and inspected it closely. "Aye, this is superior work. The stitches are invisible, and every cut has been done with precision. Ye are truly skilled at yer craft, Davita," he told her. "This is beautiful Cordovan leather and ye have done it justice."

"Thank ye," said Davita with a slight nod. "I have been helpin' my faither in the shop since I was a child. He taught me everythin' I ken."

"However," he added, and Davita knew this didn't sound good at all. "Ye ken that a woman is no' allowed to run a cordwainer's shop. Without yer faither even here, I'm afraid this goes against our rules."

"But that is why Gavin is here," she told him. "So there is a man in charge, until my da is healed and returns."

"My friends are here as well," added Gavin. "So, ye see, there are plenty of men here, and no rules are bein' broken. Archy," he called out. "Please bring some refreshments for our guests."

"I'll help him." Aila ran to help her brother pass out seedcakes, sweetmeats, and heathered ale. They even offered some to Clyde and Gregor. Gregor took it graciously but Clyde snarled and refused.

"Stop tryin' to bribe them," snapped Clyde. "It willna work."

"Mmm, I love seedcakes," said Fergus taking a big bite, ignoring Clyde's comment altogether.

"How about a little heathered ale to wash it down?" Gavin poured some into a cup and handed it to him, and then did the same for Hector.

"I'd like some, too," said Nash, but Gavin threw him a nasty look and turned his back to him.

"I've never had heathered ale before," said Hector, taking a sip and smacking his lips together. "It's rather guid."

"It's brewed usin' heather that grows wild in the Highlands," explained Gavin. "The MacKeefe's Mountain Magic is brewed in the Highlands as well, but I'm afraid the tavern doesna have any of that right now."

"I could go for regular whisky," mumbled Nash, tangling the thread and holding up the shoe that dangled from it.

"Get back to work, Nash," Gavin said under his breath.

"They're tryin' to bribe ye. Canna ye see that?" asked Clyde.

"Now, Clyde, that isna a nice thing to say." Gavin smiled dearly at him, although Davita knew he was ready to rip Clyde's head off right about now. "After all, we are just sharin' a wee bit of food and drink with our visitors."

"They have a lassie runnin' the shop with no qualified man here at all," Clyde complained to the head guild masters. "They need to be shut down, and the business given to me instead."

"The food and drink is guid," said Hector, licking his lips. "But Clyde is right about the rules."

"I agree," said Fergus. "Davita, I'm sorry, but ye broke the guild rules and ye ken it."

"I have the dues right here, for ye." She pulled coins out of a pouch and held out her hand to Fergus in one last desperate attempt to save the business. He looked at the money but sadly shook his head.

"I'm afraid that without a qualified male here, yer shop will have to be shut down," said Fergus.

"But my faither will return soon. Canna ye please just wait until he is able to work again?"

"By the sounds of it, yer faither willna be healed and returnin' anytime soon," said Hector.

"Please. Take the dues," she begged them, holding out her hand with the money. Davita was starting to panic. Gavin's plan wasn't working, and she didn't have a plan of her own. It looked like there was no chance in staying in the guild now.

Fergus slowly shook his head and Davita's hand closed and fell to her side.

"All the shoe business will come to my shop now," said Clyde happily.

"This has been our family's business for as long as I can re-member," said Davita. "My siblin's and I will have to move if we dinna have the cordwainin' business to pay our bills. Canna ye find it in yer heart to let us keep it? Please, I beg ye. My faither will return soon."

"Didna ye have a journeyman here workin' with yer faither?" asked Hector. "Where is he?"

"He died," said Davita, dreading telling them this, but they had to know.

"Then that is another rule ye're breakin'," said Fergus. "Each shop needs to have at least two qualified workers. If ye had at least one here, I could overlook the fact that yer faither will be gone for a short while to heal. But without yer journeyman, that leaves ye with no one."

"That's right," Clyde spoke up. "I have my apprentice, so I am no' breakin' any rules. Now ye'll pay for yer deception."

"I ken the craft, as ye can see," said Davita, pointing at the Cordovan boots. "Plus, my siblin's can help until my da returns and is able to find another apprentice or journeyman."

"Nay. Ye dinna have a qualified male in the shop, and ye canna run it, bein' a lassie." Clyde chuckled under his breath. "Face it, Davita, it is over."

Just when Davita was feeling as if she'd lost everything, Gavin came to her rescue.

"Now, wait a minute," said Gavin, lifting a hand in the air. "It is far from over. We do have a qualified male workin' here, that everyone has overlooked."

"Who? Ye?" Clyde laughed again. "Qualified to kill, but that's about it."

"Nay, no' me." Gavin glared at Clyde. Then he smiled and motioned to the other side of the room. "We have an apprentice who is about to become a journeyman. Ethan."

"What?" Clyde shouted. "Nay, he is my nephew and no' a cordwainer, but a cobbler. Besides, he works for me."

"Nay, I dinna," said Ethan stepping forward. He'd been so quiet all this time that Davita had almost forgotten he was there. "Ye fired me and threw me out, if I am no' mistaken."

"That's right." Aila came to Ethan's side. "Just because I'm pregnant, ye said we were no' welcome in yer shop anymore, even though we are gettin' married."

"Now, I was only jestin'," said Clyde, looking concerned.

"Nay, ye werena," Gregor spoke up. "Clyde, I might work for ye, but I willna let ye lie and ruin another man's business." He looked over at the head guildsmen. "He did fire Ethan, and Davita hired him and took him into her home."

"That's right," said Ethan. "Even though I am a cobbler's apprentice, my late faither taught me well. I ken enough about the business of shoes to learn cordwainin' easily."

"I will teach him anythin' he needs to learn," said Davita. "So, that should satisfy ye and fill the position of the qualified male in my shop after all. Please, dinna close us down."

"I kent yer faither well, Ethan," said Fergus. "He was a guid cobbler, and I am sorry to hear he's passed on."

"Thank ye," Ethan answered with a nod.

"Well, I suppose . . ." Fergus looked over to Hector and they conversed softly. Everyone else waited silently for the decision.

"We agree no' to close down yer shop since ye do have a qualified male workin' here, as well as Davita and her siblin's," Fergus finally announced. "That should be more than enough until Graeme recovers and comes back to work."

"Yay!" shouted Archy. "Da will be so happy."

"Thank guidness," mumbled Cam, putting down the shoe. "Can we be done with this nonsense now?"

"How about some ale?" asked Nash. "I could really use some ale."

"However." Hector put a finger in the air and the room became deadly silent. "Both ye, Davita, and ye, Clyde, broke rules that canna be ignored. Ye will both have to be fined."

"What rules are those?" asked North.

"Only cobblers can repair shoes, and cordwainers are the only ones allowed to make new shoes with new leather," Fergus explained.

"What if they both agreed to do that from now on?" asked Gavin. "It could be a fresh start."

"That would be fine with us," said Hector, as he and Fergus nodded at each other.

"What about the fine?" asked Davita. "I only have enough money for my dues right now, and no extra to pay." She held out the coins in her palm and, this time, Hector took them.

"We'll accept yer dues, and the fine will be minimal," said the man. "Ye can pay it when ye have the funds."

"Guid," said Clyde, not wanting to pay it. "I'll do the same."

"Besides the money, ye will both have somethin' extra to do

as part of yer fine as well," explained Fergus.

"What do ye mean?" spat Clyde. "What extra?"

"Clyde, ye'll have to repair all the shoes in that trunk for free," Fergus told him.

"What?" snapped Clyde. "Those are shoes from the castle. They can afford to pay me to fix them."

"Would ye rather we close ye down for breakin' the rules?" asked Fergus, shutting the man up quickly. "Ye two have just agreed that the cobbler will repair shoes and the cordwainer's shop will construct the new ones. So, it's yer job."

"Fine," grumbled Clyde, looking over at the huge trunk of shoes and shaking his head.

"Och, guid. Then it's over." North got up and brought the shoes he was repairing, plopping them into Clyde's hands. "I didna like the job anyway."

"This was doitit, I agree. We're warriors, and this work is for the birds." Cam followed, shoving his shoes at Clyde next.

"Does this mean I can have ale now?" whined Nash, putting his shoes on top of the pile that Clyde was holding.

"No' yet," said Gavin. "We still need to hear about Davita's fine."

"Yes, what is the extra part of my punishment?" Davita asked the head guild masters, feeling very nervous.

Fergus and Hector conversed in soft voices again, and then Fergus answered.

"Yer fine will be to invite us to this lovely couple's weddin'," he told them, motioning to Ethan and Aila.

"Also, to have plenty of Mountain Magic for us to enjoy while we're there," added Hector.

"That's no' a fine," complained Clyde, but no one was listening to him anymore.

Everyone laughed, and Gavin looked over to Davita. "I'd say that's a fair sentence . . . I mean fine. Wouldna ye agree, Davita?"

"Nay, I dinna agree," she said. Suddenly, the laughter died and everyone's smile disappeared except for Clyde's.

"So, ye're finally seein' it my way?" asked Clyde.

"Lass, what are ye sayin'?" whispered Gavin. "Take the offer. It's a guid one."

"I willna accept it, unless both Hector and Fergus will come to a double weddin' instead," she said, seeing Gavin's frown turn into a smile when he realized what she meant.

"Double weddin'?" asked Aila. "Oh, Sister, does this mean what I think it means?"

"Gavin and I are betrothed," said Davita, proudly announcing it to all. "Aila, that was the excitin' news I wanted to tell ye."

Aila ran to Davita and they hugged and laughed with excitement.

"We accept," said Fergus. "When and where will these weddin's take place? After all, we'll only be in town for a few more days."

"Then I suggest we marry immediately," said Gavin.

"I agree," added Aila, taking Ethan's hand in hers.

"Me, too," said Davita. "Gavin, where will we have the weddin'? The church willna allow my sister to get married there since she is already pregnant, and this shop is just too small."

"Then there is only one place I can think of that has more than enough room, as well as enough Mountain Magic for everyone. We'll be married at Hermitage Castle."

"The castle?" asked Cam. "Gavin, we're outcasts, in case ye've forgotten."

"That's right," added North. "Ye may be redeemed, but we have yet to even get our sentences."

"They'll never allow us to come to the weddin's," added Nash.

"Let me talk to our chieftains, Storm and Ian," said Gavin. "I am sure I can get them to agree."

"I hope so," said Nash. "Because if there is goin' to be a celebration with lots of Mountain Magic, I dinna want to miss it."

"Neither do I," said Gavin, making Davita wonder exactly what he meant. After all, he'd gone a long time without even a sip of whisky. Being around so much of it was going to be very tempting.

❖◆◇◆❖

CHAPTER TWENTY-FIVE

"HERE ARE YER boots, Callum," said Gavin, two days later, standing inside Hermitage Castle. He had to wait a day for Callum to get there from his tavern in Glasgow. Now, Gavin's sentence should be complete.

"I'm nervous," whispered Davita, holding his hand so tightly that his fingers were getting cramped. Storm and Ian sat on chairs atop the dais, while their wives and many of the castle's occupants waited and watched.

"Dinna be nervous," Gavin told her. "Ye do fine work, lass. Some of the best. Callum is sure to love the boots."

"Hrmph," snorted Callum, inspecting the boots carefully, rubbing his fingers over the surface. "They look excellent. But will they fit me?"

"I hope so," mumbled Davita.

"I'm sure they are just yer size," Gavin told the old man, sounding so confident that even Davita believed him. Still, they'd only guessed at the size of the man's feet. If they didn't fit, they might not be accepted, and Gavin would still be an outcast of the clan.

One of the clansmembers helped the old man sit down and assisted him in donning the boots.

"Well?" asked Storm from the dais. "Grandda, do ye approve of the new pair of boots that Gavin brought ye?"

"Did ye make these, Gavin?" asked the old man, holding up

one foot, turning his head side to side, still sitting on the bench.

"Nay," Gavin answered honestly. "It would have been impossible for me to do it. I am a warrior, and dinna have the skills of a professional cordwainer. Davita, the cordwainer's daughter, is the one who made them. She has a true skill and does fine work."

"Oh, Gavin," Davita whispered. "Ye should tell him ye helped me at least."

"Did ye?" asked Callum, having overheard her. For such an old man, nothing seemed to get past him. "Did ye help the lass make these boots?"

"I canna lie. I did no' really help her at all," said Gavin. "Actually, I was more of a hindrance than anythin'."

"Hrmph," snorted the old man, rubbing the long beard on his chin.

"Gavin was so much help in many other ways," Davita spoke up. "He wanted to assist me in constructin' the boots, but it takes years and years to learn and develop the skill. He was afraid the boots wouldna be to yer likin' if he was makin' them. Ye see, he wanted the best boots possible for ye. He only cared about pleasin' ye, Callum."

"I see," mumbled the man, looking like he was in deep thought.

"Gavin did go with me to the tanner's to get the leather," Davita continued. "And he told me what kind of boots ye wanted . . . and what size to make." She looked over to Gavin and made a face. Perhaps she shouldn't have said that until they found out if the boots fit him.

"It would be better if ye didna try to help me so much, sweetheart," Gavin mumbled under his breath.

"Did ye have even a drop of whisky to drink while ye were there?" asked Callum.

"Nay, he didna. I swear it," Davita blurted out.

"She made a deal with us to keep him out of the taverns," Ian reminded his father, looking piqued and a little under the weather.

"That's true. I did," said Davita, nodding her head. She looked over to Gavin but he was shaking his head at her.

"Ye'd better tell them the whole truth, lass," said Gavin.

"What truth?" asked Callum. "I want to hear everythin'."

"Well, he did go into the tavern, but it was only to get food and some ale," Davita admitted. "Ye see, it was my fault he had nothin' to eat that day, even though he did cook the meal for the rest of us while I was workin'."

"Ye cooked?" asked Storm, chuckling.

"My dear," said Lady Wren to her husband. "Gavin is a very good cook, but since you rarely bother yourself with such a skill, you wouldn't know it."

Storm scowled and looked the other way. "Sorry about that," he said and cleared his throat.

"So, is my sentence finished? Am I redeemed?" asked Gavin, hoping to hell the answer would be yes.

"I am satisfied," said Storm, looking over at his father. "How about ye, Da?"

"I guess so", mumbled Ian.

"Grandda?" Storm spoke to Callum now. "It is up to ye. Will Gavin remain an outcast, or has he done enough to redeem himself? Will he be accepted back into Clan MacKeefe?"

"Mmmph," mumbled Callum, getting up and stamping his feet on the ground like a crazy man, staring down at the new Cordovan leather boots.

"Oh, my!" gasped Davita, holding her hand over her mouth. She wasn't sure the old man wasn't going to bust the stitches, being so forceful.

"That's just Callum's way of checkin' out the boots," Gavin explained to her. "Or at least, I think it is."

"These are the best pair of boots I've ever had," said Callum.

Gavin heard Davita release the deep breath she'd been holding.

"What about repairin' the trunk full of shoes?" asked Callum.

"Those are bein' repaired by the cobbler, as part of his fine from the head masters of the cobbler and cordwainer's guilds," Gavin explained.

"I see. Well, I suppose ye did stick to the deal of no' drinkin' any whisky," said Callum.

"Then is he redeemed, Grandda?" Storm asked again. "Since ye gave him the punishment, ye will have the final say."

"Will ye respect the rules of my tavern from now on?" asked Callum, stomping just one foot on the floor now as he looked over at Gavin, squinting one eye.

"I wouldna dare be careless enough to ignore them again," promised Gavin.

"Then ye're redeemed," said the old man, waving his hand through the air.

"Och, Gavin, I am so happy," said Davita, kissing him right there in front of everyone. "Now we can get married."

"Married?" asked Callum.

"That's right," came a voice from behind them.

DAVITA TURNED AROUND to see a clansmember pushing her father who was in a wheeled chair. His arm and leg were still in splints, but the color had returned to his face and his scratches and stitches seemed to be healing nicely.

"Da!" cried Davita, running to him and putting her arms around him in a gentle hug. She gave him a big kiss on the cheek.

"Careful, Daughter. I am still healin'," said her father.

"Gavin told me that he asked ye for my hand in marriage."

"That's right. And I said yes. I will admit, I wasna crazy about Highlanders, but I've spent a lot of time talkin' and eatin' with them since I've been here. They are no' so bad after all. Ian and I have a lot in common."

"He's a guid man," said Ian with a nod.

"Chieftains, will ye grant us permission to get married at the castle?" Gavin asked Ian and Storm. "Along with Davita's sister and her betrothed as well?"

"So soon?" Callum didn't seem to like the idea.

"My sister is pregnant," Davita explained, going back to Gavin's side.

When Gavin had told her father about this yesterday while Davita and her siblings stayed back in town, he was very angry with Aila at first. But Gavin had been able to calm him down. Since her father knew and was friends with Ethan's late father, it helped him to accept the fact that Aila and Ethan would be married. Plus, her father had also been tickled to learn that Clyde's nephew was now his apprentice instead of Clyde's. That sweetened the deal.

"It is important she gets married right away," Davita continued.

"I suppose ye're pregnant, too?" asked Callum, looking disgusted.

Davita glanced up at Gavin and smiled. "I could only hope to be so lucky as to be carryin' Gavin's bairn. But nay, to my knowledge, I am no' pregnant."

"I would be delighted if ye were, lass." Gavin bent over and kissed her tenderly.

"I think it would be exciting to have a double wedding here," said Lady Wren. "There hasn't been a wedding inside the castle in a while now."

"I agree," added Ian's wife, Clarista. "What this place needs is a true celebration."

"Well, I guess that answers yer question," said Storm. "If the ladies want a weddin', I dinna think any of us could stop it even if we wanted to."

"Thank ye," said Davita. "That makes me so happy."

"Aye," said Gavin, but he sounded rather sad and Davita thought she knew why.

"Excuse me, Chieftains and Callum, and Ladies," she said, gaining their attention. Gavin looked at her in question. "Trust me," she whispered, before continuing to address the rulers of the castle. "Would it be possible to invite a few people from town to the weddin', includin' two men who are the heads of the cobbler and cordwainers' guilds? We sort of promised we would."

"Of course," Lady Wren answered for her husband. "All are invited. We have plenty of room."

"Then Gavin's friends, Cam, North, and Nash can come to the weddin' as well?" she asked, once again holding her breath and waiting for the answer.

"We'll need to discuss this one," said Callum, walking over to his son and grandson, looking at his new boots as he walked. They talked quietly between them. Then Callum turned around.

"Aye, what the hell," he said, throwing his hands in the air. "They can come to the weddin'. While they are here, the next in line will be given his sentence as well."

"Thank ye," said Gavin.

"Welcome back to the clan, Gavin," said Storm. "Ye are no longer an outcast."

"It feels guid to be back." Gavin sounded so relieved and happy. "Damned guid to be back with the MacKeefe Clan where I belong."

Suddenly, Davita didn't feel as good as she did moments before. She could see how important it was for Gavin to be with his clan. However, as soon as they married, he would be staying in town with her, and not be with the MacKeefes anymore. Had she just made him an outcast of his own people, even though she'd never meant to do it?

CHAPTER TWENTY-SIX

TWO DAYS LATER, Gavin stood inside the great hall, waiting for the priest to wed him to Davita. Aila and Ethan were next to them, and behind them were a roomful of MacKeefes. There were so many people attending the wedding and celebration afterwards that they decided to get married in the great hall instead of the castle's chapel.

Some of the townspeople were there, including Bram and his family. Also in attendance were some of the shop owners such as Grace, Keithen, Iver, and Tomas, the tanner. The head guild masters, Fergus and Hector, showed up as well. As a measure of good faith, and since Clyde was Ethan's uncle, they had invited Clyde and Gregor, too.

Of course, Clyde almost didn't make it to the wedding since he and Gregor were so busy trying to repair and return the trunkful of shoes to the castle before the ceremony.

The priest said the vows for Aila and Ethan and then it was Davita and Gavin's turn.

Gavin loved Davita, but getting married was a frightening thing to him. He needed a drink, but decided he wouldn't have one until after the vows were said. He wanted to have a clear head when he made Davita his wife. This would be the most important thing he ever did in his life.

"Do ye, Gavin MacKeefe, take Davita, the cordwainer's daughter, for yer wife?" asked the priest.

Davita didn't have a surname. None of the commoners did, only the nobles or those from a clan. If one wanted to refer to them, they would either use the place from whence they came, or their profession. However, as soon as they were married, Davita would be a MacKeefe, the same as Gavin.

"I do," he said, holding Davita's hand, giving it a squeeze.

"Gavin, no' so tight," she whispered, making him realize that he was so nervous that he was all but crushing her with his grip. His hold slackened.

"Sorry," he whispered. "I'm nervous."

"Me, too," she answered.

"Ye are?" Thoughts of doubt shot through his mind. Mayhap Davita didn't really want to marry him after all. Then when she smiled at him, he relaxed and all his fears faded away. There stood the most beautiful lass he'd ever seen, and she was about to become his wife.

Davita wore her hair long today, at his request. The two sides were braided with flowers interwoven, and then wrapped around the rest of her long hair, similar to the way a noble lady might wear it. Fresh flowers were woven into a grapevine headpiece, and bright ribbons trailed down her back. She wore the MacKeefe plaid today. It was something else that Gavin had insisted upon. He was proud to make her a member of his adopted family. And on her feet, she wore a brand-new pair of silk shoes that she had made for the wedding. Tiny little colored flowers and butterflies were stitched in colored thread, gracing the sides and toes of the shoes. They looked magical and perfect for such an angel like Davita.

"Do ye, Davita of Hermitage, take Gavin MacKeefe to be yer husband?" asked the priest. The fresh summer wildflowers of purple thyme and yellow primroses that Davita gripped in her free hand shook, telling Gavin that she was trembling.

"I do," she replied, letting out a deep breath afterwards.

"Dinna tremble, lass," he told her. "Save that for tonight when we consummate the marriage."

"I think we've already done that," she whispered, flashing him a smile.

"The rings please," said the priest, causing Davita's eyes to shoot up to meet his.

"Och, Gavin, We forgot about that. We've been so busy with everythin' that I –"

"Shhhh," he said, putting his finger to her lips. "Archy, bring the rings please."

"Archy has them?" She turned around to look, seeing her little brother heading up to the dais, carrying two rings carefully on a velvet pillow. He walked slowly, his eyes fastened to the rings, looking as if he were afraid he would drop them. Archy wore a MacKeefe plaid today as well. It hung all the way down to his ankles. "What is he wearin'?" asked Davita with a giggle.

"He insisted, and none of the MacKeefes minded. Yer brathair is infatuated with my clan," said Gavin.

Gavin took the rings from the boy. "Thank ye, Archy."

"Dinna thank me," said Archy. "I had a little help."

"Ye did?" asked Gavin.

"Aye. It seems Hamish is gettin' married, too." He pulled out a toad from each pocket and held them up. "I found Hilda under the toad house with him this mornin'."

Gavin, Davita, and those around them laughed.

"Ye'd better go sit down now, lad," Gavin told him. "Mayhap hide the toads. We wouldna want to scare the lassies."

"Aye. I will." Archy put the toads back into his pockets and had a seat.

Gavin and Davita exchanged rings, and then the priest said the words that made it final. "Ye are married, and may kiss the bride."

"Gladly," said Gavin, grabbing Davita and holding her tightly. He dipped her backwards, kissing her deeply, making a big show.

"I want a kiss like that," said Aila, her eyes and mouth opening in surprise.

"Ye asked for it," replied Ethan, doing the same to his new

wife.

Everyone clapped and cheered. Gavin's friends yelled out a few things that were probably not appropriate for the ears of lassies but, today, Gavin didn't care.

"Ye are my wife, lass," he said, feeling as if he'd made the right decision. He would spend the rest of his days with the girl he loved.

"Ye are my husband." Davita never looked so beautiful and glowing as she did today. Gavin truly was a lucky man.

"Bring out the Mountain Magic," called out Callum. The musicians up in the gallery started up a lively tune, and the whisky flowed freely.

"Och, this is a fine *uisque baugh*," said Nash, walking by with a tankard, finally having gotten his drink.

"Here's one for ye, Gavin," said Cam, handing him a tankard. "Ye waited a long time for this, so enjoy it."

"I will," said Gavin, raising the cup to his mouth, savoring the taste of the MacKeefe's famous whisky. "Dinna worry, lass," he told Davita. "I swear I will never eat or drink too much again. I've learned my lesson."

DAVITA SMILED AND her heart swelled to see how happy Gavin was to finally be able to drink whisky again. Not to mention, he was back with his clan and no longer an outcast. She realized how important family was to him. He'd sacrificed so much agreeing to live in town and to help her with the cordwaining business even though she knew he had no desire to make shoes. He had come to her as naught but a drunkard and a glutton, but he'd changed so much in that short time. Now, he was even promising not to eat or drink too much ever again. Davita believed that he would keep his word.

"Did the chieftains tell ye who would be next to receive his sentence?" Davita asked Cam, wondering what type of punishment Gavin's friends would have and need to complete in order to be accepted back into the clan.

"Aye, they did." Cam took a good long swig of Mountain Magic, not volunteering any other information.

"I'm guessin' it's ye," said Gavin.

"It is," Cam admitted with a shrug of his shoulders. "Well, at least I'll get it over with faster than the twins."

"What is yer punishment?" asked Davita curiously. "That is, if ye dinna mind me askin'."

"Well, I canna say. Ladies Wren and Clarista decided this is a day of celebration and that the chieftains shouldna give me my sentence until the morrow. They didna want to ruin yer special day."

"That's lucky for ye," said Gavin with a chuckle. "Just one more day of freedom, my guid friend."

"That's right." Cam's head turned and his eyes followed a busty serving girl walking by with a tray filled with cups of Mountain Magic. "Speakin' of freedom, I think I am goin' to make the most of it while I still can. Now, if ye'll excuse me, I need to go catch that wench with the whisky." He hurried after her without breaking his stride.

"It seems Cam likes whisky as much as ye," said Davita innocently, not realizing just what Cam was hunting down.

"Aye, whisky and a little somethin' on the side." When Gavin winked at her and pinched her bottom, she finally understood what he meant.

"Oh!" she cried, her hand going to her bottom, and her eyes opening wide.

"I canna wait . . . for later, my love."

"Neither can I," she agreed. "But for now, Gavin, let's go talk to my faither."

"All right," he said, putting his arm around her, stopping several times along the way as people congratulated them and made small talk.

"Da," said Davita, reaching down to him in his chair to give him a quick hug and a kiss. "When will ye be able to come home? I miss ye."

"Your father has been healing nicely," said Lady Wren, walking up with her husband, Storm.

"Aye," answered Storm. "I think the time he spent drinkin' with my da was guid for him. Verra healin'. I just wish it had helped my faither as much as it did yers." Storm's eyes glanced over to Ian. The man sat quietly in the corner, his face emotionless and stone-like.

"I dinna understand. What's wrong with him?" asked Davita.

"No one is sure," Storm answered. "Physically, he is no different than any man of his age."

"Actually, even better," added Wren.

"No' as spry as Callum," stated Gavin. "Then again, we all expect Callum to outlive us all."

"He's got a guid start," agreed Davita.

"It's Ian's mind that seems to be ailing," Wren told them. "I am going to keep trying to heal him with herbs. I won't ever give up."

"My best wishes to ye," said Davita. "I ken how hard it is to see a parent suffer." Her eyes flashed back to her father, and thoughts of him almost dying in that ditch filled her head.

"Enough of this gloomy talk," said Storm. "Today is a happy day and one to celebrate. Ye two are married!"

"I still canna believe it," said Gavin. "I am the luckiest man ever."

"Well, Davita is lucky to be married into such a great, strong clan as the MacKeefes," said Storm. "Let us drink to Gavin and Davita, the new members of Clan MacKeefe," Storm shouted to get everyone's attention. He lifted his tankard high in the air.

"To Gavin and Davita!" yelled North.

"Aye!" added Nash. "The lucky sot is also done with his sentence and no longer an outcast of the clan."

"Be patient. Ye'll get yer turn to feel the wrath of Callum as well," Gavin yelled back.

"I heard that," shouted Callum from the other side of the room.

"God's ears, that man hears well," mumbled Gavin.

"So, tell us, Gavin. Will ye take Davita to live at our Highland camp?" asked Storm.

"Nay," said Gavin, sounding very sad, staring down at his empty tankard.

"Oh, you two will stay here at the castle then," said Wren. "That will be nice."

"I canna believe that." Storm looked at Gavin curiously. "After all, everyone kens how much ye like the Highlands and livin' in nature, Gavin. I'd think stayin' locked up at the castle would be like hell to ye."

"We will make our home in town," said Gavin softly.

"What did ye say?" asked Storm. "It is noisy in here and it sounded like ye said ye would be livin' in town."

"I did," said Gavin. "We'll live at the cordwainer's shop."

Just as he said that, Nash and North walked up. No one responded at all.

"That will be nice for Davita and her family," Lady Wren finally said.

"Gavin, what are ye thinkin'?" asked North.

"Ye're really no' comin' back to the Highlands?" asked Nash. "We're goin' to miss ye."

"I agree," said Storm. "It willna be the same without ye."

"Davita's life is in town. So is mine, now," Gavin told them. "I'm her husband, and will stay at her side always." Gavin seemed to be biting the inside of his cheek.

"Gavin, I had no right askin' ye to stay in town." Davita held on to her new husband's arm.

"Nay, it's fine." He flashed her a smile that didn't meet his eyes.

"Now that Ethan will be livin' with us, I dinna think my help will be needed as much anymore," said Davita.

"What do ye mean?" Gavin looked at her from the sides of his eyes.

"What she means," said Aila, walking up with Ethan and

Archy, "is that I will be workin' in the shop, too. When Archy is old enough, he'll be an apprentice and someday take over the business."

"I dinna want to make shoes," complained Archy. "I want to live in the Highlands and be a warrior like Gavin."

"Haud yer wheesht, Archy," scolded Aila. "Ye ken we discussed this and it is what we are goin' to do to help Gavin."

"To help me? I dinna understand," said Gavin.

"Gavin, I canna ask ye to be somethin' ye are no'," said Davita. "I was only thinkin' of my family when I asked ye to live in town and ye so graciously gave up all ye loved to do it."

"I didna give up all I love. But I would do without any of it, just to be with ye." He put his arm around her and pulled her closer.

"Gavin, ye and Davita canna live with me," said Graeme. "There is no room now that Ethan and Aila will be there all the time, and with a new bairn comin'. It will be too crowded in that wee shop."

"I canna? We canna?" Gavin seemed so confused that Davita thought she had better explain quickly.

"My da is comin' back to the shop, and will be able to instruct Aila and Ethan until he is totally healed and able to make shoes again," she told him.

"I have enough years of experience that Graeme is goin' to make me a journeyman soon," said Ethan proudly.

"Is yer uncle all right with that?" asked Gavin.

"My uncle made a mistake no' acceptin' us, and he will have to pay for it," answered Ethan. "However, mayhap we can make amends. Either way, I will no' work for him ever again. I belong to the cordwainer's guild now," he said, lifting his chin and standing straighter.

"So . . . are ye sayin' we can live with Clan MacKeefe?" Gavin asked Davita.

"I am sayin' that I would welcome a change and be happy to live in the Highlands or at the castle with ye," Davita answered.

"It is yer choice, Gavin. As long as I'm with ye, I dinna care where we live."

"Really." A smile lit up Gavin's face. Then he looked at Archy who was sulking and his smile disappeared. "I dinna ken, Davita. What about yer family?"

"My family will always be there. We can visit them whenever we want."

"Then we'll swap off, stayin' in the Highlands sometimes, and at the castle other times," Gavin decided. "When we are at Hermitage Castle, we'll be able to visit yer family often since we will be so close to town."

"I'm goin' to miss ye, Gavin." Archy looked like he was about to cry.

"Nay, ye're no'," said Davita. "I talked to Da and he agreed that ye can stay with us in the Highlands durin' the summer. That is, as long as the MacKeefes agree."

"I can?" asked Archy, sounding so excited.

"He can?" repeated Gavin, then he nodded. "Aye, ye can. Why no'? Storm?" he asked, just to make sure.

"Of course," said Storm. "Archy looks guid in the MacKeefe plaid."

"Yay!" cheered Archy, becoming very happy. "What about the plaid? Can I still wear it?" the boy asked.

"No' in town," said Gavin. "But ye can wear it when ye come to visit. I'll even teach ye how to use a sword and how to fight."

Davita cleared her throat and gave him a warning look as Archy jumped up and down with excitement.

"Well, mayhap we'll have to do it a wee bit at a time or yer sister is goin' to have my head," said Gavin with a chuckle.

"It'll all work out," said Davita. "And now ye willna have to make shoes the rest of yer life, Husband."

"Och, I dinna ken. It wasna that bad. I am sure I could have learned it. Eventually."

"Who are ye tryin' to fool?" asked Davita.

"All right, I admit I didna like it that much, and never want to do it again," admitted Gavin. "I'm a Highlander, and ye canna expect me to make shoes."

"Nay, I canna," agreed Davita. "Ye may never be a cordwainer, but ye'll always be a *Highland Soul*."

From the Author

I hope you enjoyed Davita and Gavin's story and will take the time to leave a review for me. I loved learning about medieval guilds and some of the trades. Cordwaining was a skill that took years to learn. I am fascinated by shoes of the medieval times. I never realized how many different types there were, or how shoes also denoted one's status. I hope to have shared my enthusiasm with you through information about cordwaining and guilds woven into this story.

Be sure to follow along with Gavin and his friends with Cam's story which is next in *Highland Flame*.

If you enjoyed the members of the MacKeefe Clan and would like to read their personal stories, you can find them in some of my other series. I have listed them for you.

Storm and Wren MacKeefe – ***Lady Renegade***, Book 2 of *Legacy of the Blade Series*

Callum MacKeefe – ***Lady Renegade***, as well as other books including ***Keeper of the Flame*** – Book 5 of my *Second in Command Series*

Ian and Clarista can be found in ***Lady Renegade*** as well as in the *Highland Chronicles Series*, along with the other MacKeefes

Aidan MacKeefe from the beginning of the book and his wife Effie are from ***Aidan*** – Book 2 of my *Madman MacKeefe Series*

<u>Coira</u>, Effie's sister, has her own happily-ever-after in ***Scottish Rose: Coira*** – Book 3 of my *Second in Command Series*

If you'd like to find out more about my other series, please stop by my website at elizabethrosenovels.com, or take a look at my amazon author page as well.

Elizabeth Rose

About the Author

Elizabeth Rose is an Amazon All-Star, and bestselling, award-winning, author of nearly 100 books and counting! Her first book was published back in 2000, but she has been writing stories ever since high school.

She is the author of contemporary, western, paranormal, and her favorite – medieval romance. You'll find sexy, alpha heroes and strong, independent heroines in her books. Sometimes her heroines can even swing a sword. She loves adding humor to her work, because everyone needs to laugh more in life. Her **Bad Boys of Sweetwater: Tarnished Saints Series,** was inspired by people, places, and things in her own life. The location is the lake and small town of Michigan where she grew up visiting her grandparents.

Living in the suburbs of Chicago with her husband, she has two grown sons and one granddog – so far. A lover of nature, Elizabeth can be found in the summer swinging in her "writing hammock" in her secret garden, creating her next novel. Her secret garden is what inspired her series, **Secrets of the Heart**, which of course centers around a secret garden too!

Elizabeth's current and upcoming books will be published by *Dragonblade Publishing* and independently too under *RoseScribe Media Inc.*

Social Media:
Elizabeth's Website: elizabethrosenovels.com